RECKLESS KNIGHT

KNIGHT'S RIDGE EMPIRE #7

TRACY LORRAINE

D1603428

Editing by Pinpoint Editing

Proofreading by Sisters Get Lit.erary

Photography by Wander Aguiar

1

TOBY

Name: Jodie Joanne Walker
Mother: Joanne Rachel Walker
Father: Unknown

The folder in my hand trembles as I read the words over like I have done a million times in the past couple of weeks.

While everyone else around me was focused on what intel Jonas Ariti might have leaked about the Family, how he might have put us all at risk, my eyes were firmly set on him. On the pain he's caused behind closed doors.

On his own secrets.

Somehow, he'd managed to keep his son a secret from the Family all this time, and I was betting his existence was only the tip of the iceberg.

No one else knew the extent of the abuse we suffered, only the two of us who lived it. And even if they did, they still wouldn't understand.

The parts I've told my friends, my sister, my real father, all just skirt around the edges of the torture Mum and I have suffered over the years.

And he needs to pay.

In the most painful way possible.

I've found the perfect person to make it happen.

It took a lot of digging, but eventually, Joker led me right to her front door.

Dropping the folder that contains every single piece of information our PI found for me about her life, I rub my hands down my thighs and stare up at her bedroom window.

Every morning without fail, her light turns on at 07:02. At exactly 07:15, the front door opens and she steps out. Dressed in leggings and an oversized hoodie with the hood up, she secures her headphones before pulling the door closed behind her and taking off down the street. Not once does she ever look up and show me her face. She runs for thirty minutes.

For the first couple of weeks, I sat here in the shadows watching, waiting, taking notes. But as the days passed, my need to see more only grew, and I quickly found myself pulling my own hood up and taking off after her.

Before the funeral, she didn't spend much time at home, preferring to work or be with her cousin. But since that day, she only steps out of the house for her run, leaving me with her social media to try to discover more about the woman who allowed me to take so much from her on Friday night.

I might have had a folder detailing her life, but it didn't tell me much about the person she really was. But the second she locked eyes with me across that bar for the first time, I knew. I felt it in a way I couldn't when watching her from a distance.

And then, when she got up on the stage with Brianna, I knew she was going to fall right into my hands. Almost literally, when I finally made my move.

Pulling my phone from my pocket, I open my secure app and go through the facial recognition and passwords before pulling up the video.

Stretching my legs out, I push my fingers through my hair as the image of an empty room at Hades appears on the screen before me. But it won't be empty for long.

There were so many things that could have gone wrong with my plans that night. Hell, I expected them all to crumble around me. It was pretty much the way my life was going. What was one more thing to batter my hope of ever getting back to normal again?

My blood heats the second the door opens and Jodie stumbles in with me close behind her.

The way her mouth falls open and her eyes widen at everything surrounding us makes my cock swell. I regretted not seeing that look on her face when it happened, but hell, this makes up for it.

Reaching down, I tug at my jeans, trying to find some more space for my dick. I fucking need it when she gets on her knees for me.

I might be able to replay every second of this video in my head from the number of times I've watched it over the past few days, but the effect it has on me never lessens. The effect *she* has on me never lessens. Just looking at her sates something inside me that's been shredding me to pieces since the truth about the man I called my father all these years came to light.

She's going to be the one to finally put the raging need for revenge burning within me to sleep. She's the one who's finally going to set me free from this endless fall into the abyss.

My fists curl on my thighs as she takes all of me. Allows me to use her for whatever I need. To take my hate out on her, to claim her. To make her mine in ways she's never going to understand.

If only you fucking knew who I really was, Jodie.

If only you knew half as much about the monster you spent that night with as I do about you.

You'd have run as fast as you could.

But it's too late.

Because I've got you.

It might not happen tonight, or even tomorrow.

But I will make you mine.

My ultimate revenge.

T here's no movement as I step into the room later that afternoon, and it's not until I slam the heavy door closed behind me that he finally jolts awake, his swollen eyes barely opening to see who's come to play with him.

His dry, cracked lips part, but no words come out. I'm hardly surprised.

He stopped talking a while ago.

Probably trying to protect her.

Fair play if he is, because quite honestly, after all these years, I wasn't actually aware that he was capable of caring about anything.

And someone who doesn't even share his blood. Tsk.

The guys were right the night we discovered that Jonas had another son—or rather, a son seeing as it turned out that I didn't share an ounce of DNA with this motherfucker—thank fuck. But there were no others. And while that might be true, there is another out there who stole his dark and twisted heart. A girl. A girl I'm sure he wants me far, far away from. At least, with the lengths he went to to cover her up seem to point that way.

Too bad for him that the Cirillo PI is better than Jonas and all the attempts he made to protect her, to sever any connection between Joker and his own family.

His eyes follow me as I walk across the room, but he still doesn't move. Probably too weak after all the time he's spent down here, being our personal punching bag.

Most of the bruises and cuts that litter his body are courtesy of my own fists, but not all.

The guys—even Damien and Evan, and obviously Galen—have happily joined the little party we've been having down here in the depths of our building. Hell, even Stella finally convinced me to let her down here one night when Seb was out, and she unleashed her inner monster on the man who wanted her dead. It was beautiful. Really fucking beautiful. His shock at the sheer brutality behind the woman he tried to ruin only made the whole experience that much sweeter.

I pace for a few minutes, hoping to unnerve

him. Although, from the way his body trembles, I'm not sure it's really necessary.

Stopping, I take two steps toward him before lowering to my haunches, just out of reach.

Holding his eyes, I roll her name around in my head, trying to predict his reaction.

"You think you're so clever, don't you, Jonas?" I start. "You think you've tied up all your loose ends, hidden all your secrets. But you forgot one important thing." His brow lifts slightly, but it's the only reaction I get. "You trained me. You taught me all the tricks. How to find people's biggest weaknesses, and how to use them against them. I watched—experienced—you do it time and time again."

The vein in his temple starts pulsating. As a kid, that was the most terrifying sight in the world, because it meant that whatever was coming next was seriously going to hurt. It might not have been physically, but it would hurt all the same.

Pulling my phone from my pocket, I open the photos I took only this morning while I was out on my morning run. It's been my favourite part of the day for a while now, and I do love to capture the beauty of it.

"I've got a new hobby," I tell him. "I thought you'd enjoy it too. That maybe we could bond over it. Things have been a little strained recently, after all," I mock. "I think this one is my favourite. The lighting is perfect, my subject..." I turn the screen around, showing him the image of Jodie. "Mouth-watering."

"No," he cries, proving to me that he still does have a voice in there somewhere. "No."

Pulling my phone back when he weakly tries to reach for it, I stand with an accomplished smirk playing on my lips.

"Too late, old man. And let me tell you, she's not just mouth-watering," I taunt. "She's fucking delicious."

Some kind of pained groan rumbles in his throat as he finally pushes himself from the cold slab of concrete he's using as a bed.

"Stay away from her," he pleads, proving to me just how much of a soft spot he has for this woman.

"Sorry, can't do that. But, I do need you to tell me something." He stares at me. "Aside from the obvious," I use my hands to mimic her curves, "what makes her so much better than me? Neither of us is yours, so why protect her over me?"

His fingers curl around the edge of the concrete, a move that should really hurt, seeing as he's missing more than a few fingernails right now.

"Stay away from her," he begs again.

A smile curls at my lips as I take in his thin frame and heaving chest.

"How the mighty fall, old man. It's been fun chatting, but I've got a date... and an itch that needs scratching." I wink at him before marching for the door, my smile only growing when his cries for me to stop hit my ears seconds before the door slams and the locks engage behind me.

2

JODIE

I stare at the TV screen, but I don't see any of it.

It's been a week since the funeral. A week since I had to say goodbye to the second man in my life after only doing the same to my brother last year. And it hurts as much as it did the day we discovered they'd gone.

I know it takes longer than seven days. I expect the pain to last a lifetime, to feel the black hole within me for the rest of my days. But I'd hoped that I might be able to breathe a little easier by now.

Maybe I would be, if I didn't also feel like I was losing my mum right along with my brother and stepdad.

While I might worry that I'm not coping. I know for a fact that she isn't.

She hasn't left her bedroom since the day of the funeral.

The food I take in barely gets touched, and every time I look at her, I can't help feeling like a little bit more of her has died.

I get it. She's lost almost everything. Her son, her partner.

But I'm still here. And knowing that I'm not enough right now is killing me.

I want to help. But how can I when all she wants to do is drown?

My life restarts tomorrow. My compassionate leave is over. I have to rejoin the rest of society, plaster a fake smile on my face, and pretend that, behind my façade, my entire life isn't falling apart in front of my eyes.

My phone lights up beside me and my heart jumps in my chest in hope.

But it quickly withers and dies. Something else to feel guilty about, because I shouldn't be disappointed to see my best friend's name staring back at me. But ever since last weekend, I've craved to see his name light up my phone once more.

It's hopeless. It was a hookup, and my fickle heart read too much into the messages I found the next morning.

Bestie Bitch: How's it going? I'm

drowning in textbooks. MAKE IT STOP!

A smile pulls at the sides of my lips. This was always going to happen.

Jodie: I told you not to leave it to the last minute… AGAIN.

Shaking my head, I tuck my phone into my pocket and head for the kitchen.

I need something. Anything to dull the ache and loss that constantly squeezes my heart like a vice.

My phone buzzes again.

Bestie Bitch: All right Goody Two-shoes. Feel free to come help.

Jodie: It's your career, not mine. Enjoy your all-nighter.

Truth is, I'd quite happily go hang at her place and just watch her write the assignment that's due by 11:00 tomorrow if I thought it would help. But all I'll do is end up distracting her and forcing her to miss another deadline.

She might leave literally everything to the very last minute, but she's worked too hard to get to where she is for me to swoop in with my grief and misery and ruin it for her.

I pull the fridge open and stare at the depressing contents: milk that I'm pretty sure is fermenting in the bottle, some cheese, butter, one egg, and some seriously questionable veggies in the bottom drawer.

Pretty much sums up my life right now.

Giving it up as a bad job, I pull the freezer open instead.

The only thing of any interest is a bottle of vodka I stashed behind the peas a few days ago. But, trying to be a sensible adult who needs to get back to reality tomorrow, I push the drawer closed and force it and the oblivion it could offer me out of my mind.

I rummage through the rest of the drawers, but when I find nothing containing any decent sugar, I let out a groan and swing the door shut as if it's personally offended me.

Storming out of the kitchen, I look toward Mum's bedroom door. But with a pained sigh, I turn in the opposite direction, shove my feet into my Uggs and reluctantly turn to look in the mirror in the hall.

"Holy shit," I mutter, dragging the scrunchie out of my hair and redoing my messy bun—not that it makes a lot of fucking difference.

I'm a mess. The dark circles under my eyes are a stark contrast to my pale complexion, my lips are dry and cracked, and I'm starting to break out on my chin thanks to the amount of takeout and general shit I've consumed this week.

Dragging on my coat, I pull my lip balm from my bag and attempt to fix at least one of my issues.

The bitter January air hits me in the face the second I step outside the front door and I suck in a sharp breath, which I instantly regret when it makes my lungs hurt.

Tugging my fluff-trimmed hood over my head, I snuggle into its warmth and push forward.

It might only be a few minutes' walk, but I can barely feel my face by the time I get to our closest shop, my breaths coming out as white clouds around me.

"Oh my God," I hiss when the heat inside the shop hits me. I rub my hands together and head for the freezer section.

I grab my poison, feeling excited for the first time all day, and I keep my head down as I turn toward the checkout to pay. Only, I don't get very far, because I slam straight into a solid body.

"Shit," I hiss, my tub of ice cream taking the brunt of our collision. "I'm so so—" My apology is cut off as his scent hits me.

My heart slams against my ribs and my palms begin to sweat despite the fact that I'm holding a tub of freezing cold ice cream.

It's not. It can't be. No, I tell myself as something other than grief consumes me for the first time in a week.

I've heard nothing from the guy from that night. Not one single text after I replied to his the next morning. I was left with nothing but some hazy memories, a sore body, and his jumper that smells exactly like...

No. Fate isn't that much of a bitch. Is it?

"S-sorry," I say, trying to duck around him without looking up.

Even if by some miracle it is him, I look like the back end of a dustbin lorry. Running away is the best option here.

It's the only option here.

I step around him, my tub tucked into my chest protectively as I focus on paying and getting the hell home.

That doesn't happen, though.

Instead, the world around me comes to a grinding halt as his large hand reaches out, pressing against my stomach, and a deep, "Jodie?" fills my ears.

Fuck.

Fuck.

I hesitate, desperately wanting to run, but also having this weird desire to turn back into his body in the hope he just holds me.

Stepping closer, he reaches out and tugs the

hood of my coat down, stopping me from hiding from him.

My stomach knots as he moves in front of me and ducks down.

I want to hide, turn away—anything—but I quickly find myself lost in his blue eyes, and suddenly it's a week ago and I'm handing myself over to everything he can offer me.

"Toby," I breathe, his name falling from my lips without instruction from my brain.

His brows pinch in concern as his eyes drink me in.

Shame burns through me, and the desire to tuck my head into my coat like a freaking turtle almost becomes too much to ignore.

I hate that I've turned into this pathetic, broken girl.

Brianna would be ashamed of me right now.

"Are you okay?"

Sucking in a deep breath, I mentally pull on my big girl pants, square my shoulders, and try to own the fact that I look like a fucking mess.

"Yeah, of course. It's good to see you." I force a smile onto my face, and he stares at me like I've just grown a second head before his eyes drop to the ice cream and then lower, taking in my leggings and Ugg boots.

Christ, could I look any more pathetic right now? At least he can't see that I'm not wearing a bra.

Reaching out, he tugs the ice cream from my hands, much to my irritation, and throws it back into the freezer.

"What the hell are you doing?" I ask, sounding embarrassingly horrified by his actions.

"Come on, Demon." He winks, taking my cold hand in his "We can do better than that."

Too shocked to do anything, I let him tug me away from the freezer section, looking back and mourning the loss of my ice cream.

The second we're outside, he pulls me into his side and wraps his arm around my shoulder.

If it were any other night or any other guy, I'd probably fight it. But with him, I quickly find that I don't want to be anywhere else but surrounded by his warmth and familiar scent.

"So, what are we being depressed about? Some dickhead make the stupid mistake of dumping you or something?"

Risking a glance over at him, I find an arrogant smirk tugging at his lips.

"So you think I'm the kind of girl who'd have spent the night with you despite having a boyfriend?"

Thankfully, his smile slips.

"I ain't one to judge, Demon."

I blow out a long breath. "My stepdad died," I blurt.

Toby's step falters. "Oh, shit... I, uh..."

"Don't say it," I snap. "It wasn't your fault, so why apologise for it?"

"I wasn't going to."

He turns us down the next street and I happily follow, just like I did the last time he took me somewhere.

Something stirs within me, a twisted desire to repeat that night. To lose myself in the intensity of this guy beside me.

"Where are we going?" I ask when he continues down the road before stopping at a really fancy BMW. The lights immediately come on, making it look like some kind of spaceship.

"This is not your car?" I gasp in shock. Although, when I think about it, it makes a lot of sense. He walked us into Hades as if it was any normal kind of club, so it stands to reason that this guy has more money than sense.

He smiles at me and actually looks a little embarrassed.

"It was a gift," he explains.

"Wow, someone clearly loves you."

He scoffs, although quickly covers it with a cough before agreeing. "Yeah, something like that."

Pulling the passenger door open, he gestures for me to get in.

"I'm not sure I'm dressed for a trip in this."

He stops me by capturing my chin between

his thumb and forefinger, lifting my face so my eyes meet his.

His touch burns and releases a million butterflies in my belly as my body remembers that night and the things he did to me, even if my head is still a little fuzzy about the events.

"You look beautiful, Jodie."

My cheeks heat. He's lying. I genuinely look a mess.

"I'm not looking for compliments."

"Didn't think you were. I was just telling the truth." His hand twists until he's cupping my jaw, his thumb rubbing along my bottom lip. His eyes darken as he stares down at me, and I'm immediately taken back to the hazy memories I have of that night.

"Do you remember?" he asks, his voice raspy.

"Some of it," I admit. "I was pretty wasted."

He nods, but I don't miss the grimace that briefly passes over his face. "Do you regret it?"

I suck in a breath. "No. Not at all. Why? Do you?"

He chuckles, closing the space between us, allowing his body heat to warm mine.

"I had the best night of my life with an incredible girl who shocked me at every turn." My lips twitch at the honesty in his tone. "The only thing I regret is leaving you in someone else's bed."

My heart soars and my entire body heats as

the chemistry that I remember all too well from that night crackles between us.

His thumb brushes across my bottom lip again and my mouth waters for him to kiss me, but he never does.

"Get in, Demon. I'm going to turn your night around."

"What if I'm busy?" I argue weakly.

"You were in the shop buying a single tub of ice cream," he points out, quirking an eyebrow.

"I guess I looked about as pathetic as I feel, then," I mutter.

"I already told you that you look beautiful. Now get in. Unless you're still longing for a night in with your cold friend," he teases, releasing me and jogging around the front of the car.

His eyes find mine before he gets to the driver's side and I see the challenge in them.

I drop down into the seat before he even has his door open.

3

TOBY

I didn't want to wait a week to see her again. But between school, work, and her never leaving her house aside from her morning run—which I have no intention of ruining just yet — I didn't have a lot of choice.

I could have reached out, I know that. I had her number in my contacts. Hell, I've spent enough time over the past few days staring at it as I've debated the best way to play this. But I knew that it needed to be in person.

It would be too easy for her to cast me aside and put our night down as the best one-night stand of her life and move on.

But that wasn't how things were going to go for us. I had bigger, better, and more enjoyable plans for our future.

And the first of those was reminding her just how electric we were together last Friday.

I might have planted myself in the middle of her night out with her cousin, but there's no denying the chemistry between us. That was something I could have only hoped for, prayed for.

The car rumbles to life beneath us a beat before the side of my face burns with her attention.

"I really hope you're not expecting me to be impressed by that, because I should warn you, I'm not really into all the flashy stuff."

A smile pulls at my lips and a laugh falls free.

Of all the girls in the city, I manage to find the one who's going to be suitably unimpressed by all the things I could offer her. Figures that the universe doesn't want to make this easy for me. I should probably take that as a sign that I should be backing away from this plan, but I won't.

I need it.

I crave it.

"So fancy restaurants are out then?" I quip, pulling from the space and gunning it down the empty street.

Jodie lets out a little squeal as she's thrown back in the seat by the power of my engine, and I glance over.

"Okay, so maybe I am a teeny bit impressed by that. How fast does it go?"

"Should have guessed you were an adrenaline junkie."

"I have my moments," she mutters.

"I remember," I confess, shifting in my seat as my thoughts linger on the events of that night a little too long.

Jodie doesn't say anything else as I make my way toward our side of town, but the silence isn't uncomfortable as she sits there, picking at her nails.

Her sadness is palpable as she loses herself in her thoughts. But even her misery isn't enough to cut through my anger.

"Where are we?" she asks, looking out the window when I pull to a stop on the side of another street.

"Wait and see. I think it'll hit the spot."

Climbing out of the car, I get to her side just as she pushes the door open. Scowling at her for doing it for me, I reach for her hand, unable to stop myself from wanting to touch her again, to convince myself that spark that shot up my arm when I twisted my fingers with hers in the shop wasn't a figment of my imagination.

She gasps the second her hand slips into mine, and I can't help but smile down at her.

Hell yeah, it's real. And she feels it too.

After leaving her in Brianna's flat in the early hours of Saturday morning, I couldn't help wondering if I'd made it all up. That I wanted it so badly that my mind had run away with me and let me believe she was everything I could have ever asked for. It wasn't hard to convince myself of that, because I haven't exactly been of sound mind over the past few weeks.

But as I pull her to her feet before me, I'm reminded of just how real it was.

It makes my head spin.

"Let's see what you've got then, hotshot," she taunts, showing me a little more of the sassy girl from last weekend instead of the sad one I first found tonight.

Taking a step back, I pull her out of the way and close the door, quickly directing her to the waffle shop Stella's told me about.

"Oh my God," she moans as we step inside. "That smells insane."

"Better than a tub of ice cream?" I ask, pulling her into a booth at the back of the café.

"Jury's still out."

"Ouch," I moan, pressing a hand to my heart as if her words physically hurt me.

"The company is definitely an improvement," she adds with a sly smile.

"I'll take that." Reaching for the menus, I slide one over to her, watching as she immediately looks down, her eyes widening in delight.

I have no idea if Jodie is aware of my

attention, but she doesn't look up once while she drools over the menu.

"What can I get for you both?" a waitress asks, startling me.

"Please could I get the salted caramel waffle and a luxury hot chocolate?" Jodie says happily, making a cold, dark part of me begin to warm up a little.

"Of course, and for you?"

The waitress turns to me. Her attention burns the side of my face, but I still don't look up.

Jodie's eyes finally turn my way, and a smile immediately pulls at my lips.

"I'll have the same, thank you."

In all honesty, I've already forgotten what she's ordered, but we're in a waffle shop... how bad can it get?"

The second we're alone, Jodie starts fussing, folding the menus away and tidying up.

"Stop," I demand, reaching over the table to grab her hand.

She immediately falls still, her eyes locked on mine.

"I'm sorry. I... I'm not really myself right now."

"You're perfect. Stop worrying. You're allowed to break a bit when you lose someone you love." I force the final few words out through clenched teeth, the weight of the real reason I'm sitting here right now knotting my stomach painfully.

"I know, I just...I'm annoying myself. I've got to go back to work tomorrow and..."

"You're not ready."

She shrugs. "I don't know. It's probably what I need to drag me out of this rut, but the thought of talking to people all day long, pretending that everything is okay... It seems like hard work, and I'm not even there yet."

"So take more time," I suggest, not really knowing what else to say.

"I can't. The thought of staying home longer is worse." She drops her head into her hands and lets out a long sigh. "I'm sorry, I'm sure this isn't what you were expecting when you ran into me."

"It's totally okay." I squeeze her hand in support. "We can't spend all our time together getting so lost in each other that we forget the world exists."

Her eyes darken as I drag up memories from that night.

"Can't we?" she asks hopefully.

"I mean, if you wanna go now, we can..." I start to slide from the booth. I'm joking, I think, but she doesn't see it that way.

"No, no," she gasps in a panic. "I'm not exactly..." She looks down at herself once more and cringes.

"You're not getting it, are you?" I smile,

twisting my fingers with hers and pulling her so she's leaning across the table, her lips only an inch from mine.

Her sweet floral scent washes over me, causing the ache that started the second I saw her walk out of her house tonight to grow.

"You don't need makeup and a skimpy dress, Jodie. And it's okay to break. To need a sugar fix."

"Well, if I knew this was going to turn into an impromptu second date—assuming we can call our first encounter a date—then I'd have at least put on a bra."

My eyes immediately drop to the sweatshirt she revealed when she pulled her coat off, and they narrow as if it'll help me see through.

It's not necessary though, because now she's pointed it out and knows I'm looking, her nipples are more than obvious, pressing against the fabric.

Slouching down, I widen my thighs, giving my quickly swelling dick some space.

Memories of our time together this time last Friday have been the only thing that have gotten me through this week. Well, that and waiting for her, watching her. Generally obsessing over everything I know about her.

My friends are all studying me through concerned eyes and walking on eggshells around me as if I'm about to blow at any minute—which, to be fair, is probably wise. But being with her...

it's been the first time I've been able to forget about the nightmares that are haunting me day and night. When I was with her, I was me again. Okay, so maybe a darker version of me, but still me.

"I can't really see the issue, Jodie." I smirk, still staring at her tits.

"No matter how much you might wish for it, my sweatshirt isn't going to vanish."

"Damn it," I mutter. "Thankfully, I vividly remember what every inch of your body looks like," I confess, sitting forward once more and holding her stare.

Her eyes darken, her cheeks heat, and she bites down on her bottom lip.

"You're making me hard," I breathe, my voice deep and raspy.

"T-Toby, you can't—"

"Here you go, luxury hot chocolates. I'll be right back with your waffles," the waitress sings, shattering some of the tension around us. "T-thank you," Jodie says politely, pulling her hands from mine and dragging her mug closer. But I'm not ready to abandon our previous conversation.

"You don't believe me, do you?"

"We're in the middle of a café. You can't just announce— What are you doing?" she gasps when I hook my foot around the back of her calf and lift it until I can tug her boot off. "Toby," she hisses quietly, trying to pull her leg out of my grasp.

Just as the waitress walks back over with two plates in her hands, I press her foot against my crotch, proving to her that I wasn't lying.

"I haven't stopped thinking about you," I tell her shamelessly. "Can you tell?"

I sense the waitress look between us, but she must realise we're too distracted and eventually just backs away from the table without a word, leaving our waffles in front of us.

"We're in a public place," she argues, although I'm not actually holding her foot that tightly. If she really wanted to put a stop to this, she could.

A chuckle rips from my lips. "Nice try, Demon. You loved the risk of being watched, of being caught."

Her lips part, but desire washes through her eyes.

"Deny it, go on."

"T-Toby—" she stutters.

"Nothing to be ashamed about, baby. Own what you want. It's fucking sexy."

Knowing that I've more than proved my point, I allow her to pull her foot from me before I'm really at risk of coming in my pants in public. That's low even for the depths I've sunk to recently.

"I've never done anything like that before,"

she confesses, pulling her plate closer while I quickly rearrange myself and do the same.

"You want to do it again though, right?"

"I... um... Oh my God," she suddenly moans. "This is amazing." Her eyes roll a little, and I can't help but laugh.

"*That* good?"

"Close. Try some."

I do as she suggests and lift my fork to my lips.

She's not wrong, it's pretty incredible.

"Not bad. I know something I'd prefer to be eating, though."

"You, Toby..."

"Doukas," I offer.

"You, Toby Doukas, are wicked."

"Something tells me you wouldn't have it any other way," I quip, diving back for more.

She watches me as if I'm the most fascinating creature in the world. "What?" I mumble around a mouthful.

She shakes her head, her blush deepening.

"Jodie, I think we're long past the point of either of us being embarrassed. You know more about me than people I've known all my life."

"So not everyone knows about your nocturnal activities then?"

I shake my head. "No. Mostly just Nico."

"And some girls, I'm assuming. Not that I'm judging if you and Ni—"

"We're close, but we're not that close," I laugh.

"Shame, I'd probably pay to watch you tie him up and have him at your mercy," she says innocently, while I damn near spray her with half-eaten waffle.

"What?" I blurt once I manage not to choke.

"Just saying, he doesn't seem like the kinda guy who'd let go like that. He's like, pure alpha."

"Oh, I don't know. He can be... generous. With the right person."

"Brianna certainly had no complaints."

"And what about you?" I ask, turning the conversation away from where my best friend sticks his cock. That motherfucker has zero morals when it comes to women.

"From what I can remember, it was... okay."

A smirk pulls at my lips. "Okay? I guess it's a good job that my memory is better than yours then, huh?"

"Or you're just that arrogant."

A laugh rumbles in my chest.

"You think I'm bad, you should meet the rest of my friends," I mutter, but I instantly realise my mistake when she looks up with genuine interest.

I've never introduced a girl to my friends. Not that I've ever had one I was even remotely interested in turning into a long-term thing. But I can hardly drag Jodie too deep into my life.

Nico might know the truth, but I can't risk

anyone else discovering what's really going on with her. Or worse, them giving Jodie too much information, which will allow her to put two and two together.

Jodie is my dirty little secret, and that's the way it's going to have to stay until I get what I need from her.

"I think you might be more than enough for now," she jokes.

"So..." I start. "Tell me something. Something real."

"Other than that I'm currently drowning in grief and my family is falling apart around me?"

"Yeah, other than that," I say, needing to keep clear of any talk of families for now.

"Okay... uh... I finished sixth form last year with all A's and an offer from my top university, but I freaked out and deferred. Now I'm working in a coffee shop while secretly harbouring a desire to forget it all and become a stripper."

I damn near spray her with the mouthful of hot chocolate I'd just sipped.

"You okay?" she asks when I start coughing up the bit that went down the wrong way.

"I wasn't expecting that."

She shrugs. "I'd hate to be predictable. What about you?"

"Similar. Well, aside from the stripping thing. Not sure I've got the rhythm for that."

She smiles. "Bullshit, you're a good dancer."

"Glad you think so. But seriously, I'm still in sixth form. Doing my third year because—"

"You're scared of the future too?" she guesses.

"Yeah, something like that. I want uni but..."

"It's terrifying?"

4
_____

JODIE

"This is me," I say sadly as Toby indicates and pulls to a stop outside my house.

He'd offered to take me somewhere else after our waffles, but I refused, knowing that I really needed to get back for Mum. It's probably wishful thinking that she'll emerge from her room, but still. I know I need to be here just in case.

"Cute house," he says, looking past me at the small terrace building.

"It was my stepdad's," I say sadly, unease about my future trickling through me.

With him gone and Mum being eaten alive with grief, I have no clue what's going to happen now. Did he own the house? Are there mortgage payments that need to be made? Can we even afford them on just my wage?

I need answers, but I'm not sure where to even start to try to find them.

I blow out a long, painful breath and close my eyes.

"I'm sure everything will be okay," Toby assures me, reaching over and squeezing my thigh.

Ripping my eyes open, I stare into his intense blue ones. I get sucked in immediately, just like I did last Friday night.

What is it about this guy that's different from anyone I've ever met?

"Yeah, I'm sure it'll all work out."

Pulling my key from my pocket, I shift, ready to get out. Already regretting this decision to come home.

Part of me is tempted to invite him in, but I know I can't.

"Thank you for tonight, for the waffles," I say sincerely. "I must have some kind of luck on my side, right?"

Glancing over, I lose myself in his eyes once more as they sparkle with something that makes butterflies erupt within me.

"Can I see you again?" he asks, his eyes bouncing between mine.

Biting down on my bottom lip, I fight to stop myself telling him that I'm free tomorrow night. Hell, I'm free every night when I'm not working. But I can't. I can't lose myself in him in the hope that he'll stop me from drowning when I've got more important things to be dealing with.

"I'll message you," I offer.

"That sounds like a brush off," he says with a smirk. "I can't accept that."

"It's not, I promise. My life is just... a fucking mess right now."

"I get it."

"I'm working all weekend and then—"

"It's okay," he says, reaching over and cupping my cheek. "We'll figure something out," he promises. "But I'm going to need something to tide me over."

"Oh yeah?" I ask, my eyes dipping to his mouth as he drags his teeth over his bottom lip.

"Yeah," he confirms before slipping his hand around the back of my neck, pulling me closer and slamming his lips on mine.

A deep groan rumbles in my throat as his tongue finds mine with deep licks.

I sag in his hold, kissing him back just as fiercely.

After the past few hours of relentless flirting and reminders of our first time together, I've been damn near panting for this.

Every single nerve ending in my body tingles as his fingers gently tighten on the nape of my neck as if he can't get close enough.

My body burns as his kiss continues, and I am fucking here for it.

Everything around us vanishes as I lose myself in him, realising that I probably made a mistake not taking him up on his offer for more tonight, but equally knowing it was the right thing to do.

A few minutes later, I reluctantly pull away, but he only lets me move an inch.

Opening my eyes, I gasp at the hunger staring back at me.

"What I wouldn't give for another night with you, Demon."

I swallow thickly in an attempt to stop myself from begging for exactly that.

Keep your head, Jodie.

"Soon," I promise.

His brow rests against mine, his eyes still holding mine captive.

"Call me if you need anything."

"Anything?" I ask, quirking my brow.

"Anything," he confirms.

"I should probably..." I point over my shoulder.

"One more." He has our lips together before he even finishes talking.

That one kiss turned into many as we both kept caving to our need to continue. But as much as I expected him to up the ante, he never did. I'm not sure if I'm impressed with his willpower or disappointed that I couldn't shatter it. I can't deny that I was all for another cheeky grope to feel exactly what I was doing to him. And I know he was hard, because even in the dim light of the front of his car, I could see the bulge in his jeans.

Eventually, he lets me escape, and I walk toward our front door on shaky legs.

After stepping inside, I wave him off and shut myself inside before I change my mind.

I've barely got my coat off when I feel my phone buzz.

A smile twitches at my lips as my heart begins to race.

Toby: Thanks for the second best night of my life.

I can't help but laugh.

Jodie: Thank you for being exactly what I needed. Again.

With a smile still playing on my lips and my skin still tingling with desire from his kiss and innocent touch, I kick my boots off and head deeper into the house.

The last thing I want to do after the past few hours is check in on Mum and have my reality come crashing down around my feet, but I know I don't have a choice.

"Fuck, Mum," I gasp the second I push the door open and find her curled up in a ball on the floor beside her bed, still clutching a bottle of vodka. The bottle of vodka I clearly didn't do a good enough job of hiding in the freezer. "Mum?" I ask as I flip on the light. But she doesn't react.

Stepping up to her, I pull the bottle from her hands, discovering that she hasn't actually drunk all of it because she's sopping wet.

"Jesus Christ," I mutter, my entire body aching to walk back out of the house and get back into Toby's car, demanding he take me away from all of this and forget it all exists.

"Mum," I shout, taking her cheeks in my hands. "I need you to wake up and help me." But it does nothing.

Tucking my hands under her armpits, I suck in a deep breath and haul her from the floor before sliding her onto the bed.

The second I release her, she falls back.

I stand there staring at her with my heart in pieces.

I don't even recognise her.

I understand how much she's hurting. I'm hurting too.

But I'm still here, and I selfishly can't help thinking that she's forgotten that fact.

A silent tear runs down my cheek and drips from my chin.

"I don't know how to fix this, Mum," I confess on a sob. "I need help."

But I get nothing.

My heart starts to race as panic begins to set in.

I shouldn't have gone out tonight, and I certainly shouldn't have agreed to a date—or whatever that was—with Toby, leaving Mum alone to do this to herself.

Using every ounce of strength I've got, I manage to sit her up, but she's completely soaked through.

"Mum?" I say loudly, in the hope of waking her up. "Mum," I snap, my despair and panic melding into some kind of anger that I can't control. "I'm going to need you to wake up and help me," I tell her, but it's pointless.

"Fine," I hiss. "Don't say I didn't warn you."

By some freaking miracle, I manage to get us both to the bathroom without us crashing to the floor.

She might not look awake, but I'm pretty sure she's putting some effort in.

"Ready?" I ask, although I already know I'm

not going to get a response as I turn the shower on and allow us both to get blasted by freezing cold water.

Mum jolts the second it hits her skin and her eyes fly open.

"Jodie?" she slurs, her glassy eyes staring into mine.

A thick ball of emotion lodges itself in my throat, and I have to swallow a couple of times before I'm able to speak again.

"You need to stop doing this, Mum. It's not going to bring them back."

She drops her head, resting it on my shoulder, a pained whimper falling from her lips.

"I know, baby. I'm sorry."

I help her clean up and then guide her back to her bedroom, finding her a clean nightie and getting her into bed. The whole time, tears cling to my lashes as I fight to keep the emotion inside. Seeing me fall apart isn't going to help her.

"Tomorrow will be a better day," I promise her, knowing that I'm lying to both of us. Tomorrow will just be another day like today, full of pain, heartache, and indescribable grief.

Turning the light off and slipping from her room, I discard the bottle before walking straight back into the bathroom and stripping out of my wet clothes.

I turn the shower up as high as it'll go and step under it, wishing I could wash everything about my life right now down the drain with the water.

Well... maybe not everything.

Images of Toby smiling at me from across the table tonight flicker through my mind.

He's like a beam of light in all my darkness.

My relief from the grief.

My life raft in the middle of my pool of despair.

What are the chances of him finding me twice when I needed him most?

Maybe fate isn't so bad after all.

I lay in bed long after I should have rolled over and closed my eyes with my phone in my hand, debating whether to message him again or not.

I'd hoped that I might find something waiting for me when I got back from sorting out Mum, but I was disappointed.

My message to him had been read, but that was it.

It's been a while since I've met anyone I wanted more than a quick hookup with, and I'm not sure I like the need bubbling beneath my skin for him to text me back.

We've had one night together—a night in a freaking sex club—and one waffle date, and I'm already turning into one of those annoying girlfriends.

I really need to get a grip.

Abandoning my phone on my bedside table, I finally curl up, ready for sleep to claim me. But it never does.

Images of my time with Toby tonight blur with those of finding Mum passed out and covered in her own poison, and I soon find myself drowning once more as my tears and grief soak my pillow.

My heart clenches as I think about everything I've lost: my brother's cheeky smile, my stepdad's calm support, Mum's compassion and endless love.

She might still be right down the hall, but I've never felt so lonely in all my life.

Loud, ugly sobs rip from my throat as I let it all consume me, once again wishing I'd let him drive me away from here. If I'd gone with him, all of this could be a distant memory right now.

5

TOBY

"**D**ude, it's Friday night. Where the fuck are you?" Nico barks through the speakers of my car. "I swear to fuck, if you're out getting laid without me then—"

"I'm just pulling up."

"Where the fuck have you been?"

"Out," I snap, wondering when I started having to report my whereabouts to my best friend. "I'm coming up now. Open your door for me."

"No need, man. We're in your place."

"You're... of fucking course you are." I roll my eyes, pulling into my space in the underground garage beneath our building.

Everyone else seems to be here, so I'm half expecting to find the whole gang sitting inside my flat.

I get that they're trying to help, trying to

cheer me up, to drag me from the pits of hell I've fallen into, and I appreciate it, I really do, But I don't think some vodka, weed, and a night out will really cut it.

Being balls deep in Jodie might just, though...

Fuck. Why did I let her out of my fucking car?

Reaching down, I squeeze my lingering semi.

It's been the same all week. One thought of her and up he pops like a fucking junkie thinking he's about to get another hit.

Pulling my phone out, I stare down at her message as I step into the lift and head to our floor.

The building we live in is still empty. Hell, it's still a building site other than the basement, garage, and top two floors—exactly as it should stay, as far as I'm concerned. I love that this is our little haven and ours only.

The good, the bad, and the downright fucking filthy happens here, and no one knows about it. It's perfect.

Theo and Nico, the Cirillo family heirs, have the two penthouses on the top floor. The rest of us occupy the four flats beneath.

All of us bar Alex have properly moved in. He's still flitting between here and his dad's place. Fuck knows why—he never used to want to be there. His dad has probably got a new housekeeper he's screwing every chance he gets or something equally as fucked up. He's just as bad as Nico. Fucking dogs.

Tapping the side of my phone, I debate messaging Jodie back, but I finally decide against it, figuring that I'd rather be talking to her in person and knowing that I'm probably about to be distracted by Nico's bullshit.

I let myself into my flat, expecting voices to hit me, but it's weirdly quiet. Well, that is until a loud moan fills the air around me.

"I swear to fucking God, if you're screwing someone on my—"

I burst into my living room, more than ready to put a bullet through my friend for using my flat as a fuck pad, but I come up short when both Nico and Alex fall about laughing as I realise the moaning is coming from the TV.

"What the fuck?" I bark. "Since when did I say you could let yourselves in to watch fucking porn?" Reaching for the remote that's sitting on the coffee table between them, I turn it off.

"Well, clearly you weren't out getting laid," Nico quips.

"Or beating anyone up," Alex adds, looking down at my fists.

My teeth grind as I stare at the two of them.

"Come on, we're going out," Nico says, hopping up, Alex quickly following him.

"I'm not in the mood."

"Bro, I need to pay you back for last weekend."

"What happened last weekend?" Alex asks, picking up a row of beer bottles he'd been collecting on the floor.

"It was fucking epic. Tobes found us these two girls and we—"

"Nic," I warn, not wanting him to go into details about Jodie.

His eyes find mine before he rolls them. Dickhead.

"We took them to Hades," he says proudly.

"Fuck off, did you."

"For real, bro. That place is off the fucking hook."

"Well, what the fuck are we waiting for? And, by the way," Alex adds, glaring at me, "why the fuck wasn't I invited? You know how badly I've wanted to check that place out."

"It was an impromptu thing," Nico says, trying to dig me out of a hole that he happily threw me into only moments ago.

"I'll come, but we're not going to Hades," I state.

"Oh, come on. I wanna get all kinky and shit," Alex whines like a little bitch.

"We'll go to the Avenue and find a girl to share. How's that?" Nico offers.

"Share? Fuck you, man. I need a girl's full attention tonight, thank you very much."

"Tobes?" Nico offers.

"I'm not sharing shit with you," I mutter, heading back toward my front door once more.

"You're still gagging for a repeat of last week, huh?" he mutters behind me. "Whoa, wait... that's where you've been, isn't it?"

"I don't know what you're talking about," I shoot over my shoulder.

"Fuck me, man. You're the shittest liar I've ever met."

Flipping him off, I reluctantly head out, ready for a night being a wingman for those two dickheads. I guess it beats being home alone and drowning in my own head.

Rolling over, I groan as I rip my tongue from the roof of my mouth and my stomach twists.

But that's nothing compared to the shock that rocks through me when I bump against another body.

What the—

I sit bolt upright, my room spinning around me as I stare down at the person I'm sharing a bed with.

"What the actual fuck, bro?" I bark, shoving Nico so hard that his naked arse rolls out of my bed and he wakes as his solid weight collides with the floor.

"Dude," he groans. "Was that fucking necessary?"

"Yes," I hiss, swinging my legs over the side of the bed as his head appears.

"You were more fun when you were drunk."

I scrub my hands down my face as I try to recall the events from the night before.

"I don't remember."

"Hardly surprising. You were fucking wasted."

"Jesus."

"Fucking awesome night though, man," he announces, finally getting to his feet and stretching his arms over his head.

"Fucking really?" I hiss, getting more than an eyeful of his morning wood.

"Surprised he's got any energy left. That girl last night sucked like a fucking—"

Stalking across the room, I swing my bathroom door closed, cutting him off.

"A fucking vacuum," he bellows.

I take a piss before stopping at the basin, wrapping my fingers around the edge and hanging my head as it pounds rhythmically.

I really hope it was a fucking good night for how much it hurts.

I just look up when my door swings open and

a still butt-fucking-naked Nico strolls in with his cock in his hand.

"Fuck off home," I bark.

"And leave you lonely with no memory of last night? That girl you were with was banging, by the way," he says, relieving himself.

"What girl?"

"Fucked if I know. I fucked mine in the alley and I have no idea what her name was."

"Tell me I didn't do anything," I beg, feeling uneasy as images of Jodie flicker through my mind.

Fuck knows why. It's not like we're together or I owe her anything. But still, it feels wrong.

"Hell if I know. You had your tongue down her throat when I left."

"God damn it."

"What?" he asks, leaning into my shower and turning it on.

"Oh sure, help yourself," I mutter, reaching for my toothbrush.

"When don't I?" he deadpans. "So what, you kissed some chick? What's the big deal? It's not like you actually want Jodie. She's a game, right?"

"Yeah," I agree after spitting out my toothpaste. "Just a game," I confess, hating the way those words twist up my insides.

"So do what you need to do. Get all this shit, him, out of your system. Then, we can start looking forward. There's a whole world out there,

Tobes. A world full of hot women just gagging for a piece of us."

Dropping my toothbrush into its holder, I turn to look at Nico as he makes use of my shampoo.

"What?" he asks. "Wanna join me and scrub my back?"

My top lip peels back in disgust.

"No. Just wondering why I'm friends with such a horny dickhead," I say before taking off.

"You love me and we both know it. Remember that time we—" I swing the door closed on him for the second time in ten minutes, find a pair of sweats, and head toward my kitchen for coffee. Coffee and painkillers. I'm going to need plenty of both if Nico's going to insist on hanging around.

I find my phone on the floor next to one of my shoes, a not-quite-empty bottle of vodka, and what I think is Nico's shirt... along with a pair of bright red knickers.

"Brilliant," I mutter to myself. Picking up my shit and leaving his shirt and the underwear that I'm sure has something to do with him for him to deal with.

I'm watching my liquid gold fill my mug when his heavy footsteps head my way.

"Ah, my prize," he announces. "Oh, and so damn sweet."

I grimace, knowing exactly what he's doing without needing to turn around.

"You're disgusting."

"Tell me, Tobes, what did you do with the pair you stole from Jodie last weekend?" he asks smugly while my fingers curl around the kitchen counter. "Don't lie to me now," he teases.

"Then you know exactly where they are, and we don't need to discuss it."

"She's really got you all twisted up, huh?"

"It's not like that," I hiss.

"No? So what is it like? Wanna tell me some details yet?" he asks, marching up to me and stealing my coffee.

Resting his ass back against the counter, he sips it, burning his mouth.

With a smirk, I grab another mug and start the process again.

"Don't have one," I lie, hating that I feel guilty for it.

"So last night's video bootycall wasn't planned, then?" It takes a couple of seconds for his words to register. But when they do, my heart drops into my feet.

"Last night's..." In a rush, I drag my phone from my pocket and open my chat with Jodie, my heart racing at a mile an hour.

Whatever's left of last night's alcohol in my stomach almost makes a reappearance when I find the evidence of a video call.

"Oh my God," I breathe. "What did I say to her?"

"Fuck knows. I went and crashed in your bed."

"Shit. Shit. Fuck."

There are no messages after our call ended.

That's got to be a bad thing.

"Shit."

"I'm sure it's fine. You probably just told her how much you wanted to tie her up and fuck her again or something," he suggests with a shrug.

"Yeah, maybe," I whisper. Or I told her fucking everything and ruined my plan before it's even really begun. "I need to talk to her."

"I fucking knew she'd got you whipped already. Was she really that good a lay?"

My lips part to agree, because she was fucking epic. But then I think of the bigger picture, and the memories from that night begin to twist and morph into darker thoughts of a man not so far away.

"I just want to get some truth."

"Bullshit," he spits. "You want to hurt him. And you're going to use her to do it."

I stare at him, my mouth opening and closing like a fucking goldfish.

"I know you, Tobes. Better than you know yourself. Talk to me. Hell knows I'm not going to judge you for any of it. If it helps get your head back on straight, then I'll even help you.

53

"I hate seeing you like this. I hate knowing you're suffering and we can't do anything about it."

"Fuck, Nic. That's deep for you."

"Bro, you're my ride or die. I'd raise hell for you and you know it."

I smile at him. "I know, and I appreciate it. But this is something I need to do myself."

"So... I don't get to fuck her friend again then?"

"O-oh, now it all makes sense," I tease.

"She was hot, man. Best I've had all year."

I make a show of looking at the calendar hanging on the wall beside me that Mum bought me for Christmas and quirk a brow.

"I know it's early, but I'm telling you, it's gonna take a lot to top her."

I shake my head at him.

"Don't you judge me, Doukas," he laughs.

"Been doing that for years, mate. Doesn't make you change though, does it?"

"As if you would want me to," he scoffs. "Can't top perfection, my friend. Right, I'm out. Theo and I have a meeting with the old men."

He drains his coffee, dumps the dirty mug into my sink, and takes off.

"Out again tonight?" he shouts before letting himself out.

"Fuck no. I've got plans."

"Grovelling, you mean. I'm sure you didn't embarrass yourself that badly."

"That's the least of my worries, mate," I shout back, but the door slams before I get an answer. "Shit."

I scrub my hand down my face, desperate to recall some memories from the night before, but there's nothing. Well, nothing after a few too many shots at the bar at the Avenue and Alex disappearing with some blonde.

What the fuck did I say to her?

6

JODIE

My feet ache and my movements are getting slower, but I feel better than I have in weeks. And I know exactly why.

I might have been scared to walk back into this place today and have to force the smile on my face, but it's been nowhere near as bad as I was expecting.

Matt, my manager, has been incredible, and so have the other girls I've worked with today. None of them looked at me in sympathy. None of them pitied me coming back to work after another devastating loss that's turned my world on its head. They just got on with it and dragged me right along with them, allowing me to lose myself in being normal.

It was nice. Almost enjoyable. And a little mid-afternoon visit from my favourite person in the world to check in on me didn't go amiss either. Even if she was half asleep after predictably pulling an all-nighter.

Bri kept me company on my break and then eagerly headed off, warning me that she was going for a nap and then we were going out tonight.

As much as I wanted to complain about my feet and that I wanted to stay in, my need to find the old me was too strong to ignore, and I quickly found myself agreeing.

I didn't tell her about Toby. I don't know why. It wasn't intentional. The words just got stuck in my throat. I felt weirdly good about having something for myself for once. I'm not sure I'll be able to keep the secret for long, especially when we start drinking later, but for now, I'm enjoying the rush.

Saturday might be one of the city's busiest days of the week, but on our side of town, things begin to slow down not long after the sun sets. Especially at this time of year.

Trisha and Paula, who work part-time shifts, have already left for the day, leaving me and Matt to finish up for the night.

We've only got three customers when I push through the door with a box of disposable cups in my hands, ready to restock everything for tomorrow.

There are a couple of young women locked

in a heated discussion, and there's what I assume is a guy sitting on one of the sofas by the window with his hood up, staring at his phone.

Hoping that none of them are expecting to hang around for the long haul, I join Matt behind the counter and open my box.

"Any exciting plans for the night?" he asks as he cleans the coffee machine.

"Going out with Bri," I say with a smile, more than ready for a standard Saturday night with my girl. "You?"

"Same. But with the guys," he quickly adds.

Matt's great. I couldn't ask for a better manager. And despite his slightly rough exterior, he's been more than supportive with everything that's happened over the past few weeks. He's allowed me to have the time I've needed and given me something of a safe haven when I've returned. This place is my home away from home, and I know that most of that is because of the way he runs it.

We fall into easy conversation about our plans for the night as the two women bring their mugs over to help us out before leaving. Both of them openly eye-fuck Matt, making me roll my eyes. It's a pretty common occurrence. He's hot, and he has the bad boy look down to a fine art. The only difference is that I know that under it all, he's a good guy.

"One down and then we lock up, yeah?"

Matt asks, his eyes shooting over to the guy by the window once his admirers have left.

"Sure thing, boss." I salute him like an idiot before heading back out to the stock room for more refills.

"Motherfucker," I hiss when the bottom of a box falls out, depositing hundreds of disposable lids all over the floor.

Dropping to my knees, I set about picking them all up as my mind drifts to the video call last night.

A smile twitches at my lips as I think of Toby's drunk face as he smiled at me through the phone. He was wasted. Beyond wasted. It's the reason I've told myself over and over not to put too much weight on all the things he said to me. But it doesn't matter how many times I repeat the words in my head—my heart keeps running away with itself.

When I finally return, the coffee shop is empty and Matt is just twisting the key in the door before turning the sign to closed.

"We're good to go," he says with a smile.

Pulling his phone from his pocket, he reads whatever's on it before barking out a laugh.

"You can go. I've got this," I say, knowing that he's already done all the important stuff.

"Nah, it'll only take a few minutes."

"Honestly, Matt. You've already done enough for me. Go and enjoy your night."

He wants to argue, I can see it in his eyes, but he's also more than ready to get his weekend started. Unlike me, he doesn't work Sundays, so he's free to get as trashed as he wants tonight.

"Are you sure?" he finally asks.

"Yes. Bugger off," I joke.

"You're the best, Jo. It's good to have you back."

He smiles at me as I quickly return it, although I don't have the reaction to him most women do on the receiving end of that grin. He's hot—sure, there's no denying that. He's just... my boss. And nothing more.

"It's good to be back," I tell him honestly as he makes his way toward the staff-only door at the back of the shop.

"I'll let myself out. Thanks, Jo," are his parting words before the door slings closed behind him.

Silence settles around me as I take a moment to suck in a breath and ground myself.

I'd been dreading this shift for days, but now it's over I can't help feeling ridiculous for ever thinking it would be anything other than exactly what I needed.

Yeah, I'm worried about Mum and the state she might have got herself into while I've been gone. But there's no alcohol in the house, so unless she's strong enough to leave, or even order more, I'm hoping she'll have had a few hours detox at least.

Maybe me coming back to work can be the beginning of things slowly getting back to normal. Whatever 'normal' looks like these days with half of my family gone.

Blowing out a long breath, I banish those thoughts from my head and focus on the good in my life. A night out with Bri, and maybe, if I'm lucky, another late-night chat with Toby.

I'm smiling like an idiot at memories from last night again when a door closes behind me.

"Did you forget somethi—" My words falter when I turn around, not finding who I was expecting.

Instead of Matt rushing back in, I find the guy who was sitting on the sofa not so long ago.

Well, I'm assuming it's the same person, because he's wearing a black hoodie.

"What the hell are you doing in here?" I ask in a rush, my brow wrinkling with confusion as I stare into familiar intense blue eyes.

He closes the space between us and my heart begins to gallop in my chest at the longing on his face.

I back up, bumping against the counter as he continues to prowl toward me like a lion stalking its prey.

"Funny story," he starts, reaching up to push

the hood from his head as the rapid movement of my chest starts bordering on embarrassing.

"Toby," I breathe, already beyond turned on but also slightly afraid of the glint in his eye right now.

He doesn't stop until his hands land on either side of my waist on the counter and his breaths are racing over my face.

"When I looked at my phone this morning, I found evidence of a thirty-minute video call with you last night." He moves closer, his rough jaw brushing against my cheek and sending a bolt of electricity shooting straight to my clit.

His lips brush my ear and I have to stifle a groan as my body grows hotter and hotter with the heat of him seeping into me.

"I need you to remind me what I might have said," he growls in my ear.

"Oh my God," I breathe when he nips my ear.

"Y-you..." I stutter, barely able to get my brain to function as his lips brush the sensitive skin of my throat.

What is it about this guy? He manages to disarm me at every turn by knowing exactly what I need.

I've been burning for this since climbing from his car last night. And then listening to his filthy words through the phone a few hours later. How I managed not to reach for my vibrating little friend the second the call disconnected is beyond me. I deserve a fucking medal for that shit.

"I what, Demon?" he growls, the timbre of his voice hitting me exactly as I'm sure he intends.

I quickly realise that there are two sides to this man. The restrained, sweet guy who looked after me last night, and then this darker, demanding side that turns me to a desperate ball of need. And I'm more than happy to take this one right now, because fuck...

"You told me all the things you wished you could have done to me last night instead of driving away."

He pauses with his lips against my pulse point, and they pull into a smile.

"Go on," he demands.

Oh my God.

I squeeze my eyes closed as the pure filth that came from his lips comes back to me.

"You said... you said you wanted to eat me until I screamed your name."

A deep growl rumbles in his chest as he kisses down my neck.

"Keep going."

"You said you wanted me to choke on your dick, wanted me to take your cum like a good little girl."

His hands move and he unties my apron before pulling it over my head and discarding it somewhere behind him.

"Did I tell you how I'd fuck you?" he asks, his lips grazing my collarbone before his fingers flick open the top few buttons on my shirt, exposing my bra.

"Any way you could get me. Over and over."

"Sounds about right," he whispers, suddenly tucking his fingers into the cups of my bra and exposing me.

Finally, he pulls back, his dark and dangerous eyes finding mine.

"Say yes, Jodie," he demands, his voice commanding and dominant.

"Yes," I breathe despite my better judgement.

His lips crash against mine as his hands find the backs of my thighs and my feet leave the ground.

He carries me over to where the counter is lowest and rests my arse on it as his tongue dives past my lips, giving me little choice but to join in—not that I'd want to be doing anything else, of course.

The best kind of pain shoots down my spine when he drags my band from my hair and twists his fingers in the lengths, angling me exactly as he wants me.

"Oh my God," I pant like a desperate whore when he finally releases me, and I fight to catch my breath as he descends my body in search of my aching breasts. "Toby, fuck," I cry when his lips close around one of my nipples. "Oh Jesus. Fuck."

"He's not going to help you right now, Demon," Toby growls as he switches sides.

"W-we should— shit," I gasp when he bites down on me. "We should g-go somewhere."

"I'm good right here."

"B-but..." I look over my shoulder at the floor-to-ceiling windows that cover the front of the shop.

Releasing me, he twists around, searching for something.

He finds what he's looking for and slams his hand down on the light switches, plunging us into darkness—or as dark as it's going to get with the emergency lighting above us.

"Better?" My eyes still remain on the empty street outside as my stomach twists with nervous excitement.

Toby was right last night when he told me I liked the risk of being caught, being watched.

His fingers grasp my chin and he turns my head back so I have no choice but to look him in the eyes.

"The only people who watch will be jealous as fuck. They'll be out there, wishing they were lucky enough to be standing where I am, tasting what I am."

"You're crazy," I tell him honestly.

"Oh, baby. I'm a lot worse than that, trust me."

Any response I might have had is quickly forgotten when his lips find mine once more and his fingers go for my waistband.

I should tell him no, force him to back up and at least go out the back where we can have a bit of privacy, but I don't. I can't find it in me to even form the words as he kisses me so deeply, I forget my own goddamn name.

Lifting my hips, I help him out as he tugs my jeans and knickers over my hips and drags them down my legs.

My Converse hit the floor with a thud and my clothing quickly follows.

"Oh fuck," I moan, my back arching when he runs two fingers through my pussy.

"You've been thinking about everything I said last night all day, haven't you?"

"Yes," I cry. "Please. Toby, please."

"Did you get yourself off to images of all the things I told you I wanted to do to you?"

I shake my head. "No."

"Why?"

"B-because it wouldn't have been the same. I wanted you. I needed you."

"Right fucking answer, baby."

He rewards me by pushing two thick fingers inside me and curling them to hit the most blissful spot.

"Oh my God, oh my God," I chant as he works me, remembering just how incredible he was last weekend and all the reasons I've been dreaming of a repeat ever since.

The angle changes, and when I rip my eyes open, I discover why.

His knees hit the floor, and he leans forward, swiping at my swollen clit with his burning hot tongue.

Holding myself up on weak arms, I watch every second of him working me higher and higher with perfect precision.

In only minutes, I'm balancing on the edge of what I know is going to be an earth-shattering release.

Every single one he gave me last time was nothing if not mind-blowing, and I know this time is going to be no different.

He doesn't let up until he's dragged every second of pleasure out of me.

"Just as sweet as I remember," he confesses, wiping his mouth with the back of his hand, hiding his grin.

Reaching out, he grabs the bottom of my shirt and tugs harshly. The remaining few buttons fly off, pinging around the shop as they come to a stop.

His fingers grip my hips and I'm dragged off the counter and placed back on my feet.

My shocked gasp rips through the air when

his fingers collar my throat, a whimper of need ripping from my lips.

His head dips and my lips part, ready for the kiss I so desperately need... but he never gives it to me.

"Turn around and bend over. I want to see your pretty pussy before I fuck it so hard you'll be feeling it for the rest of the weekend."

"Yes," I moan, quickly following orders as I gasp, a shudder ripping through me as I press my heated skin to the cold counter.

7

TOBY

I've done a lot of fucked-up shit in my life thanks to the family I was born into, but never has any kind of revenge mission been quite so pleasurable and... addictive.

I take a step back and admire the sight before me.

Jodie is folded over the counter, her arse in the air and her greedy, slick cunt right there, begging to be taken, ruined by none other than me.

Giving her boss the slip and shutting myself in the bathroom instead of leaving was a risk. I'd watched her for long enough before the funeral to know that she often sent people away so she could lock up and have a little quiet time alone. But knowing that this could be the reward, it was a risk worth taking.

My mouth waters as I stare at her. My desire

to make her come over my face again is strong, but not as strong as my need to sink as deep inside her as her body will allow.

Now knowing what I said to her last night, it's no wonder I woke up in such a shitty mood when I discovered the naked body in my bed was Nico. I've been horny and frustrated all day. And now I know why. No amount of jerking off was ever going to sate the need burning through my veins like the real thing will.

"I've been dreaming about this pussy for a week," I tell her honestly, stepping back up to her and rubbing her arse with my palm.

Her back arches as she offers herself to me.

"You like a little pain with your pleasure, don't you, Demon?"

"Anything. Toby, please."

My cock aches at hearing her cry out my name, precum leaking from the tip with my need for her.

Lifting my hand, she gasps, predicting what's coming next.

Crack.

She howls beautifully as the pain blooms and my fingers twitch to go again.

"More," she begs.

"You're a filthy girl, Demon," I growl before raising my hand again.

Her reaction is just as blissful the second time, but as much as I could continue to ensure my handprint is glowing bright red on her arse, my need to take her is stronger.

Ripping my fly open, I push my jeans down my hips and quickly line up with her entrance.

"This is going to be hard and fast. Are you ready?"

"For you? Alwaaaaays," she screams when I drag her back, my fingers digging into her hips as I impale her on my cock.

"Yessss," I hiss as her heat surrounds me and her muscles try sucking me deeper despite having bottomed out in her. "Fuck, yes. My little demon," I groan before giving it to her exactly as I promised.

***

"Holy shit, I needed that," she forces out between her heaving breaths as I pull out of her.

A laugh falls from my lips, but I can't help but agree. A week has been far too fucking long.

"Toby," she moans when I quickly replace my cock with my fingers, needing to feel my cum inside her.

"You're so full of me, Demon. Can you feel it?"

"Pretty sure I'm going to be feeling it for the next few hours," she deadpans.

Ripping my fingers from her body, I grab a

handful of her hair and drag her from the counter so her back is to my chest.

"Open," I demand, pushing my two fingers into her mouth. "See how sweet we taste."

A moan rumbles in her chest a beat before someone starts hammering on the windows.

"Oh fuck," Jodie gasps, and before I know what's happening, she's ducked beneath the counter, leaving me still standing there with my semi still proudly on display.

"Toby," she hisses. "Someone was watching."

Shrugging, I tuck myself away before moving around to get a better look.

If it's some dirty old man standing there with his own cock out, then he might very well regret it in about ten seconds' time.

But as it is, a laugh rips from my throat when I recognise the face smooshed against the glass.

"You can come out," I say to Jodie. "I think our spectator has seen it all before."

Walking over to the door, I flip the locks open and let her in.

"That was fucking hot," Brianna announces, rushing inside. "Seriously, I thought this place was about to go up in flames."

"Bri, what the hell?" Jodie snaps, finally popping up from behind the counter, her cheeks glowing red even in the dim light. "I thought you were meeting me at mine."

"Yeah, well. I thought I'd surprise you. It

seems I was the one who got a shock." She fans herself. "Where's your friend?" she asks, turning to me. "I could sure make use of him right about now."

"I left him at home, playing with himself," I quip.

She gets this faraway look in her eyes, and her teeth sink into her bottom lip as if she's imagining him at home doing just that.

Jesus.

"You going out tonight, Tobias?" she asks once she's got over herself and Jodie has emerged from the counter, looking almost put back together.

"You ruined my shirt," she says, holding open flaps where the buttons are missing.

"Whoops. I'll buy you a new one."

She waves me off.

"And, I don't know. I'm sure Nico could be convinced, though," I say to Brianna.

"We're probably going to hit The Spot again, if you fancy it," she offers, my eyes finding Jodie to see what she thinks about the suggestion. "What do you say, Jojo? Want a do-over of last weekend?"

Jodie's lips part, her eyes darkening as she remembers.

"Uh..."

"We'll take that as a yes. She'll message you when we're there. But it might take a while.

Looking this good takes effort," she says, pointing to herself.

"I'm sure it does," I mutter, beginning to understand why she and Nico got on so well.

Turning my back on her, I step up to Jodie and wrap my hand around the back of her neck.

"You want us to come meet you tonight? Or have you already had enough of me?"

"I guess that depends," she breathes, tilting her head to the side.

"On?" I ask, more than curious about where she's going with this.

"Will you reappear as the Toby who kisses me sweetly in his car and lets me walk away frustrated, or tonight's Toby, where you take me no matter what?"

My grip on her tightens as I dip down to kiss her.

"I wouldn't want to ruin the surprise, baby."

"God, you two are so sweet, it's sickening."

"You just watched him fuck me silly over the counter, Bri. Not sure we're all that sweet," Jodie jokes.

"It comes no sweeter than that, girl. You find a man who can't wait to even get you in the stock room to fuck you, then you hang onto him."

"Sound advice there, baby. You should probably take it."

"Jesus, you two are as bad as each other," she

mutters, accepting another kiss before pushing me away. "Go, I need to clean up."

I glance back over at the counter, trying to imagine just what Brianna saw.

"Sure. Message me, yeah? We'll be ready," I promise.

"So will we," Brianna says suggestively.

I flip the locks on the door once more, Jodie following so she can lock them both inside.

"Oh, and don't worry too much about the security cameras," I say loud enough for Brianna to hear. "Your boss seemed like a decent guy. I'm sure he'll be able to overlook it."

Jodie's face drops, all the blood draining out of it before she spins around, her eyes darting between the cameras. A little more guilt than I was expecting trickles through my veins as I watch her reaction, but I quickly force it away.

"Oh my God. Oh my God. Oh my God. He's going to sack me. Fuck. Toby," she whines, smacking me in the arm. "I need this job."

"It'll be fine. Relax. I'll see you later, yeah?" She lets me kiss her once more before I drag myself away from her and down the street with a smile on my face.

She doesn't need to worry. The only person who's going to see that video is me. She just doesn't need to know that.

"Nico," I bark after letting myself into his flat and marching toward the living room. "I've got a present for you. Polish your dick, we're—" My words falter when I emerge and find a face smiling at me that I wasn't expecting. "Sis, how's it going?"

"Good. Although your plans sound like they might be better," she deadpans.

"Uh..."

"Yes, bro," Nico booms from down the hall. "Please tell me it's what I think it is."

"What do you think it is?" Stella asks, already more than invested in finding out our plans.

"Nic," I warn.

"What? Your sister needs to learn sooner or later what a dirty dog you are."

"Jesus," I mutter, scrubbing my hand down my face as I fall onto the opposite sofa to my recently-discovered sister. "Don't listen to him, he's talking out of his—"

"Fuck off, am I," Nico scoffs.

"Toby, Toby, Toby," Stella mutters, making me cringe. "I thought you were the sweet one."

"Tsk. You need to get to know your brother better, Princess. Spoiler alert: He's not. He just plays a good game to cover up all his filthy kinks."

"Jesus fucking Christ." Dragging my eyes from my sister, I stare up at Nico, my eyes hard with frustration. "Forget what I said. I've retracted your invite. I'm more than man enough to take your place."

76

His mouth drops as Stella sucks in a shocked breath.

"Sorry to ruin the image, Princess. But I'm about as nice beneath the surface as the rest of these motherfuckers. I'm out."

Flipping Nico off, I march from his flat, unsurprisingly with Stella hot on my heels.

"Toby, wait," she calls, but I don't stop. I also don't take the lift down to the next floor for fear of being trapped in an enclosed space with her. I really don't need that intense level of interrogation right now.

I'm halfway down the stairs when she finally catches up with me.

"Toby, for fuck's sake," she hisses, her fingers wrapping around my upper arm to stop me. "I don't care about any of that," she says softer.

I pause, my chest heaving with frustration, my head swirling with confusion.

She's right, I used to be the nice one. As nice as it's possible to be when you're trained to maim, kill, and torture people from as young as you can remember, and you've lived a life full of stifling abuse.

I fought it. The darkness.

Everyone around me dove headfirst into the depravity we're surrounded by until they were swimming in it.

But every day, this life, my experiences have destroyed a little more of the lightness in my soul.

And this is the outcome: a man hell-bent on revenge on the man who tried to ruin everything around him, no matter the cost.

"You should," I spit, tugging my arm from her grip and continuing forward.

She doesn't say anything else, but that doesn't mean it's over. I know she's still following me instead of heading for her and Seb's flat.

I let myself in, leaving the door open for her.

"This life doesn't scare me, Toby. *You* don't scare me."

I turn to her, my nostrils flaring as I take in her blue eyes. Eyes so much like my fucking own. I have no clue how I didn't suspect something sooner. My breathing is erratic as she silently challenges me to talk, to let go of some of the anger that's eating away at my insides.

"He tried to fucking kill you," I boom, her small frame flinching at the volume of it.

"But he didn't win, Toby. We're all here. We all survived."

"Barely," I scoff.

"He's the only one suffering now. He—"

"Really? That's what you think?" I ask. "I might as well be locked in that fucking cell with him," I confess, although quietly.

"I know you're hurting," she breathes, taking a step closer, albeit hesitantly. "You have every right to be. All that shit with—" She cuts herself off before his name passes her lips. "It was fucked up. Everything has changed, and trust me, I know how hard that can be.

"But I hate this. I hate seeing you drowning. Refusing to really talk to anyone."

Lifting my hands to my hair, I tip my head back to look at the ceiling.

"I can't, Stella. If I talk—" *I'll explain my plans, and you'll all see the monster I really am.*

"It doesn't have to be one of us. Anyone. Please, Toby."

Releasing a breath and some of my anger with it, I step up to her and wrap my arms around her shoulders.

Things were weird for quite a while for me after discovering Stella and I were actually related. I played it off, scared that if I freaked out too badly about how I was feeling before that huge bomb was dropped, I would scare her off. And I needed her.

From the moment she turned up at Knight's Ridge, she was like a shining ray of light. I knew in my heart that she'd been sent for me. I just never could have guessed it was because she was my fucking sister. Something I really wish I'd known about before both jerking off to thoughts of her. And then kissing her.

Jesus, I'm just as screwed up as the rest of them.

Her arms slip around my waist as she rests her head on my chest. Her warmth seeps into my bones and I sigh in contentment as her strength surrounds me.

"Everything is going to be okay, Toby," she whispers, squeezing me tighter.

I grit my teeth as the words hit my ears. I fucking hate it when people say that, especially when they have no idea what the fuck I'm going through.

With Stella, it's not quite so bad, because I know that she does understand, to a point. Jonas Ariti tainted her life, too. Not as badly as mine, but she's experienced some of his wrath. It's only helped forge our bond. I just wish we could have connected in a way that didn't involve pain for both of us.

"So what are you doing tonight, then?" she asks when she finally pulls away.

A smile tugs at my lips as I rub at the back of my neck.

There's a part of me that really wants to confide in Stella about Jodie. She'd understand. I'm sure she would. But can I risk the chance that she doesn't?

Stella's smart. Smarter than all of us motherfuckers she's found herself in the middle of. I have no doubt she'd come at the whole thing from a different angle and try to talk me out of it.

She won't be able to, though. And then she'll just look at me like a monster when I continue with my plan.

"I'm assuming there's a girl involved," she says happily, curling herself into the middle seat of my corner sofa, looking like she's in for the long haul with this conversation.

"Uh... you want a drink?" I offer, feeling like I'm going to need one—or five—for this.

"Sure. Surprise me," she says with a smile that helps settle the unease within me that has only been growing since I walked away from Jodie earlier.

My phone damn near burns a hole in my pocket. My need to message her and to find that security footage from the coffee shop earlier is almost too much to ignore.

It was just pure luck on my part that she just so happens to work in a Cirillo-owned business. And pure bad luck for her that it's given me even more access to her life. Something I fully intend on making use of.

Spotting the cranberry juice Stella insisted I buy for her in my fridge when she, Seb, Alex, and Nico turned up one night for an impromptu housewarming slash cheer-Toby-the-fuck-up party, I pull it out.

After making her drink, I grab myself a beer and head back over.

"So..." she prompts the second my arse hits the cushion.

"You're like a dog with a bone," I point out, much to her amusement.

"I've always wanted a sibling to torture. Humour me with all your dark and dirty secrets, Tobes," she teases.

"You asked for it," I mutter, deciding to just dive in headfirst with this conversation. "Ever heard of Hades, Princess?"

Her brow crinkles. "The Greek god? Yeah, obviously." She takes a sip of her drink. "But I'm not thinking that's what you're talking about."

"Hades is a sex club a few streets away." I gasp when she sprays my brand-new light grey sofa in fucking vodka cranberry.

"Shit, I'm sorry. Get me some tissue or something."

"Jesus Christ," I mutter lightly as I stalk toward the kitchen to find something to attempt to save my sofa from being turned pink.

"Okay. Sex club. I'm totally listening."

"I thought you might," I quip. "Surprised Seb hasn't taken you."

Her eyes widen at my comment. "Well, he's going to be now that I know about it."

"I do love having a sweet and innocent little sister," I deadpan.

"Fuck off. You wouldn't have it any other way."

I can't help but smile at her. She's right. She's exactly what I need.

"Well, Nic and I met a couple of girls last

Friday night. We took them there for a bit of fun. Nico is gagging for another chance with his girl."

"That's... unlike Nico," she points out.

"Yeah, there are only a couple who've seen his shrivelled-up, overused dick more than once."

"Ugh," Stella shudders. "The image," she says before faux gagging, making me laugh. "And you don't want a repeat?" Her brow lifts accusingly.

"Hell yeah, I do." A downright wicked smile pulls at Stella's lips. "Last Friday was... yeah." I rub the back of my neck awkwardly as I get as close as I have yet to talking about it honestly.

"You can talk to me, Toby. Nothing you say in confidence will ever leave my lips again."

"I know. I know. I trust you, Stel. I do. It just... I don't even know how to process it all, other than to turn it into anger, let alone talk about it.

"She was amazing," I confess in favour of avoiding talking about feelings. "The whole night was pretty insane, to be fair."

"Oh my God, you've fallen for her." Stella grins.

"What? No. It's been a week, and I've only seen her twice since."

'Oh my God,' Stella mouths excitedly, bouncing on the sofa.

"Do not do that," I say, pointing at where her

arse is actually leaving the cushion. "We're just having some fun. She's a good..."

"Lay?"

"Distraction," I say with a laugh.

"She's a good lay too though, right? I mean, she let you take her to a fucking sex club on your first night. She must be hella kinky."

My lips part to agree, but all I end up doing is laughing.

"This," I say, gesturing between the two of us, "isn't fucking normal."

"Fuck normal, Tobes. Nothing about our lives is normal. You might be my brother, but you were my friend first, and I don't want things to get all fucked-up and awkward just because we share some DNA. We like sex, so fucking what? Hell, you've seen me at it enough. You shouldn't feel weird telling me about some wild night."

"Jesus, Stella."

"What? I'm just saying, own it. None of us give a shit if you're into some kinky stuff. And clearly, your new girl must be more than willing." She wiggles her eyebrows at me. "I'm going to need to meet this girl, by the way. I think we could be friends."

"Yeah, no. That is not happening."

"Spoilsport." She pokes her tongue out at me and I laugh.

"If you convince Seb to take you to Hades— not that I think he'll need all that much convincing—make sure you tell me when. I am not walking in on that... again."

"Prude," she snorts.

"Oh yeah, that's the issue," I mutter before draining my beer. "You hanging out or..." I glance down toward my bedroom, more than aware that I need to shower before heading back out to find Jodie.

"I'm hanging, but don't think that you're going to get away without answering more of my questions."

Pushing from the sofa, I drop my bottle in the kitchen and immediately grab another. "Knew I should have shut the door in your face."

"Charming," she mutters, her voice closer than I was expecting.

"What are you doing?"

"Well... you're making me another, and then we're going to do a quick-fire round about your new girl while you shower."

I stare at her, waiting for her to laugh or tell me she's joking. She never does.

So, exactly as she described, we spend the next twenty minutes with me in the bathroom and her chilling out on my bed while shooting a million and one questions to me about Jodie.

Some I managed to dodge. Others seemed innocent enough that I answered honestly. When I refused to tell her the details of our night in Hades, her voice got that dangerous tone I've heard her use on Seb before, and I seriously thought she was going to march into the room and torture the information out of me.

"Looking good, Doukas," she teases when I finally emerge.

Being referred to by that name still feels weird, despite legally changing my name being the first thing I did after discovering the truth about who my father really was.

It felt weird, claiming the name of a man I barely knew, but it was a fuck load better than using the name of the cunt who'd tried to destroy every bit of light in my life, so I just went for it.

"You think she'll approve?" I ask, looking down at myself.

"You look like a Greek god, Tobes. She won't be able to resist you."

"Two times in one day. I must have something working for me."

Her chin drops at my words.

"You've already seen her today."

A smirk curls at my lips.

"Might have." I wink.

"And I thought Nico was the dog," she quips right as the man himself shouts through my flat.

"Down here, asshole," Stella bounces back.

"Bro, I don't think Jodie will be all too pleased to find out you've had another woman in your bed."

"Good to see you've come to apologise."

"For what? Letting your sister in on all your secrets? Mate, she deserves to know who she's related to."

"Whatever."

"It's okay. He's told me all about his kinks. And he's totally invited me to visit Hades."

Nico's eyes widen, instantly finding mine.

"I didn't invite her to join us," I confirm.

"I was gonna say... I'm down for all the freaky shit, and I know it wouldn't be the first time... but she's your sister, man."

"Christ, are you ready to go?"

"Hell, yes. I'm all fresh, clean, and ready for action." He thrusts his hips forward, making Stella's face twist.

"Have fun, boys. Don't do anything I wouldn't do."

"No worries there, Princess. You're as bad as the rest of us."

"Can't beat 'em, join 'em, right? I'm gonna go talk to Seb about this sex club." She flounces out of the room, shouting, "You know where I am if you need me, big bro," while Nico just stares at me.

"What?"

"You told her about Hades?"

"Was that not what you intended when you mentioned it?"

"I was just yanking your chain, man. I didn't exactly expect you to tell her that you had Jodie trussed up on that cross with whip marks across her body."

"I didn't tell her that, no. But I'm pretty sure she read between the lines."

"Just don't tell Calli, for fuck's sake. I'm happy for her to think that a pair of handcuffs is purely for coppers."

"Oh yeah, that's totally what she thinks. You did just watch her best friend walk out of here, right?" I ask, knowing full well that Stella won't keep the details of that place secret—especially once she visits.

"My little sister is never having sex," he declares.

"She's right, know you." His curious stare burns into my back as he follows me down to the living room. "You're a hypocrite."

8

JODIE

"Mum?" I gasp, coming to a grinding halt the second I round the corner into the kitchen and find her sitting at the table, hugging a mug.

"What the—" Brianna slams into my back, sending me tumbling forward. "Joanne," she blurts. "It's so good to see you up," she says, sounding as shocked as I feel.

Mum's eyes find mine, and my heart shatters in my chest at the pain staring back at me.

Walking over, I pull the chair out beside her and sit down, wrapping my hands around hers, letting the heat of the coffee warm my chilled skin.

"I'm sorry," she sobs, one of the tears she's desperately trying to hold in falling from her lashes.

I shake my head, my throat too thick with emotion to force any words out.

"It's okay," I finally manage. "You have nothing to apologise for."

She blows out a breath, her head dropping, severing our connection as the weight of her grief weighs her down once more.

Bri's hand squeezes my shoulder.

Glancing up at her, I say words that make my heart ache even worse. "I should stay home tonight."

I expect Bri to argue, but when someone speaks, it's not her voice that hits my ears.

"No," Mum says sharply before lifting her head once more.

This time, it's not just grief I see swirling in her dark depths but also determination.

"You are not staying in to babysit me. Your dad, Joe... they wouldn't have wanted that," she chokes out.

My heart twists at the agony in her words as she mentions them. She might as well have just pushed a knife into my chest.

"And they wouldn't want you alone," I point out.

"Jodie," she sighs. "Don't put your life on hold because of me. If there's one thing the past few months have taught us, it's that life is short. Too short to waste."

I bite back my immediate response to tell her

to listen to her own advice, because I don't think it would do her any good right now.

"Go out with Bri. Let her show you a good time. Smile, laugh, have fun. It's what I want."

I look back up at Bri, my body feeling like it's being ripped in half by the two most important women in my life.

"It's up to you, Jojo," Bri says softly. "We can order takeout and just chill here," she offers.

"No," Mum says again. "I want things to be normal. Please," she begs. "I want to listen to your music while you get ready. I want to watch you get dolled up. I want to see you both smiling, laughing. I want to wave you off, knowing that you're about to have the time of your lives. I want you to be young and living. Not stuck here drowning with me."

"But—"

"No buts, Jojo. Your mother has spoken."

My lips part in shock at the authority in her voice when she's barely said more than a few words in the past few weeks.

What changed?

"You're right," Bri says, squeezing my shoulder to stop me from arguing. "But if Jojo does this, she's going to need something from you in return."

My brows pinch as I look between the two of them.

"We know everything is hard as fuck right

now," she says bluntly, one of the many reasons why I love her, "but if you want Jojo to try to restart her life once more, then she needs to see you trying to do the same. I'm not asking for anything crazy, just... get up and get dressed every day."

Mum sighs heavily, as if Bri just requested she climb Kilimanjaro. But after a couple of seconds, she agrees.

"We can get through this, Mum. Together," I assure her.

"We will, baby. We will."

Brianna rushed home to grab everything she needed while I showered, so she didn't have to go out wearing my clothes for the second weekend in a row. I put my music on loud as Mum requested and pretended it was a year ago, Joe was just living his life, Dad was away on business, and Mum was downstairs watching *Strictly Come Dancing* with a glass of wine.

With no alcohol in the house, I have little choice but to stick to Coke, but fuck it. Shit could most definitely be worse. They *had* been worse, only last night, actually.

Mum's up. She's left her room and made herself a coffee. I need to celebrate small miracles right now, and I'm taking that as a pretty fucking significant one.

I'm curling my hair when Bri finally reappears with bags weighing her down and a wide smile on her face.

"I brought supplies."

"How is she?" I ask, ignoring her comment, knowing she just passed Mum.

"Watching TV. She's going to be okay, Jojo." She smiles at me encouragingly, but her words don't lessen my worry at all.

Right now, she might look like she's coping. But what about in two hours, after we've left?

Grief is a fragile, unrelenting thing that drags you into its dark clutches when you least expect it. I should know, it's been happening to me for weeks now.

While I might have been able to keep plastering a smile on my face, under the surface, I'm hurting like I've never experienced before. I'm just not letting everyone see for fear it'll eventually lead me down the same road Mum is currently on.

I can't allow that. Dad and Joe wouldn't have wanted it, and I need to do this for them. I need to live. For them.

"Okay, so I grabbed these," she says, holding up some bottles of cocktail mixes. "I know they're not much, but I thought it would be rude having hard liquor while your mum is trying."

I nod at her, thankful that she cares about my mum as if she were her own. It's understandable, seeing as her own mother is a useless piece of shit I'm ashamed to call an auntie.

"And I got snacks. No getting wasted too early tonight. I think that boy of yours might just have plans."

I groan, dropping my head into my hands at the reminder of what went down earlier.

"I can't believe I let him do that, Bri," I mutter into my palms.

"It was hot, and I only got there at the end. What I want to know is... how did you end up bent over that counter with that god behind you in the first place? Where the hell was Matt?"

"He's going to fire me, Bri. How I got into that position isn't the biggest issue right now."

"Girl, you have nothing to worry about with Matt."

I spin around so fast on my stool that I nearly fall off.

"Bri, tell me you haven't," I beg.

She winces, guilt written all over her face.

"Um... about that."

"You fucked my boss? Seriously? When?"

"A few months ago when you were sick. I came to meet you, but obviously you weren't there. He was... one thing led to another. That chair in his office, though... good things can happen on that."

"Oh my God. Bri, you're a whore."

She shrugs, not giving a single fuck about my assessment.

"He was worth it. Not Nico level of fucking, but decent."

"Pretty sure we're at the point where you need to start pointing out who you *haven't* been with."

She nods, thinking about it. "Might actually be easier."

"You're something else," I mutter, focusing back on my hair.

"Living my best life, Jojo. Exactly what your mother thinks you should be doing. So what are you wearing tonight?" She pulls my wardrobe open. The move reminds me so much of her actions last weekend that it makes my head spin.

"Just jeans and a top, I dunno."

"Firstly, no. Secondly, fuck no. You aren't coming home until that boy has been between your legs, at least once, and that means jeans are firmly out of the question. You need easy access."

When she turns around, she's holding up a short leather skirt and an almost sheer white top.

"Perfect," she announces before throwing both at me.

My lips part to argue, but she cuts me off before I even get a chance.

"I know you're suffering, but that wild girl

still lives inside you, Jojo. Keep digging, you'll find her again."

I look down at the outfit in my hands as memories of the first time I wore it out flash through my mind.

Bri booked us a weekend away at a holiday park, and I bought this for our first night. It was wild, like nothing I'd ever experienced before. I was barely seventeen and mostly naïve to the kind of nights out Bri used to go on, assuming her crazy stories were always exaggerated. I was wrong. If anything, she toned them down for me.

I wasn't a virgin before that weekend, far from it. I gave that baby up to my first boyfriend one night in his bedroom when we were both fifteen, but that was the first night I fully embraced the meaning of meaningless sex.

I'm pretty sure I was more myself that weekend as I let my hair down and released my inhibitions than I've ever been in my life. Well... until last Friday night.

Being tied up on that cross was the closest I've come to the freedom I experienced that weekend. Letting go of everything and handing myself over to someone else.

It's a heady feeling.

One I'm more than happy to experience again and again when it comes to Toby.

It hits me that that is exactly why I allowed him to take me so publicly earlier. The second he's close to me, everything else vanishes. It's like he sucks all the misery and grief right out of me, allowing me to be free, to be me. That and when he touches me I burn like I've never experienced before.

"That was some weekend, huh?" Bri asks, her head clearly going to the same place. "We should book another. It's been too long."

I nod, although I can't help feeling weird about a weekend filled with nameless, faceless guys when right now there's only one who's taking up my headspace.

"Yeah," I murmur absently. "What are you wearing?" I ask, dragging my head from filthy memories of Toby this evening.

Fuck, that boy really has some talent.

"Aw, you two look beautiful," Mum says with a smile when we finally emerge.

The pain in her eyes still makes me question this, but I can hardly argue after what she said earlier.

"I was going for sexy," Bri teases, "but I'll take beautiful."

Mum shakes her head at her in amusement. "Oh to be young and free again."

Grief threatens to get its claws into me as the

reality of her being single for the first time in her adult life.

"Are you sure this is okay? We could still sta—"

"I'm sure," she says confidently before I even finish talking. "This," she says, gesturing to us standing before us, "this makes me so happy. Go and enjoy yourselves."

"I've got my phone," I tell her. "If you need any—"

"I won't." She holds my eyes, daring me to argue.

"Come on, Jojo. Time to find some playmates to buy us some drinks."

"Have fun, and stay safe. I won't expect you home until morning."

"See, even your mother thinks you need to get good and laid again," Bri whispers in my ear, making me burst out laughing.

"I'm not sure that's exactly what she meant."

"Sure it is. Let's go find those boys."

The second we step outside, Bri pulls a small bottle of vodka from her clutch.

"Down the hatch, Jojo," she instructs after swallowing a shot.

"I thought you stuck with the soft stuff," I mutter, happily taking the bottle from her.

"Yeah, inside the house. It's all to play for now we're out." She winks, bouncing toward the Uber waiting for us.

By the time we pull up at The Spot, I've got a nice buzz and my belly is full of erratic butterflies.

"Look at you," Bri shouts as we step into the main bar. "He's got you all kinds of crazy for him, huh? I mean, I get it. I could almost feel how good that was earlier, but damn."

"Can you please stop reminding me that you watched us like a live porno?" I ask, although I'm pretty sure it's pointless.

"When I've got someone giving it to me that good, I'll let it go."

I shake my head at her, heading straight to the bar.

"Ladies," Eden shouts. "How's it going?"

Turning away from the manager, I let Bri chat with her while my eyes scan the bar, desperate to find him. But I come up empty.

"They're not here," I shout in Bri's ear once Eden has disappeared.

"He'll be here, Jojo. Don't stress. Drink, then dance. They'll find us."

With the vodka warming my belly, Bri takes my hand and leads me right into the middle of the dance floor. I let the beat flow through me, tip my face toward the ceiling and finally just let go of everything.

A squeak of fright passes my lips when a pair of hands land on my hips a beat before a hard body presses against my back.

I don't need to see Brianna's smile to tell me who it is. I feel it. My body relaxes back against him as if it was made to align with his as his scent surrounds me.

Resting my head on his shoulder, I twist so my lips are right beneath his ear.

"You came," I shout, the slur to my voice more than obvious.

"You thought I wouldn't?" he asks, almost sounding offended as his hips start moving with mine in time with the music.

I shrug, not wanting to appear vulnerable, because I was seriously starting to think they weren't going to show.

"Plus, that one was like a dog with a bone after I suggested he might get a second shot with your friend."

I can't help but laugh as Nico greets Bri by smacking her ass, grabbing her by the throat, and slamming his lips down on hers.

"He looks pretty desperate."

"He's always fucking desperate," he mutters, making me laugh.

"Match made in heaven," I mutter.

"What was that?" Toby asks, spinning me around to face him.

"I said, they're a match made in heaven."

"Funny," he murmurs, dipping his head so close our noses touch. "I thought you were talking about us."

Toby steals my breath as he captures my lips, kissing me as if he hasn't seen me in a week, not just a couple of hours as his hands slide from my waist and down my arse, hauling me against his body.

Our kiss goes on and on. The songs change around us, people move, even crash into us, but we never come up for air, too lost in each other. My hands roam over his body, learning his curves and the way his muscles ripple as he moves.

9

TOBY

"W e're getting out of here," Nico shouts in my ear. "You coming or what?"

"Is that a trick question? Hell yes, we're coming."

I watch as he steers Brianna toward the exit with his hands firmly on her hips.

"What's going on?" Jodie asks, her dark chocolate eyes staring up at me with a lazy smile playing on her lips.

"They're leaving. Do you wanna—"

"Yes," she says enthusiastically. "Where are we going?"

"I'll take you wherever you want to go, baby," I growl in her ear.

"Why do I get the feeling you're about to offer to take me to heaven?"

A deep laugh rumbles in my chest at her words.

"Again?" I quip, lifting a brow and shamelessly running my eyes down her body as memories of how it felt to sink inside her earlier assault me, making my dick swell. "If you beg, I could make it happen all night long."

"Big words for a guy who's not dragging me out the door."

"Demon," I hiss in her ear, delighting in the shudder that rips through my body as I grab the back of her neck and steal a quick kiss. "Let's go, then. Heaven will only wait so long."

Her laughter fills the air around us as we rush to catch up with the others.

The air turns bitter as we climb the stairs from the basement bar and soon, spray from the rain that's pounding on the pavement splashes us.

"Oh my God," Jodie cries when we emerge, the downpour soaking her white sheer blouse in seconds.

"If I'd brought a coat, I'd have offered it to you," I tell her, letting her know just what a gentleman I could be if the situation were different.

"Quick, get in. We're going to my place," a familiar voice shouts over the rain, and when I look up, I find Brianna and Nico in the back of an Uber on the other side of the road.

"Come on, baby." I grab Jodie's hand to race across the street, but she doesn't move. "What's wrong?" I ask, looking down at her. Her hair is already sodden and sticking to her cheeks, her dark makeup making tracks down her face.

"No," she says quietly like she's talking to herself and not even aware that I'm here. "We'll walk," she suddenly shouts, before tugging on my hand and dragging me down the street.

The rain is relentless, but her steps don't falter.

"Are you crazy?" I shout over the lashing rain.

"Yeah, probably." Her hand slips from mine and she turns to face me, her arms out wide. "Doesn't it make you feel alive?" she asks, a wide, honest smile on her face. As I look at her, something inside me loosens, and I can't help but smile back at her.

She's right.

"Come on," she says, tugging her heels from her feet and taking off. "Bri only lives a few streets away," she calls.

Shaking my head, my smile firmly in place, I run after her. Her manic laughter gets louder as I close in on her.

The second she's in reaching distance, I wrap my arms around her waist and lift her off her feet.

She squeals in delight as I spin her around.

"Toby," she screams until I stop and press her up against the building beside us.

Both our chests are heaving as we stare at each other.

The torrential downpour continues. Rivers run down both our faces as it lashes against our bodies.

"You're something else," I mutter.

"Anything to stop me from drowning." She sucks in a breath the second she finishes talking, as if she regrets letting in any kind of reality.

"Not tonight, Demon," I whisper, capturing her mouth and pushing my tongue between her lips.

She can remember all that tomorrow. Tonight is about forgetting, about pushing reality aside and just enjoying whatever it is we've found here.

I lift her off her feet, wrapping her legs around my waist as our kiss continues.

"Can't get enough of you, baby," I groan into her kiss.

"Toby," she moans, rocking her hips to find some friction.

"Jesus, Demon," I groan against her throat. "You'd let me fuck you right here, wouldn't you?"

"You make me crazy," she moans when I copy her move, grinding my hard length against her cunt.

"So you were totally sane before me, huh?" I mutter, kissing and nipping down her neck.

"Tota— oh shit."

Her head falls back against the rough wall behind her as I hit the perfect spot. Her fingers claw at my shoulders as I continue.

"Fuck, you're mesmerising," I breathe, completely lost to watching her fall apart in front of me.

"Toby," she cries, her voice loud enough to drag attention our way—not that I'm sure anyone has missed us. "Oh shit, shit."

She's right on the edge when a loud siren cuts through the rain surrounding us.

Our eyes lock a second before we both bark out a laugh.

Putting her back on her feet, I grab her hand and pull her along with me, both laughing as we escape the scene of the almost-crime.

"You're going to get me in trouble, Tobias," she forces out through her panting breaths as she slows down in front of a building.

The siren has long faded away, but my high and the adrenaline pumping through my veins hasn't.

Jogging up the stairs to the building, my eyes are locked on Jodie's arse as she digs around her bag for the keys.

"Shit," she barks when they fall from her frozen fingers and straight into a puddle.

Scooping them up, I wrap my arms around her from behind and push one of the keys into the lock. Luck must be on my side, because I choose the right one.

A violent shiver rips through Jodie's body as my warmth hits her.

"Fuck, you're freezing."

"I'm good, can barely feel it," she argues, but the second we get inside and swing the door closed behind us, it becomes quickly apparent that she's lying.

Her teeth begin chattering, her body trembling before we reach the stairs.

"Come here, Demon," I say, sweeping her off her feet, holding her against my chest.

"Her flat is on the fourth floor. You can't—"

"Watch me, baby. Then I'm going to get you nice and warm.'"

"Now that sounds like something I can't argue with."

By the time Jodie stops me outside Brianna's flat, I can't deny that my arms aren't aching—not that I'm going to tell her that.

"Put the key in the lock, Demon."

"We could be about to walk into anything."

"I've seen Nico at his worst, and we already know Brianna doesn't care, if the night in Hades was anything to go by."

Jodie laughs, letting me know that I'm right.

"Let's do it, then. We'll just have to bleach our eyes later."

With a laugh, I throw the door open and march inside.

"Thank fuck for that," I mutter, finding an empty living room, although it soon becomes clear that they're not too far away because Brianna's screams for God fill the air around us.

"Baby, you're freezing," I say when the shivers wracking her body only get stronger.

"Maybe making out in the rain was a bad idea."

"I've got a better one. Where's the bathroom?"

Jodie points to a door on the other side of the living room, and I take off toward it.

The second we're inside, I kick the door closed and lower her arse to the counter.

"What are you doing?" she asks when I turn my back on her.

"Exactly what I promised. Warming you up."

Leaning into the shower, I turn it on before stepping back between her thighs.

"Arms up, baby," I demand, quickly wrapping my fingers around the bottom of her sodden blouse and pulling it up her body. The rest of her clothes quickly follow until she's standing before me, completely bare.

"Jesus," I breathe, getting lost in her sinful curves, but the second I take in the goosebumps covering her skin, I remember what we're meant to be doing.

"Get in," I demand, spinning her around and slapping her arse to get her moving.

"You'd better be joining me," she warns, shooting me a wanton look over her shoulder.

"You're about to be naked with water running all over you. I'm there, Demon."

Reaching behind my head, I try to pull my jumper from my body, but the motherfucker is stuck to me like glue.

Jodie's laughter hits me as I try to wrestle myself out of my soaking wet clothes, although her amusement is soon cut off when I push my boxers over my hips, letting my hard cock spring free.

She backs up when I step into the shower with her and a smile twitches at my lips.

"It's a little too late to run, Demon."

Her eyes hold mine before a gasp of shock rips through the air when her back collides with the cold tiles.

"I've got you now, and I'm not letting you go."

"I'm not sure if that's meant to be a threat or a promise," she teases.

"Maybe it's a little of both," I say honestly, crowding her. "And unfortunately for you," I murmur, pressing my forearms against the wall on either side of her head, "it's too late to do anything about it."

With the shower pounding down around us, the rest of the world ceases to exist as I slam my lips down on hers and pick right back up from where we left off—only this time with significantly fewer clothes and much more chance of getting what we both need.

"Toby." My name rips from her lips as a gasp when I sink my teeth into her neck before quickly soothing the bite with my tongue. "Oh God. I need—"

"I know exactly what you need."

I hoist her off her feet and she quickly wraps her legs around me, mimicking our position from earlier.

"I'd have fucked you right out on the street for everyone to see, I hope you know that," I growl in her ear as my cock brushes against her cunt.

"Yes, yes," she chants, rolling her hips forward in the hope of getting what she needs.

"And you'd have let me too, wouldn't you? My filthy little demon."

"Yes," she cries as I shift our position, pushing just the tip inside her. Her muscles ripple, trying to drag me deeper. "Toby," she whimpers.

"Beg," I demand, the monster inside me wanting to hear her say the words.

"Please, Toby. Please."

"Please, what?" I ask, my voice scarily empty.

Not that she notices. She's too desperate for what I can offer her.

"Fuck me. Please, fu— yes," she screams when I thrust forward, filling her in one quick shift of my hips.

My teeth grind as her burning velvet walls encase me, sucking me deeper both literally and figuratively into this twisted thing with her.

To her, I'm the perfect stranger, the perfect distraction. She has no idea that really, I'm her worst fucking nightmare.

Threading my fingers into her wet hair, I drag her head back, claiming her lips in a brutal kiss that fills my mouth with the taste of copper. I have no idea if the blood is mine or hers, but I also don't really care as I fuck her with complete abandon until she's screaming her release and I'm emptying myself deep inside her.

"You nice and warm yet, baby?" I ask as I slip from her body and reach for a bottle of shower gel on the side.

10

JODIE

A loud moan falls from my lips, Toby's thumbs digging into the tension knotting my shoulders as he washes every inch of me.

It's the most mind-boggling yet content moment of my life.

This guy is... almost too good to be true.

He fucks like a savage, yet his sweetness, his tenderness makes a lump form in my chest.

It can't be real. It just can't.

I'm not that fucking lucky.

I can barely hold myself up by the time he's finished working my back, and when he turns me around, I find his gaze dark and hungry once more and my stomach clenches despite the exhaustion claiming me.

Ripping my eyes from his, I take in his body, my gaze lingering on the scar high up on his chest before dropping lower. His defined chest, his cut abs, that V that leads to... All the air rushes out of my lungs when I take in his straining cock.

My mouth waters for another taste of him and my hand reaches out without instruction from my brain. But I never manage to make contact.

His fingers wrap around my wrist, stopping me.

His other hand turns the shower off before I'm tugged out. In seconds I have a towel around me and I'm watching him wrap another around his waist, his cock tenting it.

"Don't you w-want—"

My words falter as his lips find my neck, kissing and nipping down the damp skin.

"More than I can put into words, Demon. But I can wait."

"But I—"

"Come on," he murmurs, taking my shoulders in his hands and steering me out of the bathroom and back toward the living room.

He gently pushes me down on the sofa and grabs the blanket that's hanging over the back of it. And after dropping a kiss on my head, he walks away again.

"Where are you going?" I ask in a panic.

"Does Bri have a dryer?" he shouts over his shoulder, and I damn near melt into a puddle when he returns from the bathroom with our clothes in his arms, even thoughtfully pulling my leather skirt and his jumper from the pile.

"Y-yeah, it does both," I say, my eyes flicking to the machine in the small kitchen.

I watch, enthralled as he empties his pockets and shoves our clothes inside before figuring out how it works.

He continues pottering until he's found us both a cider—not his kind of drink if the way his nose wrinkles is anything to go by—and he stalks back over with them in one hand and the contents of his pocket in the other.

"Put something on," he instructs, passing me the remote control. "Something tells me we're going to need all the noise we can get to drown them out."

I chuckle, turning the TV on and finding reruns of *The Inbetweeners* on whatever channel it's already set to.

"I love these," I say, taking the rhubarb cider from him.

"Really?" he asks, looking sceptical as hell.

"Really. Trust me." I tip the bottle to my lips as something flashes in his eyes, but it's soon gone when they drop to my lips as I lick up a couple of drops of sweetness.

"I'm changing my mind already," he mutters.

"You haven't even tried it, you idiot."

Tipping the bottle to his lips, I watch the

muscles of his neck pull and stretch as he swallows.

Hmm. Delicious indeed.

"It could be worse," he confesses, taking another sip.

I roll my eyes at him, and the smile I get in return would knock me on my arse if I weren't already on it.

"So... what now?" I ask almost nervously. I hate that I sound unsure. I'm not usually like this with guys, but then I guess those guys aren't Toby, and they usually are just only one night. We're currently on night two and everything is changing between us.

Yes, I'm still sitting here practically panting for him to take me again, but there's so much more than that.

Just looking at him makes something settle inside me. His touch has the power to burn me right down to my soul. And when we're together, nothing else in the world exists. It's—he's— exactly what I need right now.

"Now," he growls, placing his bottle down by mine and turning to me with a hungry and downright filthy look in his eyes which makes my heart gallop in my chest.

He rises up and looms over me, making me feel like a tiny mouse about to be captured by the big bad hunter.

Grabbing my calves, he tugs me down the

sofa, my towel barely holding on as I move, before falling over me.

"Now," he repeats, his nose—and more importantly, his lips—only a breath from mine. "Nothing."

He drops down beside me, squishing his large frame between me and the back of the sofa, and I let out a shocked and disappointed laugh.

"Baby," he sighs. "I know what you're doing. And while I might be more than happy to oblige, I also know something you need more than sex."

"Not possible," I sulk.

"When was the last time you slept properly?" he asks, and my entire body tenses up as I try to come up with an answer. "Exactly," he whispers, the rush of his breath against my neck making my entire body shudder. "I could spend all night doing a million and one things to you, making you forget your goddamn name, but I won't."

"Why?" The word comes out needy as I try to bite back my pleas for him to do exactly as he described.

I stare into his dark blue eyes as I wait for his response. His fingers tickle as he wraps his hand around the back of my neck, pressing his brow to mine and anchoring us together.

"One, because I want you to be able to walk tomorrow. I have plans to take you out for breakfast."

"Oh," I gasp. This thing really isn't just a one-night stand for him either, is it?

Hope foolishly begins to soar within me as I consider that this may actually be the start of something good after all the shit that's been thrown at me recently.

"And two, you need to sleep." His lips find mine before I have a chance to argue, and he kisses me until my toes curl. My hands roam around his insane body beneath the blanket he pulled over us, and I shamelessly tug the towel from him so I can reach around and grab his arse. His cock rubs hungrily against my thigh, but he never tries for more as his own hands roam, branding himself on my skin.

Hushed voices somewhere close fill my ears as I begin to rouse from sleep. Reaching out, I mindlessly search for Toby without opening my eyes. My last memory from our night together was having my limbs tangled with his and his lips on mine.

Perfect.

"What?" a familiar voice gasps. "We were not that loud."

"Wanna tell that to your neighbour who came to knock? She thought you were being maimed in your sleep," a deep voice rumbles, one that makes a wide smile spread across my lips.

"Well, she was. Her neck is nothing, you should see her ti—"

"I'm good," Toby says, and Bri squeals as if Nico was actually going to show off the mess he's made of her chest.

"Bro, you can criticise all you fucking like, but don't think we didn't hear you both in the shower," Nico starts.

"For like, fifteen minutes. You two went all fucking night."

I don't need to look over to know that both Bri and Nico have probably got smug-as-fuck grins on their faces.

"You could have done the same, man. Didn't you have the stamina?"

Silence cuts through the room.

"Yeah, or I could have let her sleep and give her half a chance of being able to deal with the shit that's going on in her life right now," Toby says, ignoring Nico's jibe.

More silence falls as I melt into a puddle once more for this unbelievable guy.

"How much has she told you?" Bri enquires.

"Enough to know she's drowning. Enough to know that I want to help."

"Ow," Nico complains.

"Why can't you be as sweet and caring as your best friend?" Bri snaps.

One of the guys—I'm assuming Nico—snorts. "You weren't complaining about it all that much last night. Good guys don't fuck like I do, Siren."

"Uh... I've seen Toby at work. I can assure you, they do."

"What are you suggesting?" Nico grunts. "You wanna switch sides? Sure, he can put on a good show. If you really want the—"

"Morning," I sigh, cutting off whatever bullshit he was going to spew next.

Wrapping the blanket around my body as I sit up, I look over at all of them drinking coffee around the breakfast bar. I have to do a double-take, because it's such a weirdly domesticated sight.

Bri never, and I mean never, does the next morning thing with guys. She's a fuck 'em and chuck 'em kind of girl. The only guy she's had repeats with in the past few years is Brad, and apparently, that's only because he has a magical diamond-encrusted cock or something. It's certainly not because she sees herself in a white dress and walking toward him in a church. I know that for a fact. So the fact that Nico is still here speaks volumes about either his personality or his bedroom abilities. Based on the limited time I've spent with him, I'd guess the latter.

"This is very... civilised."

"Aren't we always?" Bri asks, getting off

Nico's lap and walking toward the coffee machine.

I step closer, not hating at all that both Toby and Nico are both sitting there in only their underwear. I've certainly woken to worse sights over the years.

"Come here," Toby says, holding his arm out.

"I'm just gonna—" I point toward the bathroom, more than aware that I need to freshen up before getting too close to him.

I manage two steps before he reaches out and drags me down on his lap.

His eyes catch mine for the briefest moment before our lips collide. I fight him when he tries to push his tongue into my mouth, but I lose the battle when he manages to slip a hand inside the blanket and pinches my nipple.

I gasp, my lips parting and giving him the access he craves while I internally cringe at the state of my morning breath.

"It's funny you think I care," he mutters against my lips when he finally lets me up for air.

I wiggle against him, feeling his cock growing beneath me.

"Go. Unless you want more than a good morning kiss."

"Don't let us stop you," Nico adds. "I'm good for another round. See," he says, pulling Bri over and dragging her hand beneath the counter.

"Animal," she hisses.

"You fucking love it, Siren."

"Jesus. I'm going to pee. Try to keep it in your pants while I'm gone, yeah?" I say to Nico with a smirk.

"I can't keep those kinds of promises, Jojo." He winks before I turn away from them all and rush toward the bathroom.

The second I close the door behind me, I suck in a deep breath and try to get my head on straight.

I have no idea what I expected this morning. I didn't allow myself to think about it as I lost myself in Toby. But I'm pretty sure that if I had, I wouldn't have imagined us all sitting around, playing house.

Shedding the blanket, I pee before finding my toothbrush in Bri's cupboard and set about freshening up.

A knock on the door startles me, but I quickly relax when it's followed up with a feminine, "It's just me."

She lets herself in, not even batting an eyelid that I'm standing here completely naked.

"Brought you Toby's jumper to wear," she says with a smile.

It didn't escape my attention when I first looked at her that she's happily walking around in Nico's shirt.

"Thanks," I mutter, taking it from her and slipping it over my head.

It might have been soaked through last night, but when I breathe in, I realise quickly that it still smells like him. I just about manage to contain my sigh of contentment.

"So..." Bri starts, and I can't hold in the smile that appears on my lips.

"I really like him," I confess, my heart fluttering in my chest.

"I know, I can see it every time you look at him. I'm pretty sure he's feeling the same, too."

"Yeah?" I ask, hating that I sound vulnerable, but I can't help it. I need her to confirm that what I'm feeling isn't crazy. I mean, it is totally crazy but... I sigh.

"Yeah. His eyes go all soft and mushy when he looks at you. It's sweet as fuck."

As much as I want to hear more, I turn the conversation onto her in an attempt to keep my heart in line.

"And what about you and Nico? You look cosy this morning."

"Ugh." She rolls her eyes and waves her hand at me. "He refused to leave."

I rear back a little. "You tried to make him?"

"Of course I did. I don't do... that." She points at what's happening on the other side of the door.

"Aw, that's cute. He wanted to spend more time with you."

"No he didn't. He told me he wasn't leaving without Toby, and Toby refused to leave because he promised you breakfast. There's only one love story happening here, Jojo, and it's not mine."

My lips part to argue, but she sees it coming and places her hands on her hips.

"Don't even think about it," she spits. "I don't want nor need a man for any other reason than his cock... well, maybe his tongue. So stop getting these crazy thoughts about double dating and all that shit. Not happening."

I stick my tongue out at her. "Spoilsport."

"Whatever. Get your backside back out there and make that boy sitting at my counter happy. He looks like a sad little puppy yearning after you."

"Shut up, he does not."

She raises a brow at me.

"And let him take you out for breakfast so that Nico leaves my fucking flat."

"You don't mean that. You thought he was God last night."

"That was last night. This is this morning, and I've got things to do."

"Oh?"

She glares at me. "You're a pain in my arse, Jojo. Go, shoo." She ushers me out of the bathroom and is hot on my tail when I round the corner and Toby's eyes lock on me.

"See," she whispers. "That look right there. Smitten, girl. I'm telling you."

"Damn, you look good wearing that, Demon," Toby groans, his eyes eating me up.

"Okay, great. Can we go for food now, seeing as she's refusing to let me eat her?" Nico sulks.

"Jojo, go get dressed so this dog will leave my flat."

"You know your pussy will miss me the second I've gone," he counters.

"I've got a pretty decent vibrator and a guy on speed dial who can get here pretty bloody fast should I need something more... authentic."

Nico's face hardens briefly at the mention of her seeing someone else, but he covers it so quickly I start to wonder if I imagined it.

"Right, well I hope you enjoy some lame sex, because we both know that's what it'll be in comparison to what you could get with me."

She steps up to him, her hands on her hips and her eyes narrowed. She's like a viper ready to strike, and I know that whatever's about to fall from her lips is going to sting.

"Actually, Brad is better than you. You look like a two-pump chump in comparison."

Hurt flickers across his face so quickly that if you blinked you'd have missed it before he throws his head back and laughs.

"You're such a shitty liar, Siren. But whatever. I got more than what I needed last night. Brad," he snarls, "is more than welcome to my sloppy seconds."

The tension crackling between them as they glare at each other is enough to set the entire place ablaze.

"I should probably go and get dressed," I say, swiping what I assume is my coffee off the counter and quickly downing half.

"Or you could just wear that. I certainly have no complaints." Toby's knuckles brush up the back of my thigh before he grabs a handful of my arse.

"I would, when all the women start eye-fucking your bare chest," I blurt, immediately regretting it as his eyes light up with delight.

"I wouldn't notice," he confesses, his eyes running down the length of me. "I've got my eyes firmly set on only one woman."

Bri gags at his words while I swoon. Hard.

"Give me ten minutes and we can get out of your hair," I say, racing toward her bedroom.

I'm hardly surprised when she follows me.

"See, I told you," she announces happily, falling onto her bed, which is nothing more than a pile of twisted sheets.

"Why do you want to get rid of Nico so badly? I think you two are—"

"Don't," she snaps, throwing a pillow at me.

"Ew, gross. There's no way that doesn't have at least one of your bodily fluids on it," I hiss, throwing it back.

"Oh, like my sofa doesn't have any of yours," she points out with a quirked brow.

"It doesn't, actually. We didn't screw on your sofa."

Her brow wrinkles in confusion.

"So what did you do?"

"Talked a bit. Made out. Fell asleep."

"Huh," she mutters. "Maybe he's not the man I thought he was," she muses.

"Bri, the guy took us to a fucking sex club the first night we met and tied me to a..."

"St. Andrew's cross," Bri supplies when I struggle to come up with its name.

"Yeah, that," I mutter, pulling open her bottom drawer that houses my stuff.

Prior to Joe and then Dad dying, I was practically living here with her. But Mum's needed me too much, and I've been spending more and more time at home once again.

I miss it, though. The freedom, the endless nights out. Even the crazy nights in.

With a sigh, I pull on some knickers and drag a pair of leggings up my legs.

"I don't think we need to be discussing that boy's ability to do the job right."

"Maybe so... but to not fuck you on the sofa, and you were both naked. Guy must have the self-control of a fucking rock."

"He was thoughtful. It was... nice."

"Weird," she says at the same time, making me laugh.

"There are nice guys out there, Bri. Just because you're attracted to the dickheads, it doesn't mean they don't exist."

"Yeah, I'm sure they do. I'd rather have one who breaks my bed, though, and not my heart."

Pulling on a bralette, I tug a floral dress over my head and rummage in her wardrobe, hoping I left some shoes here. Hell knows I can't wear her clown shoes.

"Bingo," I hiss, finding a pair of boots I'd forgotten existed.

I should probably make some effort to do something with my hair and makeup, but that's not happening until I've had more coffee and food. Throwing my hair up in a messy bun, I turn to Bri, who's lounging in her bed, half asleep. Hardly surprising if she was up all night.

"Will I do?" I ask, holding my arms out from my sides.

"Girl, he'd still look at you like a sap if you were wearing a bin bag."

I raise my brows at her.

"You look perfect. Now go. I want those smelly boys out of my flat."

I open my mouth to tell her that the only way they smell is mouth-watering, but I quickly decide against it.

She's made up her mind, and there will be no changing it.

"Right, let's go. I need food," I announce, walking over to where Toby is dressed, bar his jumper that's in my hands. He smiles at me as he takes it and pulls it over his head.

"Thank fuck, a female who agrees with something I say," Nico barks. "Thanks for the orgasms, Siren." He winks at Bri, who's appeared in the doorway, now in her own oversized hoodie, allowing Nico to have his shirt back.

He holds the fabric to his nose and breathes in.

"You rub your pussy on this?"

"Jesus Christ," Toby mutters. Snatching my hand, he drags me toward the front door. "Thanks for letting us crash, Brianna. Sorry about this knobhead. Can't train pork," he shoots over his shoulder before pulling the door open and gesturing for Nico to get the hell out.

"Miss you already, sweet cheeks." He blows a kiss at Bri before striding toward the staircase.

"Is he always like this?"

"A dickhead? Yeah, pretty much. It's part of his charm."

"I can hear you, you know," Nico barks from a few steps below us.

"I'm more than aware. You coming for breakfast with us?"

"To watch you eye-fuck each other? Nah, I'm good thanks. I'll just catch you later, yeah?"

"Sure thing, man."

Toby wraps his arm around my shoulders and pulls me into his side.

"Where's a good place to eat around here then?" he asks while Nico hovers outside, waiting for an Uber.

"He's pissy for a guy who spent the entire night inside a more than willing pussy," I mutter as we walk away.

Toby barks out a laugh.

"You're something else, you know that?"

11

TOBY

"**H**ey, it's me." A voice rings out after a soft knock on my front door. "Are you home and clothed?" she asks with a laugh.

"Yeah, the coast is clear," I call back, not taking my eyes off the TV.

"Bro, you're playing without me?" Stella gasps when she appears, seeing that I'm on the Xbox.

"Well, yeah. I wanted to actually win."

"Fuck you, I'm still learning," she barks, falling down beside me after grabbing the second controller.

"You want me to stop, don't you?"

"What gave me away?" she asks, waving the controller in my face and putting her feet up on my coffee table.

"I thought we needed to leave," I say, aware

that I was just wasting time before heading to Galen's—Dad's—for dinner.

"Yeah, but Seb's only just got back."

"Fine," I sigh, ending my game and turning it to two player. I might make out like I'm pissed off, but really, I quite like killing people with my sister. And at least this way, I don't need to worry whether anyone is going to actually shoot her. Not that she's not shit hot with a gun, or a knife. Fuck it, even her fists are deadly. Girl's a walking fucking weapon. Something that I'm sure Damien wasn't aware of when Galen brought her home. She's one of us through and through, and I couldn't be fucking prouder.

"Ready?"

"I'm always fucking ready," she hisses as I press play.

I dive right while she goes left, hiding behind a wall waiting for the first guy she knows is going to come from the building opposite.

"Yes," she cries when she gets him on her first shot.

"Good to see you're improving."

"You might be better with a gun on the screen, but we both know I'd outdo you on the range any day, big bro."

"I think that's something I'm gonna need to take you up on," I say between shooting a few of our enemies and ducking behind a crate.

"You're on. Name the day and time. I might

even do it blindfolded to help you out. I'd hate to make my big, bad, scary brother cry."

I bark a laugh as someone jumps around a corner that she wasn't expecting and shoots her dead in one shot.

"You were saying, little sister?"

"Lucky shot."

"Sure, sure."

We're still battling it out twenty minutes later when Seb lets himself into my flat and finds us hurling insults at each other.

"Ah, bonding again, I see," he mutters, falling onto the other end of my corner sofa, watching us with amusement dancing in his eyes.

"You need to up your Xbox training with your girl, man. For a bad-arse, she's pretty shit."

"Pfft, we've got better things to do with our spare time than play games."

"Oh, I don't know," Stella mutters. "We play plenty of games. Remember the other night when we played hide the sa—"

"Enough," I bark, ending the game and throwing my controller onto the coffee table, unable to listen to any of their sexploits right now.

"How was your night, anyway? You never said if you got lucky," Stella says, turning to face me.

"It was good," I say, getting up and heading to

the kitchen for the dessert I promised Mum I would bring with me for our family dinner.

"Good? That's really all you're giving me?"

"Unlike you two, I'm not really into kissing and telling."

"Boring," Stella scoffs. "So no sex club this weekend?"

"Jesus Christ. Seb, put a lead on your woman," I mutter lightly.

"Oh yeah, because she's so easy to control. And, you're assuming that I don't also want to know about this mystery girl and your little illicit visit to Hades. Bro, that's hot. Didn't know you had it in you."

"I didn't. She had it in her, though."

"Oh burn, bro," Seb barks, holding his hand up for me to high-five while Stella mutters about us being pathetic, horny little boys.

"Please let me meet this girl so I can apologise profusely for you," Stella says once the three of us walk into the lift.

"Seriously?" I ask, hitting the button for the ground floor. "I'm not letting her near any of you. She thinks I'm a decent person right now. I wanna keep that up for as long as possible."

"Tobes," Stella sighs. "You are a good person."

"I'm sure there are plenty of people out there who would have a solid argument against that." Jodie herself, in the not-too-distant future. My stomach knots at the thought of hurting her, but I know that I can't turn back now. I'm too invested in this plan.

"Meh, fuck them. Not everyone can be right all the time."

She nudges me with her elbow.

"All joking aside, she's putting a smile on your face. So as far as I'm concerned, you can keep doing what you're doing."

"She's a good distraction."

A ripple of tension goes around the enclosed space as the face of the man I need distracting from flickers through my mind.

"I know you don't want to talk about it," Seb starts. "But don't you think that maybe you should just end it? Put it all behind you?"

"I will. But it's not time. Death is too easy."

"It's fucking with your head though, man. I'm not sure it's worth it."

The lift dings, announcing our arrival, and I take a step forward, more than ready to leave this conversation behind.

"It'll be worth it," I shoot over my shoulder. It'll be more than worth it as I rip his world right from beneath him, just like he did to us.

A wicked smile curls at my lips as I walk toward my car, although I can't ignore the painful twist of my stomach which never used to be there when I thought about my revenge.

Swallowing it all down, I pass Stella the cheesecake and slip into the driver's seat.

Heading to Galen's, and now Mum's place is weird as fuck. Seeing Mum happy with another man, despite her real husband being a monster of the worst kind, is weird, and something that's going to take a while to get used to. So is the fact that that man also happens to be my biological father, and that while Jonas was off cheating on my mum with Jodie's, my mum was also doing the dirty.

Their relationship really was fucked from the get-go. Shame neither of them did anything about it; we could have all had much easier lives if they had.

Stella and Seb thankfully turn the conversation away from the poisonous rat who's locked up in our basement on the short journey.

The second we pull into Galen's driveway, both he and Mum emerge with massive smiles on their faces. They look like picture-perfect parents.

My heart aches as I take them in. If things had been different, they could have had a lifetime of happiness together instead of living through hell separately.

My eyes lock on Mum. She looks better than she has in months, and I know that it's not just because her treatment has come to an end and she's received the news she was hoping for. It's because of him. The man at her side. My real father.

Every time I see him, I see more of myself in him, and it settles a little of the concern I have deep within me that Jonas might have poisoned me enough over the years, and that even without his evil blood flowing through my veins I might be a younger version of him.

Spending time with Galen, seeing the way he is with Mum, Stella, even the way he opened his life up to me the second he learned the truth, gives me hope for the future.

It makes me think that maybe once I've got all this out of my system, dished out the revenge that is so desperately needed, I can go back to my old life, can reclaim my title as the nice one and actually think about my future.

It's funny, because I used to hate that everyone thought I was nicer than the others. It made me feel like they all thought I was weaker. But now, with this dark monster and need for revenge growing bigger every day, I crave that normalcy.

There's nothing wrong with appearing to be nice. I guess I always was a wolf in sheep's clothing. It just took the right kind of betrayal to really bring that wolf out.

"It's so good to see you all," Mum gushes the second we're out of the car.

She pulls Stella in for a tight hug, while Galen shakes Seb's hand.

A smile pulls at my lips, seeing Mum with her daughter. If I'd had any clue she'd even existed, that she'd been ripped from Mum like she was, then I'd have raised hell to get her back sooner. As soon as they reconnected, it became glaringly obvious that it wasn't just Jonas who put the dark shadows in her eyes but also her loss. I watched them vanish as a part of my mum I never knew was missing slotted back into place when her daughter stepped back into her life.

"My babies," she says softly, gesturing for me to join them.

Seb takes the cheesecake from Stella before it gets squished between us, and I step into Mum's side.

"You're looking really well, Mum," I say, holding her tight.

She's still wearing a hat, mostly to keep her head warm than to hide the hair she's missing beneath, but her eyes are sparkling and her skin has colour instead of that grey pallor I hated seeing on her so much.

"I'm feeling good, baby. Galen's looking after me so well. I feel like a new woman."

I smile at her, reminding myself why I need to see my plan though. Fuck what that monster did to me. I can get over the years of abuse I suffered. I even understand it, to a point. I wasn't his kid, and he felt the need to torture me for that.

But Mum? She was his wife. The one he'd promised to protect, to lay his life down for.

The way he treated her, the way he controlled her. That's something I'll never forgive him for. How he managed to have an entirely separate life outside of us. How could he betray her like that when she had no choice but to do everything he said? All the while she could have been with the man who really had her heart. With her daughter. They could have supported her while she fought for her life, battling the tumour that was threatening to rip her from me all too soon.

My fists curl at the thoughts, the beast inside me rising to the surface once more.

"Come on, let's go in. It's freezing out here," Galen says, disappearing inside, quickly followed by Seb, Stella, and then Mum and me.

She turns to me the second we're in the kitchen and looks at me—I mean *really* looks at me.

My heart begins to race as I wonder what exactly she can see within my eyes.

Can she see the darkness? The need to cause pain?

Does she recognise it from *him*?

The thought of being like him in any way makes my stomach twist, threatening to bring up the breakfast I had with Jodie this morning before I had no choice but to deliver her home so she could get ready for her shift at the coffee shop.

"Sweetie," she sighs, taking my cheeks in her hands. "You look exhausted."

Over her shoulder, I don't miss Seb as he snorts a laugh.

"Well, obviously. He's got a girl on the go," he helpfully offers.

And as Mum's face splits in two with a smile, I swear to God I could put a bullet through his fucking head.

"Don't get excited, it's nothing serious."

"Yeah, not everyone needs to be moving in together and getting married at eighteen," Galen points out, dragging Emmie and Theo into this despite them not even being here.

"What? We haven't got married," Stella argues.

"Yet," Seb adds, wrapping his arm around her shoulder and kissing the top of her head. They really are annoyingly cute when they want to be.

"I mean it, Mum. I'm not about to bring a girl home to meet you or anything."

She continues to study me, her motherly instinct clearly sensing that there's more.

"You need to let it go, Toby," she whispers. "It's over."

"I know, Mum. I've got everything under control. Trust me, yeah?"

"Toby, I—"

"So what's for dinner? It smells amazing," I say, twisting out of her hold and stepping deeper into the room where Galen has a beer waiting for me.

"You promised me a roast dinner," Stella points out. "You'd better not have gone back on that."

"You think I'd be brave enough?" Galen asks.

"You've got a problem, baby," Seb mutters.

"What? I'm just embracing my inner Brit and making up for all the lost dinners."

Seb and Galen laugh at her. All the while, Mum's concerned gaze still burns into me.

"So... aside from Toby's mystery girl, who else has news?" Galen asks once we're all sitting with empty plates and more than full bellies.

Everyone looks around at each other.

"No? So everyone's lives are calm and normal?" he asks with a smirk. "That can't be right. Who's hiding something?"

"Maybe it's just time for some normalcy?" Mum says softly. "I think we've all had enough drama."

"Amen to that," Stella says, lifting what's left of her glass of wine to her lips.

She, Seb, and Mum fall into a conversation about school while Galen's phone dings in his pocket.

"Sorry," he mutters, pulling it out to read, but no one pays him any attention. Well, no one aside from me.

"What's wrong?" I ask when his brows pull together, concern obvious on his face.

"Uh..." He hesitates, looking at me across the table.

Unlike Stella and Mum, the two of us haven't really spent all that much time together yet. He's been busy with work, and I've been spending all my free time either torturing a man or stalking a woman.

"Things aren't going very smoothly with the Wolves' new leadership in Lovell," he confesses.

"Archer having issues?" I ask.

"Seems that way. Some of Luis Wolfe's right-hand men aren't impressed with the changes he's already putting in place."

"Is Damien getting involved?" I'm aware that he's been helping both Archer and Cruz in their takeovers of both the Lovell Estate gang and the MC we share our territory with.

"He's monitoring the situation," Galen says hesitantly.

"That doesn't sound good," Seb pipes up, clearly listening.

"I'm sure Archer and his boys have it under

control." My brow lifts, questioning that statement. If we know about it, then he's clearly not dealing with it well enough. "Just be ready should he need backup."

"What about the Reapers?" I ask, looking between Galen and Seb, assuming he might know more via his connection to Emmie.

"Quiet," Seb answers.

"Well, I guess that's something."

"The concern," Galen starts, "is that Ram and Luis were working together before they were taken down. Both have enough loyal followers to cause Cruz and Archer issues. Only time will tell just how loyal they were."

"They were both scumbags," I scoff. "Surely they'll see the light now one is dead and the other is behind bars."

"Only time will tell."

12

JODIE

Everything is good. For the first time in a very long time, I actually feel a trickle of hope in my veins that things might just turn around.

Mum is improving. The dark shadows still linger in her eyes, but just like she promised Brianna, she's trying.

She was already up and dressed when I got back on Sunday morning after breakfast with Toby, demanding I tell her everything about the night before. Obviously, I didn't quite do that— I'm not sure she'd have appreciated listening to my tale of Toby fucking me against the tiles in Bri's bathroom. But I gave her enough to ensure she knew we had a great night, and her smile damn near lit up her entire face when I explained about Toby taking me for breakfast.

I haven't mentioned a boy to her in... years.

Probably since school. But despite not having a clue if Toby and I were actually going to be anything, I felt that it was the good news she might have needed.

Her words that followed have lingered in my mind ever since. "If he took you for food the next morning, then he's a keeper."

I smile as I mindlessly make some coffee for a customer.

I haven't seen him since Sunday. I wasn't expecting to, and he made no promises for what might be to come for us, but we've messaged a few times. Whenever I find his name staring at me on my screen, butterflies take flight in my belly and excitement fills my veins. I haven't felt giddy over a boy for years, and despite it only being a few days, I'm already addicted to the high.

I can only hope he's experiencing something similar and the next time we're together it's full-on electric. It's been a few days now. I'm more than ready for a little time with him again.

"Jodie," a familiar voice says as I spin around with the coffee I was making.

Lifting my eyes, I find a smiling face staring back at me.

"Sara," I sing, rushing to put my customer's coffee on the tray before I spill it, and I run around the counter, throwing my arms around her shoulders. "When did you get home?"

"This morning," she says in my ear, holding me just as tightly.

"God, I missed you," I sigh.

"You too. It's so good to be home," she says, releasing me. "Are you due for a break soon?"

Glancing at my watch, I see she's in luck. "Ten minutes. Go grab a seat, I'll make you a drink. Usual, yeah?"

"Yeah," she says, a soft smile playing on her lips and happiness filling her eyes.

I watch her walk over to one of the vacant sofas in the window as contentment settles around me.

Sara's my oldest friend. We met at preschool and were pretty much inseparable until she left after year eleven, preferring to attend a local college for vocational courses while I stayed on for sixth form. We never lost touch, though.

She's since moved across town to live with her boyfriend, and the two of them took off right after Joe's funeral to spend six weeks and the holidays in Australia.

We've spoken often, and she even threatened to return early when I told her what had happened to Dad, but I refused to allow her to ruin her trip because of it.

There was nothing she could do to fix the situation, and I'd rather know she was enjoying herself than drowning in my tears.

The ten minutes until my break drag as my

excitement to hear about all the things they've been doing first-hand gets the better of me.

When Paula finally comes over to relieve me for my break, I'm more than ready to catch up with my friend.

Grabbing a sandwich from the fridge, I rush over with two fresh coffees and fall down beside her.

"You look so good," I say, taking in her bronze tan. "I'm so freaking jealous."

She smiles at me, her own excitement obvious, but I don't miss the sadness and concern in her features.

"How are you doing? And I mean, *really* doing. I know you've been fobbing me off in your messages." She quirks a brow and I groan.

"Things have been tough, but I didn't want you worrying about me while you were off having the time of your life."

"It doesn't matter where I am, Jojo. I'll still worry."

"I know. But we don't need to talk about my miserable life. Tell me all about Australia."

Her smile widens, her excitement palpable as she talks at a million miles an hour, telling me about all the things she and Jesse got up to during their travels.

"Jodie," a deep voice booms behind me, startling me and making me realise that I totally lost track of time as I got absorbed in Sara's stories about perfect golden beaches and warm blue seas.

I spin around, wincing at Matt standing behind me with his hands on his hips and a fierce look on his face.

"Shit. Sorry, boss."

"Paula was meant to go home fifteen minutes ago." The anger lacing his tone makes my stomach clench.

I barely look him in the eye as I quickly say goodbye to Sara and rush behind the counter, apologising profusely to Paula, who just smiles at me softly and says, "It's not a problem, sweetie. I know she's been away."

"I'll make it up to you," I say, despite her argument that it's not necessary.

Matt's eyes still burn into my back as I take the next order and quickly fall back into routine until the small line is gone.

I was off Monday and was able to put off seeing him after the whole sex-on-the-counter episode, but we've worked together for the past two days and I've been waiting for him to bring it up, to drag me into his office and make me explain myself before throwing me out on my arse.

I can only hope that the reason he hasn't done it yet is that the cameras don't actually work and he has no idea anything went down on Saturday night after he left. The other option is that we're already short-staffed and he can't afford to do it yet.

With a sigh, I turn to face him, swallowing down any unease that he might have witnessed me bent over the counter getting railed exactly where I'm standing now.

Ignoring my brain's demands, my cheeks burn bright red as I try to hold his eyes.

"I'm sorry, I lost track of time. It won't happen again."

"I expect better from you, Jodie," he says, disappointment evident in his tone.

"I know, I'm sorry."

"You can lock up tonight."

This time, it's not just my cheeks that burn as my blood turns to fire.

"Y-yeah, sure. Whatever you want."

He takes a step back, but I swear to God that his eyes drop to my lips very briefly before he turns around.

Oh my God, he's watched the footage.

Internally, I scream as he disappears through the staff-only door toward his office.

"That was tense," Sara says, stepping up to the empty counter now that the lunch rush has died down. "Think he might need to get laid."

"Sara, that's my boss," I gasp.

"I know. He's hot, though. He shouldn't really have an issue getting female attention."

"Oh my God. Jesse is a bad influence on you, girl."

She blushes and flutters her eyelids innocently at me.

The two of us have always been polar opposites. I think it's one of the reasons our friendship has lasted like it has. While I've always been happy to spend my Saturday nights out partying with Bri, who's older and certainly a bad influence, Sara was always more than happy to stay at home and watch TV.

I always thought she would find herself a nice, sensible guy to settle down with, move out of the city, have two point five kids and a white picket fence and be more than happy.

But then she met Jesse, the bad boy of all bad boys and fell madly in love. Her innocence and inhibitions seemed to fly right out the window as she started riding around on the back of his bike and generally shaking up her average life.

While it all might have been a shock, I can't deny that he's the best thing that ever happened to her. I've never seen her smile like she does since she's been with him, and her confidence is through the roof. And although he might be a bad boy from the estate, he's also a total sweetheart with her. I can understand how she fell so hard and fast.

"Come out for dinner with us tonight?" she asks with hope in her eyes.

"I'd love to. I don't finish here until seven, though."

"We can pick you up at your place at eight?"

"Sounds good. Give Jesse a hug for me," I say when I notice the big guy loitering outside the front doors waiting for her. "He could have come in, you know."

"He went to run a few errands, wanted us to have some girl time."

"Fair enough. I'll see you later, yeah?"

"Can't wait," she says excitedly. "I'm so glad to be back. See you later."

She damn near bounces out of the coffee shop and jumps into his arms.

Jealousy threatens to take hold as I witness the incredible connection the two of them share. They've got the kind of relationship that everyone craves, but most never find. I truly believe they've both found their soulmates in each other. I really hope that life never comes between them, because I'm not sure either would survive it.

My eyes don't leave them until they disappear around the corner, and then I drag myself out of my own head and get back to work, really not wanting to risk pissing Matt off any more today.

The thought of him sitting in his office right now, watching our little sex tape on the security feed slams into me and I shudder.

He wouldn't. He's a decent guy.
He wouldn't do that.
Would he?

I flip the sign to closed the second the last customer leaves and twist the lock on the front door after promising Matt that I'll behave, something I do with my cheeks glowing again.

I watch as he drops into a black car that's been out the front for a while waiting for him, although I couldn't see who was driving.

Despite working here for almost two years now, I still know very little about my boss. He's a total enigma, one I know that I don't want to piss off for real. There's certainly something about him that is a little terrifying, and I'd rather not have to witness any more of it than I have.

Turning the background music off, I work in silence, just listening to the torrential rain pounding down on the windows as I restock everything beneath the counter ready for the morning shift.

I'm almost done when there's a knock at the door.

My heart jumps into my throat and hope floods me that it might be Toby.

I hop up, my eyes glued on the doors, and a

little squeal of excitement passes my lips when I see him sheltering from the rain in the doorway.

My hand trembles with adrenaline as I lift it to open the door once more.

"Hey, this is a nice sur—" He forces his way inside and wraps me up in his arms, his lips finding mine. My word turns into a groan as he kisses me as if he hasn't seen me in years, not just a few days.

The door slams shut behind us as he backs me into the counter, hiking me up onto it so he can stand between my thighs.

My heart pounds and my skin burns with need for him, but I know I can't.

Fighting to keep my head, I press my palms against his chest and push him back a little, reluctantly ripping our lips apart.

His chest heaves as his erratic breaths rush past his full, parted lips, and his eyes darken with hunger as he takes in my reaction to his surprise arrival.

"Fuck, I've missed you."

"W-we can't," I stutter, really wishing that we could.

A pained laugh falls from my lips, and his brow wrinkles.

"That wasn't the reaction I was hoping for," he confesses.

"I'm sorry. I missed you too," I say shyly, my eyes dropping from his.

"Hey," he says, capturing my jaw in his warm palm and turning me back to him. "Why are you hiding?"

I stare at him for a beat, my heart tumbling in my chest.

My head tells me to keep my lips shut, to hide my vulnerabilities within, for fear that he'll only use them to hurt me.

But my heart begs for me to be open, to tell him how I really feel.

It's a battle that I'm not all that fond of.

"This," I say, letting my foolish heart take charge. "Us," I breathe. "I've never... I've never felt anything like this before."

The most incredible smile appears on his face, and it only makes my pulse pick up more speed.

His thumb brushes across my bottom lip, and I have to fight my initial reaction to suck it into my mouth. That move would certainly not help with us trying to restrain ourselves.

"Me neither. I haven't been able to get you out of my head."

He closes the space between us, ready to capture my lips again. But I can't let him. If I do, I know exactly where it's going to lead.

To me without a job and a possible criminal record.

I quickly press my fingers to his lips before he makes contact.

"Let me finish up and we can head out."

A growl rumbles in his chest. "My car is right outside," he says with a smirk.

Everything south of my waist clenches at the thought of letting him take me in the back of his car. But then a bucket of reality crashes over me, cooling my blood in an instant.

"I can't," I say, "I'm meeting a friend for dinner." It almost pains me to say it, but there's no way I'm bailing on Sara after her being away for so long. "You could come," I blurt when his face drops, showing his disappointment.

"You want me to meet your friend?" he asks as if it's the most insane suggestion.

"Sure, why not? She and her boyfriend just got back from six weeks in Australia. She surprised me by turning up here earlier." Slipping from the counter, I set about finishing up while I tell Toby about Sara's visit and my less-than-discreet telling off from Matt.

The second I mention the way he spoke to me, Toby tenses.

"That arsehole. It's not like you cost him any real money."

I shrug. "It's okay. He's been a little weird all week. I can't help wondering if it's because he saw..." My words trail off, and I shoot a look toward one of the cameras in the corner.

"He'd have said something, surely?"

"I don't know. He keeps getting this weird look in his eye."

"Weird like what?" Toby growls possessively.

"I'm sure it's nothing. He's just been tense as fuck. I'm probably reading too much into it."

"Jodie," he says, taking a step closer as a shiver runs through me at his dominant tone. "If he does anything, says anything, you need to tell me."

"Matt's harmless. I'm just paranoid."

"Maybe. But I won't have anyone disrespecting you."

"This is my job, Toby. You can hardly talk to my boss about—"

"You wanna bet?" he asks, something dark flashing through his eyes. "Someone hurts you, Demon, and I'll do whatever it takes."

"O-okay," I whisper, slightly terrified and more than just a little turned on by this side of him. "I just need to clean up and go grab my stuff from my locker."

"I can do that. Point me in the right direction."

13

TOBY

"What is it?" I ask after pulling to a stop outside Jodie's house and killing the engine.

"I... umm..." She fiddles with the zip of her coat anxiously. "I'm really sorry, but could you wait out here?"

My chin drops, but I quickly cover my shock. I'm not sure why I expected to be able to follow her, but I had.

"It's just my mum will be home and—"

"It's okay, I can wait," I say softly, reaching out and cupping her cheek. "Whatever you need."

I brush a sweet kiss against her lips before releasing her, knowing that she won't thank me for making her later than she already is.

She's already had to message her friend to tell her we'll meet them there.

"I'll be ten minutes, max."

"I'll be right here, Demon," I assure her.

My eyes don't leave her as she runs to her front door and practically flies through it.

Only ten seconds later, there's a flash of light from the window and I spot a dark figure peeking out—her mum, I assume, trying to get a look at the guy who's waiting for her.

My heart jumps into my throat as I consider the fact that I'm sitting here in a custom BMW.

I have no idea what Jodie's mum might know about the situation with Jonas. Up until this moment, I've assumed she had no idea, like her daughter clearly doesn't. But as the seconds tick on with her standing there clearly staring right at me, or the car at least, I realise just how naïve that might have been.

Joker had to have known who his dad was, what he was involved in. Jonas got him doing his dirty work in going after Stella, after all. Or was he just so enamoured by the man who helped create him that he'd do anything for him? Knowing Jonas and his superiority complex, it's certainly a possibility. Not that it really matters now. It's not like I'm going to be able to ask Joker how that really all played out.

The woman inside that house, though... I wonder what secrets she carries.

Does she know that she and her kids were only one half of Jonas's life, or did she truly believe whatever bullshit he spewed for the reasons he was never there?

My grip on the wheel tightens until my knuckles turn white.

What I wouldn't give to storm in there right now and demand some answers, expose some truths. But as much as I might want to, doing so won't help with my quest. Telling his grieving family the truth won't hurt him enough.

My eyes are still locked on the dark figure in the window when my phone cuts through the silence and makes my breath catch in my throat before I reach for it.

"Yeah," I bark after answering Nico's call.

"Pull your cock out of Jodie. We've been called in."

"You're fucking with me?"

"Nope, no fucking around here, unfortunately. Boss wants us in Lovell. Shit's kicking off, apparently."

"And that's our fucking issue why?"

"Just following orders, man. Now get a wiggle on, yeah?"

"Fuck," I bark. "I'll be back in fifteen. Wait for me, yeah?"

"Sure thing. Be a gentleman and make sure she comes before you leave."

"Nic, I'm not—" The dial tone rings out, telling me he's cut the call on that little nugget of advice. "Fucking chance would be a fine thing," I mutter to myself

Jodie pulls the door open not two seconds later. Her floral perfume hits my nose and my mouth waters. She's wearing a heeled pair of knee-high boots that expose her toned calves. Her coat hides what she's wearing beneath, but I know it's short. Short enough to drive me wild with need and makes my frustration grow about the fact that I'm going to have to bail on our night.

"I'm so sorry, but I'm not going to make dinner," I confess before I get too lost in her and end up bailing on the boss's orders instead.

"The prospect of meeting my friends that scary, huh?" she teases.

"I've been called into work," I say honestly.

"O-oh... okay?"

I pull out onto the road with the intention to drop her at the restaurant before heading home to meet Nico.

"What?" I ask, her attention making my face heat.

"Nothing," she says, and when I look over, I find she's frowning.

I lift my brow to encourage her to say more.

"I just assumed you didn't have a job."

"Is that right?" I ask, my heart racing with the confirmation I needed that she has no idea who I am, or who I'm connected to.

"You drive a custom BMW that's probably worth a bazillion pounds."

"You think my daddy pays for everything, huh?"

She cringes beside me. "I'm sorry, that was really judgmental of me."

"You're not entirely wrong. Daddy did buy the car. But not because I'm his precious little prince or anything, I can assure you." Truth is, he ordered it for me after he discovered me disobeying his orders by allowing my aunt in the house to see Mum, and he locked me in our basement for longer than I want to admit to as punishment.

For some fucked-up reason, he seemed to think that buying me this outrageously expensive car softened the blow of his punishment. Fucking deluded cunt.

"You and your dad not get on?" she asks.

"It's complicated," I grunt.

"I think that's fairly standard with families, isn't it?"

"From my experience, yeah. Although my story is particularly fucked-up."

"Oh?" she asks, clearly hoping that I'll give her something more.

"I wouldn't want to ruin your night with the truth. Maybe one day I'll share."

"I'm here if you want to talk about it," she

offers, reaching over to squeeze my thigh in support.

I look over at her and smile at the concern on her face.

If only she knew the truth. If only she knew how her family was even more fucked up than I'm sure she could imagine.

"What about your dad?" I ask, more than curious about him, seeing as he seems to not exist.

She blows out a long breath. "I have no idea. My mum and stepdad split up after my brother was born. She was seeing someone else for a brief time, and he got her pregnant. That ended and Mum and Dad got back together, sorted their shit out, and he raised me as his."

"That was big of him," I force out through gritted teeth.

"He was a good guy."

How the fuck I manage to contain my reaction to that statement, I don't know.

My fingers begin to cramp on the wheel I'm holding it so tight, and I can't help but hope that whatever we're being sent to Lovell for involves some fucking violence. I could really do with losing some of this anger on some cunt's face right now.

"Here's fine. I can walk the rest of the way," she says, completely oblivious to the rage swirling within me like a storm.

Needing to get her out of the car before I show my hand too soon, I swerve into a tight space at the last minute and peel my fingers from the wheel.

"Toby?" Jodie asks, clearly seeing through the mask I've pulled on. "Is everything okay?"

Sucking in a deep breath, I try to rein in the fury that's threatening to spill out of my features.

"Yeah," I say, forcing a smile and turning to look at her. "I'm just annoyed I've got to bail on you. I was hoping to spend the night together."

"What are you doing tomorrow night?" she asks hopefully.

Leaning over the console, I wrap my hand around the back of her neck and drag her closer.

"I'm spending all night with you," I tell her, my lips brushing hers, craving the relief she brings me from the constant burning need for revenge that lives inside me. "You get off at seven again?"

"Yeah," she confirms, her hot breath racing over my lips, making them tingle with the need to claim her.

"I'll pick you up. Pack a bag for the night. You won't be going home."

I don't need to look to see that her lips have pulled into a smile.

"I'm off Friday."

"Maybe I'll have the day off too, then. I'm

sure we can find something much more exciting to do."

"Sounds like a plan," she agrees.

I finally close the last bit of space between us when my phone starts ringing through the speakers, three seconds before it auto answers for me, but I'm too lost in our kiss to speak.

"Tobes, you there?"

"Uh-huh," I mumble.

"Where the fuck are you? We're waiting."

"Fuck's sake," I groan, pulling back from Jodie's kiss.

"I'm gonna go," she says quickly. "I'll see you tomorrow night, yeah?"

"Can't wait."

Not that I really expected him to, but Theo doesn't wait until Jodie is out of the car to address the situation.

"You dirty dog, Tobias. You've got a girl none of us know about."

Jodie's laugh rings through the air before she swings the door shut, leaving me with Theo's smug-as-fuck voice.

"She's no one. I'm on my way back now. I'll be five."

I spin the wheel and floor it from the space I'd pulled into, causing some Miss Daisy driver behind me to blast their horn.

"You were a fucking mile away," I bark,

finally able to expel some of the anger that talking about Jonas created within me.

"A *no one* that you'll be seeing again tomorrow night? And whose face you were blatantly sucking off when you answered?"

"Don't you have some more pressing issue to deal with right now?" I snap.

"Nope, just waiting for you so we can go party Lovell style."

"Wait... what?"

"Boss is sending us to their fucking warehouse."

"Why the fuck would we want to go there?"

"To help keep the peace. They're expecting trouble."

"Great," I mutter, although I can't deny the fire burning in the pit of my stomach isn't getting hotter and hotter by the minute.

Getting in the middle of a Wolves war could be exactly what I need tonight.

"I'm pulling in now."

"We'll meet you down there. No need to change."

The line cuts as I indicate to turn toward our building.

Right as I pull into my space, the others, Stella and Emmie included, burst through the door.

"Where's Calli?" I ask, knowing it'll rub Nico up the wrong way.

"She ain't partying in Lovell. I might let her hang out with you motherfuckers now, but that's a step too fucking far."

Stella and Emmie roll their eyes.

"We're gonna pick her up on the way," Emmie announces, making the vein in Nico's temple pulsate.

"Get in, Hellcat," Theo demands, holding his passenger door open for his wife.

"Jesus, you're so whipped," Nico mutters, looking utterly horrified as Theo leans in and drops a kiss to her lips.

"Leave them alone, asshole," Stella snaps, slapping him around the back of his head. "They're cute."

"Fucking sickening, more like."

"Get in the fucking car, Nico," Theo growls.

With a sigh, he finally falls into line and rips Theo's back door open.

Turning on my heels, I opt for Seb's car, hoping that with him driving I might get lucky and not have to watch him do anything inappropriate to my sister. They've got form when it comes to cars, after all.

Alex follows my lead and drops into the seat on the other side of me.

"Who got his knickers in a twist?"

A smirk plays on my lips. He's been like a bear with a sore head all week. I'm pretty fucking sure I know why, too.

"He's met a girl who doesn't take his shit," I happily announce, feeling no guilt whatsoever after he sold me out to Stella about Hades at the weekend.

14

JODIE

"Jodie, could I talk to you in my office, please?" Matt's cold, hard voice booms from behind me as I make my way down to the staff room for my lunch break—a short one to make up for my lost time yesterday.

"Of course." Wheeling around, I give him a bright smile, trying to ignore the dread that's seeping through my bones at his tone.

I slip inside after him, my heart thrashing in my chest. "Close the door, please."

The click of the latch pierces through me as I push it closed.

"What's going on?" I ask, my eyes flashing to his computer screen, half expecting the security footage of Toby fucking me to fill it at any moment.

Thankfully—I think—that's not what

happens. Although the words that fall from his lips aren't all that great, either.

"For a few weeks now, there have been issues with the daily takings," he says as if I should know something about it.

"Oh shit, really? Do you think someone has been stealing?" I ask, genuinely horrified. I always thought we had a pretty strong and reliable team. Clearly, I was wrong.

"Yes, I do. And I have reason to believe it's you."

My eyes go wide, and I take a step back as if he just physically struck me.

"What?" I screech. "No. I would never. I—"

"Could you empty your bag for me, Jodie?" he says, his voice brokering no argument, and I let it slip from my shoulder.

"Matt, you're not actually serious right now?" I ask in complete disbelief.

He looks at me, and finally, I see a slip in his cold mask as a little guilt creeps through his eyes.

"I'm sorry, Jodie. I am."

"Jesus," I mutter, dumping my bag on his desk, more than ready to upend the things and prove that I'm not taking money from the till.

I know my life might be less than perfect right now, but I'd never do that.

The contents of my bag spread out across the old chipped desk, a couple of tampons rolling off and falling directly into Matt's lap. Something that would usually entertain me, but right now I feel nothing but ice-cold dread leaking through my veins.

"See," I say, gesturing to the completely unnecessary amount of crap I've just discovered I've been walking around with.

His eyes rake over it, lingering on an old condom packet before he looks up at me. He holds my stare while my heart continues to pointlessly race, making me a little light-headed.

I swallow nervously as I start to wonder if this is all about the sex tape. Does he think it's easier to pin some bullshit stealing on me instead of the embarrassment of that thing?

"Inside pockets," he barks.

"Matt," I sigh, "I fucking swear to you. I've not been ste—"

I open the hidden zip pocket at the back that I'm pretty sure I've never used, and I gasp in shock.

A dangerous growl rumbles in Matt's chest before his hand darts out, fishing the stash of notes from the small pocket.

"I didn't put those there. I had no idea they were there." He glances up at me from counting it, and I swear, if looks could kill then I'd be six feet under right now. "This has to be a setup. I've never stolen a thing in my life."

"I think it's probably time you left, Jodie."

"Matt, please," I beg, beginning to feel the

claws of desperation wrapping around me. "I need this job. Please. I didn't do this. Check the security footage," I blurt without thinking. "I've never taken a penny from the till. I fucking swear."

"Jodie, you need to leave," he says sternly, pushing his chair back and standing, looming over me as if his sheer size will make me run.

"I'm not scared of you because you're bigger than me," I hiss, stuffing all my belongings back inside my bag.

"This could be a lot worse than just having to deal with me," he mutters. "I'm more than happy to keep you here and call the police to investigate. I have to say though; the evidence is pretty damning."

I want to stomp my foot like a toddler and demand he watch all the footage. But knowing he'll only find other damning evidence of what I actually have been doing, I reluctantly decide against it.

"You're making a mistake here, Matt," I warn, holding my head up high and looking him dead in the eyes for five seconds.

When he doesn't react, I barge past him with my pulse pounding in every inch of my body, but I refuse to cower. He's pinned me as guilty and clearly isn't listening to anything I have to say. I refuse to lower myself to begging any more than I already have.

"I'll take this as your notice, effective immediately."

"I'm destined for more than a fucking coffee shop, anyway," I mutter mostly to myself as I march away from him, desperately trying to hold myself together as I storm through the door and out into the main shop.

The door slams back against the wall, turning everyone's eyes my way. Huge mistake.

Emotion clogs my throat and tears burn red hot, threatening to spill before I escape.

"Jodie," Trisha breathes, "are you okay?"

"I-I-I'm sorry," I blurt before running for the door.

I'm instantly blasted by ice-cold air and rain that feels like tiny little knives as it hits my face.

Rushing around the side of the building, hiding behind one of the shop's huge bins, I fall back against the wall and let everything I've held inside over the past few minutes free.

A sob rips past my lips as my tears finally fall.

Anger, frustration, disappointment all mingle with the grief that is always bubbling just under the surface, and I completely lose control.

My body trembles as my back slides down the rough wall until I'm in a heap on the soaking wet ground.

The rain continues to lash at me, the cold threatening to freeze me to the bone, but I barely feel any of it and unleash all of the pain inside me.

My frozen fingers hold onto my phone, the whole thing shaking violently in my grip as I lift it to my ear. But as much as I might want to fall apart alone—it's exactly what I'd have done in the past—now, I don't want to. I want warm, strong arms to wrap around me and for him to tell me that everything's going to be okay. That he believes me, that he knows I'm not some cheapshot thief who'd risk her job over a few hundred quid.

"Hey, shouldn't you be—" His deep voice washes over me and another ugly sob rips from deep in my throat, cutting off the end of his sentence. "Jodie?"

"I-I'm sorry. I just... can you—"

"Where are you?"

Sucking in a shaky breath, I squeeze my eyes shut and try to pull myself together.

"At work. B-but not at work. I'm around the back. T-Toby, I've been—"

"I'm coming. I'm coming right now. Don't fucking go anywhere."

I hear him moving down the line and relief washes through me.

"I'm ten minutes away, okay?"

"Y-yeah. I'm sor—"

"Don't," he barks. "Don't fucking apologise for needing me."

I gasp at his harsh tone, and another whimper falls from my lips.

"Shit, I'm sorry, baby."

I don't say anything as I sit there with water seeping through all my clothes, raindrops dripping from my nose.

"I'm going to be right there. Everything will be okay."

He doesn't cut the call. Instead, it just connects to his car when he starts the engine.

"You wanna talk about it?" he asks, his wheels spinning from wherever he is. School, I guess.

Guilt assaults me as I realise that I've just dragged him from the middle of his life.

I shake my head in answer to his question despite the fact that he can't see me.

He must understand my answer though, because he doesn't ask any questions. Instead, he starts giving me a rundown of his journey, letting me know what shops and buildings he's passing, what lights he jumps in his hurry to get to me.

"Please don't get in trouble," I squeak, terrified that I'm about to hear sirens down the line as he gets pulled over for speeding.

Before I know it, he's telling me that he's turning onto the street, and in only seconds his car screeches to a stop right in front of me.

The door flies open and he's out before I

manage to even attempt to get my arse from the cold ground.

The fact that I'm dripping with water doesn't seem to faze him as he wraps his arms around me and crushes my body against his.

My sobs break free once more as his scent fills my nose and his strength surrounds me.

I probably should be embarrassed about crying all over the guy I've been seeing for only a couple of weeks, but I'm not. There was no one else I wanted when I fled the coffee shop—not Mum, not Bri, not Sara. It was just him, and it tells me a lot about how quickly this guy has buried himself under my skin.

"Shhh," he soothes in my ear, one hand holding the back of my head, my cheek crushed against his chest, while the other rubs up and down my back soothingly. "I've got you, it's okay."

I have no idea how long we stand there locked in our embrace, but it's long enough for his clothes to be soaked through when I finally find the strength to pull away.

"Oh my God, Toby," I gasp when I finally get a non-tear blurred view of his face. "What happened? Are you okay?"

"I'm fine, baby," he assures me, but it's not the truth. He can't be okay. His face is...

"Shit," I sigh, cupping his cheeks as I take in each of his bruises and cuts. One of his eyes is swollen and an awful purple and yellow colour. His eyebrow and lip are split, and he's still got dried blood on his skin as if he hasn't even attempted to clean it up. "This isn't okay, Toby. Who did it?"

A dark chuckle falls from his lips.

"No one you need to worry about, Demon. And trust me, they're in a much worse state than me right now."

Releasing his face, I lift one of his hands, inspecting his busted knuckles.

"Have you even cleaned any of this up?"

His lips part to lie, but I raise a brow at him, glad to have something to think about other than my own disaster of a life.

"Maybe I was waiting for you to get your hands on me," he growls, sending a shiver of desire racing down my spine. "Have you got to go back to work?" That question is like a bucket of reality tipped right over my head.

Fresh tears fill my eyes as I shake my head.

"Let's get out of here, then. You want to go home?" he asks, concern more than evident in his tone as he wraps his arm around my shoulder.

"No," I say sadly, lost in my own head as he closes the door on me. He moves somewhat awkwardly around the front of the car to the driver's seat, which must be soaking after leaving the door open. "I just... I wanna leave," I whisper.

"I want to just walk away from everything for a bit. Does that sound crazy?"

He straps himself in and turns to me. The state of his beautiful face makes me suck in a sharp breath.

"No, Jodie. It doesn't sound crazy. It just sounds like someone who's had too much thrown at them recently and who needs to just take a breath."

I nod, totally overwhelmed for a moment that he understands exactly how I feel right now.

The tears that are still making tracks down my cheeks might be a result of losing my job, but in reality, I'm not too bothered about that. It's just a job. Recent events have taught me that life is too precious to be this devastated about something like that. They're more to do with my soul-deep exhaustion from everything since we discovered that Joe had been killed. My life has been one big roller coaster of grief and misery ever since, a roller coaster I don't see coming to an end anytime soon despite the gut-wrenching pain that begs for it to stop.

"Did you have anywhere in mind?" he asks as if he's actually entertaining my words.

"Anywhere that's not here."

"You wanna go home and get some stuff first?"

I turn to him in shock.

"You're serious?" I ask, lifting my hand to wipe my cheek.

"Yeah. Why, aren't you?"

My chin drops to tell him that I'm deadly serious about getting out of town, but something stops me.

"This is crazy, Toby. We can't just get in your car and disappear."

"Why can't we? There's nothing in my life that can't wait a few days. Anything in yours?"

I think of Mum, who seems to be slowly putting herself back together again, of Bri, Sara, and Jesse. I've got no job. No one needs me.

"I guess not," I say sadly.

"So... do you want to go and get some stuff? Tell your mum we're heading off for a few days?"

I shake my head, not as a no, but just in total disbelief.

"Why are you so..."

"So?" he prompts when I trail off.

"Perfect," I say, a little shyness edging into my tone.

"Trust me, Demon. I'm anything but that, but it's nice to know I've tricked you," he says lightly.

Pulling the visor down, I close my eyes and take a breath before I brave looking at myself in the little mirror.

"Holy shit," I gasp when I finally take in my puffy, red-rimmed eyes.

"You look beautiful," Toby offers beside me.

"It's too early in our rel— whatever this is to lie to me," I quip.

"I'm not. Although I must admit, I'd prefer if those tear tracks down your cheeks were because you were choking on my cock."

"Jesus," I baulk, damn near choking on my own breath.

I just catch Toby's shrug as I look over at him. "What? You wanted the truth."

Ignoring the heat his words stir within me, I swipe at the dark makeup lingering under my eyes and focus on the issue at hand.

"I'd love to go home and grab some stuff, tell Mum I'm gonna be gone for..."

"A long weekend."

My eyes widen at his offer.

"Don't you have work or..."

Toby reaches over and squeezes my thigh.

"I'm all yours, baby."

A rush of excitement goes through me.

"So what are you waiting for, then?" I ask with a smirk, and he quickly delivers by pressing his foot to the accelerator and throwing me back in my seat.

15

TOBY

I watch Jodie disappear into her house before resting my head back and letting out a pained breath.

Last night, and this morning, was brutal.

So much for going for a fucking party. It might have been what we originally walked into, but it turned into a fucking bloodbath quite quickly. Too quickly. We didn't even hang around to the end. When things really turned brutal, we crowded Stella, Emmie, and Calli like a wild pack of wolves ourselves and got them the fuck out of there.

It wasn't soon enough to save any of us from some pretty savage beatings.

The girls were the only ones who left that place not bleeding or groaning in pain. Well, actually, that's not entirely true—both Stella and Emmie were sporting pretty busted-up knuckles from when they felt the need to dive into the middle of it and put their skills to use. I'm still not sure if Seb and Theo were utterly horrified or completely turned on when both of them held their own as Lovell turned into a fucking war zone full of corrupt, twisted, and power-hungry gangsters.

My ribs burn from the punches I took and my face aches like a motherfucker, but none of it was enough to stop me from bolting from Stella and Seb's place the second she called. We'd all congregated there sometime after dawn to lick our wounds and debrief after the shitshow the boss sent us into. Once the sun was up, Theo and Nico set off to go and see the man himself. From the looks on their faces, I'd say they were likely to attempt to give him a dressing down—not that I'm sure it would actually be effective in any way. They might be heirs to the family throne, but their words don't hold a lot of weight where the boss and his underboss are concerned right now.

I wince as I push my hand into my pocket, my split knuckles dragging on the fabric as I grab my phone.

Finding Nico's mum's number, I hit call and set about putting my plan into place, which thankfully, is as easy as I hoped. There really is nothing like having your life well and truly fucked up to get people to bend over backward to do nice things for you.

By the time Jodie emerges from the house with an overnight bag over her shoulder, everything is set.

Thankfully, the rain has reduced to a drizzle, so with a groan, I force my body to unfold from the seat and stalk around the car to take her bag from her.

Our one-woman audience watches every movement from the window. She's been there almost since the moment Jodie slipped into the house. I'm still torn about her nosiness. Is she just trying to suss out the guy who's captured her daughter's attention, or does she already know exactly the kind of man I really am?

"I think your mum might want to meet me," I comment after throwing her bag into the boot and swallowing down the pain that shoots from my ribs. I'm pretty sure no motherfucker broke them, but fuck me do they hurt.

"I think she's craving some excitement in her life," Jodie says sadly. "But she won't even leave the flat."

"I can give her excitement," I say in a rush, gathering her up in my arms and crashing my lips on hers.

"Oh my God," she squeaks in shock, but the second I swipe my tongue along her bottom lip, her entire body relaxes for me and she allows me to dip her low.

A laugh rumbles in her chest and my own

screams in pain, but I don't let up, especially when I shoot a glance at the window and find Joanne's eyes locked on us. But still, I can't read anything on her face.

"Oh my God, you're crazy," Jodie gasps when I drag her back up, but it makes me a little lighter, seeing a smile on her after the way I found her not so long ago.

"If they're gonna look, might as well give them a show."

A shot of red-hot desire flashes through her eyes, and I can only assume her head took her right back to Hades and whether or not all the people outside the room that night were watching us.

"You're bad," she breathes, her eyes locked on my lips.

"You have no idea, baby. Ready to get out of here?"

"Hell yes."

"Better wave to your mum," I laugh.

She turns in my arms and lifts her hand.

Her mum returns the wave, a smile playing on her lips as she watches us.

"She looks happy."

"Maybe I should corrupt her daughter some more in front of her then," I suggest.

"No, no. I think that was more than enough. Let's go."

With a laugh, I release her and allow her to

walk around to the passenger side of the car.

I stand exactly where I am for a beat, my eyes locked on Joanna's before I spin on my heel, rearrange myself while hiding behind the car, and slip inside, ready to take on the weekend.

"Ready?" I ask after breathing in her sweet scent. She changed while she was inside and is no longer in the work uniform but instead a pair of leggings and an oversized hoodie. Her face is now clear of the makeup that was staining her cheeks, and her hair is hanging damp and limp around her shoulders.

"Everything will be okay, whatever it is."

She nods, curling her legs up and wrapping her arms around them as I pull out from the side of the road, the GPS already set to get us to our destination.

"I got sacked."

"Holy shit, why?" A beat passes, but I don't give her a chance to respond. "The security feed?" I ask.

A sad laugh falls from her lips. "I actually think I'd have preferred it to be that," she confesses. "It's stupid, I'm not even that bothered about the job. I think it was just the final straw, you know?"

I nod, understanding how she's feeling. For weeks, I've been one step away from shattering into a million pieces. I'm just waiting for the final thing that's going to make me snap.

"What happened?" I ask.

She sucks in a deep breath and her lips part, ready to explain, but her shoulders sag at the last minute and she shakes her head.

"I don't want to talk about it," she mutters, her eyes drifting to the passing buildings outside the window. "I just want it all to go away. The pain, the loss, the grief."

"I know, baby," I say, reaching over and twisting my fingers with hers. "We've got a bit of a drive. Why don't you sleep?" I suggest, because she's not the only one who doesn't want to talk.

Watching her break is harder than I thought it was going to be. Seeing her tears, her pain... It's somehow managing to dig its way under the hard steel armour I've wrapped around myself in the past few months and is reminding me that deep down under it all, there is a decent human being.

It's weird, being reminded of the person I used to be. Most days it feels like he never really existed and is just a figment of my imagination. A memory from a previous life.

She doesn't close her eyes for the longest time as I drive us out of the city, the beat of the low music playing through the speakers filling the car.

Neither of us speaks, both too lost in our own heads. It's comfortable, nice even. And that realisation freaks me out even more.

We must be about forty-five minutes into the

journey before I glance over and find that she's finally given in.

The frown has finally loosened from her brow, the pain in her eyes hidden.

I blow out a long breath, my grip on the wheel tightening as my feelings over this woman continue to war within me.

My eyes find my knuckles. Blood trickles down the back of my hand from where one of the deeper splits has opened up once more, and I think back to last night, and then to the man who is behind all of this.

That's all it takes to remind me of my reasons for doing what I'm doing.

He caused this. He is making me do all this.

He has to pay.

J odie doesn't even stir when I pull up in front of the cabin we're going to be staying in. I kill the engine, plunging us into silence as the darkness surrounds us. The soft outside lights of the cabin glow in the distance along with the moon that's reflecting in the lake beyond. At some point during our journey, the rain stopped and the clouds parted, leaving a clear, star-filled sky for us. Couldn't really ask for much more as romantic breaks go. If anyone could really call whatever this is that.

I stretch out my legs and roll my shoulders, my entire body aching with my need for sleep after what we endured last night.

"Jodie," I say softly, rousing her. "We're here."

She uncurls from the seat and sits forward, blinking a few times as she comes to her senses.

"Toby," she breathes, her voice nothing but awe as she stares at the illuminated cabin before us. "W-what are... where are... wow," she finally settles on.

"You said you wanted to leave everything behind."

"Yeah," she whispers. "Where are we?"

"In the middle of nowhere."

She nods, almost as if she can't believe she's woken up here.

"Come on, I wanna show you inside."

Pushing the door open, I grit my teeth at the pain that shoots around my body while she does the same behind me.

"Are you okay?" she asks, moving faster than me and taking note of my slow movements.

"Been sitting in the car too long. I'll be fine." When she gets to me, I wrap my arm around her shoulder and walk her toward the huge wrap-around deck.

"Please don't tell me this is your holiday home or something."

I chuckle. "No, it's not. It's Nico's parents'."

"Jesus. It's like the thing of dreams."

"It's a one-of-a-kind, hand-built Canadian log cabin."

"So definitely a thing of dreams, then. I can't even begin to imagine how much something like this costs," she murmurs, dragging her fingertips along the wooden handrail as we climb the steps.

"Probably best you don't think about it. Just enjoy the escape."

"This is utterly insane, Toby. When I said I wanted to leave, I—"

Coming to a stop in front of the door, I turn to her, taking her cheeks in my hands.

"You need this. All you've got to do here is relax. Okay?"

"I don't deserve this. You."

"Let me be the judge of that," I tell her, pressing a kiss to the end of her nose.

"Seriously?" she gasps when I press my hand to the biometric scanner beside the door. "Who the fuck are you, the kid of a fucking MI6 agent or something?"

"If only. How cool would that be?" I joke as I push the door open and step inside.

Warmth surrounds us and I quickly shut us in, leaving the bitter winter night behind us.

"Wow," Jodie breathes, stepping farther into the huge open plan living space. The building is a hexagon built around a huge centre pillar that a spiral staircase wraps around.

I remember coming out here the first time with Nico and Evan when it was being built and was completely mesmerised by how it was all put together. It really is a work of art.

"Who started the fires?" she asks, coming to a stop in front of the one roaring in the living area.

"There's staff."

She glances over her shoulder, a look of total disbelief on her face.

"You live in a completely different world from me."

"Money isn't everything, baby. It's the root of all evil." And I have no doubt it's a major factor in the reasons why Jonas did many of the things he did.

"So what does Nico's family do to have a place like this?"

"His dad is... second in command of a massive company."

"And I'm assuming your dad works for them too."

I nod, not wanting to talk any more about that motherfucker.

"You hungry?" I ask.

Jodie shakes her head, sadness darkening her eyes once more.

"Drink then? There's pretty much every spirit you could ask for in Evan's bar."

That makes her face light up.

"Lead the way to oblivion."

Holding my hand out for her, I lead her toward the alcohol.

"What's your poison, Demon?"

Her eyes scan the coloured bottles.

"Tequila. There's lime and salt, right?"

"Of course." I laugh, opening another cupboard.

I make quick work of slicing the lime while Jodie fills two glasses with very generous shots.

"Lick," I say, holding my hand out for her. Her eyes darken almost immediately as she follows orders. Part of me wonders if the state of my hand will put her off, but she doesn't so much as flinch to do as she's told. Her instant submission makes my cock twitch.

Her tongue laps at my skin and I have to force myself to pull back before I shove her down on her knees to make better use of her mouth.

After sprinkling salt where Jodie licked, I grab her hand to return the favour, coating the back of it.

"Ready to get wild and reckless?"

"Fuck yes," she agrees, grabbing her glass ready.

Lifting her hand to my mouth once more, I lick up the trail of salt, eliciting a growl of desire to rip from her throat before shooting back the tequila and snatching up a wedge of lime and biting down on it.

Jodie watches my every move with her lips parted and her chest heaving.

"Your turn, Demon," I say, holding up my hand.

"Y-yeah."

She follows my steps until she reaches for her lime and finds it gone. Her eyes flick to me, dropping to my mouth where it's waiting for her.

"You're bad," she growls.

A smile twitches at my lips as I wrap my hand around her waist and pull her forward. Her body collides with mine, causing a rush of air to spill free as her lips wrap around the lime.

I release it and spit it to the counter before capturing her mouth.

Lifting her from the floor with a grunt of pain, I sit her back on the counter.

Our kiss deepens, becoming more violent with our need for each other.

The second she bites down on my bottom lip, the split rips open once more, the taste of copper filling my mouth, and a hungry growl rumbles deep in my chest.

"Moving to body shots already?" she asks as I begin kissing down her neck.

An appreciative groan fills the air around us as images of her naked and laid out before me fill my mind.

"Now you mention it..."

16

JODIE

"Oh God," I moan as Toby pulls my bralette from my body, releasing my heavy, needy breasts.

My nipples harden as he blows a stream of air across them, making my back arch, offering myself up to him.

"Fucking missed you, Demon," he growls, sending a strong wave of desire through me, making my skin tingle with the need to be touched. To be claimed. To be forced to focus on this, on him, and nothing else in my bullshit life.

"Lift up, baby," he demands, tucking his battered fingers into my waistband.

My intentions were to clean him up the second we got to wherever we were going, but he threw me for a total loop with this... this little piece of paradise he's found for me to escape to.

When I told him I wanted to leave, I never

expected anything like this. I was thinking of some shitty hotel where we could get wasted, high, and fuck until we passed out. Nothing like this. I've never seen anything like it.

My boots hit the floor with two loud thuds before my leggings and knickers are dragged from my feet.

"So fucking beautiful," Toby murmurs. "And all mine."

Leaning forward, he lets his lips brush up my stomach, over the swell of my breast until he's nibbling on my neck.

"Toby, please," I moan, wrapping my legs around his body and dragging him closer. "I need — argh," I scream when coldness suddenly hits my shoulder before running between my breasts like a river. "Oh fuck." My wanton moan echoes around us as Toby dips his head, lapping at the tequila he just poured over me.

"Yessss," I hiss when his tongue finally finds my nipples. But the pleasure is short lived because no sooner is he there than he's gone again.

Reaching out, he grabs the salt shaker, making quick work of covering both my nipples.

"Oh fuck, yes."

He pushes a lime wedge between my lips as I cry out before Toby dives for my nipples, licking up every grain of salt and driving me fucking crazy. He pours more tequila over me and drags his tongue up the length of my body until his lips brush mine as he bites into the lime.

My heels dig into his lower back and he chuckles as I try to drag his crotch against my aching pussy.

"Such a desperate little demon," he says after spitting the lime onto the counter. "I am starting to get a little hungry, though." His blue eyes flash with wicked intent, and heat floods between my legs.

Lowering back on my elbows, I watch in fascination as he grabs the salt shaker and drops to his knees before me, his eyes right in front of my pussy.

"Look how wet you are for me, Demon. You've missed me too, huh?" he growls.

I gasp as the tickle of the salt dancing on my sensitive skin sends shockwaves racing through me.

His eyes roll up my body before they lock with mine and a dark smile pulls at his lips.

Slowly, so fucking slowly, he leans in, but he doesn't do what I'm expecting and lap at the salt, at me. Instead, he runs his nose through me, breathing me in.

"Oh my God," I moan, unable to decide if I'm mortified or just completely fucking turned on. Before I can come to the conclusion, his searing tongue presses against my clit and all thoughts leave my head as he ensures every last grain of salt is gone before he upends the bottle of tequila over my belly button and laps at the river of alcohol that races down my body and between my legs.

He forgets about the lime this time, and the second he slams the almost empty bottle on the side, he dives for my pussy once more, eating at me like a starving man.

And he doesn't let up until I'm screaming out his name, my entire body quaking and trembling on the bar top.

"Holy shit, I gasp.

"Been dreaming about doing that all week."

My cheeks burn at his words, although I have no idea why. It's a little late to be embarrassed about anything around Toby. In only a short period of time, he's seen me at my best, my worst, and my filthiest. I'm not sure there's much more for him to learn about me at this point. I've given him plenty of reasons to turn his back on me and find someone else to spend time with, yet he's still here. He brought me here.

I shake my head, barely able to process all of this.

"What, baby?" he asks, wrapping his hand around the back of my neck and dragging me from the counter.

"All this... you... it's crazy."

"Just enjoy it," he says before capturing my

lips and letting me taste myself mixed with tequila on his tongue.

"You gonna share that tequila, or are you the only one getting to have some fun tonight?"

I still have no idea how long the journey was here—I haven't so much as glanced at a clock—but the dark night sky when I first opened my eyes told me I was asleep for quite a while.

"Oh, I'm all for sharing the fun, Demon."

He smirks before releasing me, reaching behind him and pulling his hoodie off in one sexy move.

"Holy shit, Toby."

I'm off the counter and on my feet before my body has even registered the movement.

My hands land gently on his sides and I take in the angry bruising on his ribs.

"Doesn't this hurt?" I ask, gently running my fingertips over the dark purple marks.

"A little," he confesses, threading his fingers into my hair. "I know what might help take my mind off it while you're down there, though," he quips.

"You should be in fucking bed healing, not... not... that," I say, waving my hand behind me at the counter I was just sprawled out on.

"There's only one thing I want to be doing in a bed, Demon. And I can assure you, it's not resting."

He tugs on my hair, forcing me to stand back up.

"I'm fine, baby. Fully functioning and more than up for the challenge of getting you out of your own head."

To prove his point, he steps closer, ensuring his hard length presses against my stomach.

"Is there a bath in this place? You need to do something about all this, Toby. I need to clean you up and make sure you don't need stitches."

"I don't. This isn't my first rodeo, Demon. I promise you I'm..."

"What?" I ask, my heart jumping into my throat, thinking that something is wrong.

He holds my eyes for a beat and panic floods me, but then a truly filthy smile splits across his face.

"I've got the perfect thing."

My brows pinch before he sweeps me off my feet.

"Toby, no," I argue, trying to twist out of his arms. "Your ribs."

"It only hurts when you fight," he tells me, but he's lying. I can hear it in his tone.

"Liar," I hiss. "Put me down, I can walk. Wait... where the hell are we going?" I ask when he marches toward a wall of floor-to-ceiling windows. "No, it's freezing out there," I squeal as he pulls the door wide, allowing the bitter air to flow over my heated skin.

Without batting an eye at the cold, he marches across the deck and around the corner. The soft lighting from around the cabin allows him to see where he's going, and the second my eyes land on a sunken covered square tucked into the corner and sheltered by low-hanging trees, I start to understand his plan.

"Is that a—"

"Sure is, Demon. You still up for a bath?"

"As long as it's warm," I say, my body beginning to tremble despite the heat coming from him.

"It'll be perfect."

He lowers me to my feet, and I hop back and forth as the ice water on the floor damn near burns my feet.

"Hurry," I whisper, wrapping my arms around myself as my goosebumps get goosebumps.

In a flash, he throws the lid of the hot tub back, and steam billows up into the night sky.

"Yes," I hiss, racing forward and stepping into the bubbling water. "Aren't you joining me?" I ask, looking over my shoulder when the water is at my waist and finding him standing there, watching me.

"I'm not a fucking imbecile, Jodie. Of course I'm getting in. Just give me a minute. I'll be back," he says cryptically and rushes back into the house.

"Okay," I sigh, finally sinking all the way under the soothing water.

Resting my head back on the side, I stare up at the dark sky and twinkling stars and let go of the lingering anger, disappointment and betrayal from my interaction with Matt earlier.

I didn't do it. I've never stolen a penny from that place. From anywhere.

If he doesn't trust me, then that has to be on him, not me.

The knot in my belly begins to loosen and my muscles relax.

I never could have imagined this when I announced I wanted to get out of London, but it's exactly what I needed.

This nothingness. This escape.

Guilt worms its way through my veins as I think about Mum sitting at home alone. She'd have loved it here. And she needs it just as much as I do.

My thoughts are cut off when the whoosh of the sliding door cuts through the silence around me, and when I look up I find the most incredible sight before me.

"Whoa, you've really pulled out all the stops, huh?" I ask as a still shirtless Toby lowers a tray to the side of the tub that contains a bottle of what I can only assume is obscenely expensive champagne with two glasses and a plate of fancy charcuterie. And as if that wasn't enough, he then digs into his pocket and reveals a baggie of weed and a pre-rolled joint.

My eyes widen and my mouth waters. For all of it.

"You look like a kid who's just been shown a lifetime supply of sweets," Toby says with amusement.

"I have. Alcohol, food, weed, and you. What more could a girl need?"

"There's the question," he deadpans as he pops the button on his jeans and pushes them and his boxers down over his hips.

"O-oh," I laugh. "That's right. You naked."

I take my time running my eyes down his insane body, trying not to focus on how much pain he must actually be in before they lock on his hard length. My teeth sink into my bottom lip as I remember exactly how he tastes.

The magnetic pull between us has me moving across the tub until I'm in front of him, his cock bobbing an inch from my lips.

Unable to stop myself, I stick my tongue out and lick up the precum that's already beading at the tip.

"Shit, baby. You really are a demon. Can't even wait for me to— fuck," he barks when I take him in my mouth fully.

I bob back and forth, my tongue teasing his head every time I pull back, and I hold his eyes the entire time. It's not until his hand lifts and presses against his ribs that I realise what I'm doing.

This guy makes me so fucking dick drunk, I forget my own damn name.

"Shit, I'm sorry. You need to get in."

"Never apologise for sucking my cock," he states so seriously that I can't help but laugh.

"Sit on the edge," I demand, taking charge for once. "You're not getting in until you come down my throat."

His eyes widen at my crass words, and his throat ripples with a harsh swallow.

"Whatever you say, baby."

He steps into the water somewhat stiffly as his body probably screams at him from the movement and props his arse on the edge.

"I'm all yours," he says with a smirk, widening his thighs to give me the access I'm so desperate for.

In a flash, I'm right in front of him with my fingers wrapped around the base of his steel length as I tease the end, sucking and licking at him as his fingers tighten in my hair.

"Keep teasing me, Demon, and you might just find my cock in your throat faster than you were expecting," he warns in a deep, raspy voice.

Heat blooms, burning me from my core at his wicked words. But as tempted as I am to see if he'd follow through on his threat, I find myself complying to his demands and sinking down on his cock.

"Fuck yeah. Your mouth is sin, baby," he praises, gathering my hair up in one hand, using it to set the pace.

I hum around him, making his cock twitch and the salty taste of his precum coat my tongue.

"You're too fucking good at this, Demon," he grits out, already on the edge of release.

Needing him to find the same intense pleasure he gave me not so long ago, I relax my jaw and take him deeper.

"Oh fuck. Fuck. Jodie," he grunts a beat before he spills his load down my throat.

I don't release him until he's finished, but he quickly takes over—unsurprisingly—lifting me from my kneeling position on the seat and sinking beneath me. My legs wrap around his waist as the water laps at our chests. The second he's settled, he grips my chin tightly and slams his lips down on mine, plunging his tongue into my mouth and probably tasting himself on me. That thought only makes me burn hotter for him.

My hips flex against him as our kiss continues, desperately seeking some friction.

"Needy little whore," he mutters lightly into our kiss.

My response is nothing more than a whimper as his fingers skim up my thigh before colliding with my swollen clit.

"Are you wet for me, Demon?"

"Yes," I cry when his fingers drop lower to find out for himself.

"Such a good little demon, and always so desperate for my cock."

His fingers curl inside me, finding the spot that drives me crazy.

"Oh fuck," I cry, my voice echoing in the miles of nothingness surrounding us.

"Louder," he demands, beginning to finger-fuck me harder. "No one can hear you here."

"Toby," I scream when he gets me right on the edge before ripping his fingers from inside me. My entire body jolts with the loss, my muscles clamping down as if they're going to be able to drag him back inside me.

"Suck," he demands, pushing them roughly into my mouth. "Fuck yeah."

I'm still cleaning him up when he shifts my position, pressing the head of his cock against my entrance and dragging me down, impaling me on his cock.

"Never get enough of this," he grunts as he holds me down so I'm fully seated on him.

His arms rest out along the sides of the tub and his eyes hold mine, challenge flashing in them.

17

TOBY

The smirk that spreads across Jodie's face makes my cock jerk deep inside her body.

We might have only been together a handful of times, but she's yet to have any kind of control over the situation, exactly as I usually prefer it. But the concern in her eyes every time she sees one of my cuts or bruises is clearly softening me, because suddenly I find that I'm more than willing to hand the hard work over to her.

My fingers curl around the lip of the tub in the hope that I can give her this, allow her to think that she's giving us what we both clearly crave and stop me from hurting in the process.

It's impossible, although she has yet to know that the real pain I have to live with isn't only skin deep. Those are the nightmares that wake me most nights in a cold sweat, the memories of seeing Mum trying to hold it together despite the fact that I heard every single scathing word Jonas had just spat at her. It's the feeling of my world falling from beneath me as the truth finally began to unravel around me, exposing the cunt's true colours for what they really were.

Jodie's fingers thread into my hair and she lifts herself off me, her inner muscles rippling and damn near making my eyes roll back in my head.

"Get out of your head, hotshot. You're showing me a good time, remember?"

"As if I could forget."

Throwing my previous thoughts aside, my arms dip back under the water before I grab handfuls of her arse and help her move.

"Just can't help yourself, can you?"

I shrug, loving the easy smile on Jodie's lips. It's a million miles away from how she looked when I found her a broken mess in the rain. "You wouldn't have me any other way, Demon."

"That may well be true," she confesses, her lips brushing mine before she bites on my bottom one, making it bleed all over again.

"I thought you wanted to fix me up, not break me further," I joke.

"Maybe I'll do both. The bad boy looks stupidly good on you," she says with a smile.

"Oh baby, if you want bad, I can do bad."

She squeals as I lift her out of the water, keeping us connected, before laying her back on the deck, leaving her arse hanging over the edge. A violent shudder rips through her body as the cold rainwater bites into her skin, but she doesn't complain.

My hips thrust forward with enough force to send her shooting backward before my grip on her hips tightens and she cries out into the night.

"Harder. Fuck me harder."

I follow her orders, ignoring the pain and focusing on the pleasure of her body instead.

"Addicted, baby. Fucking addicted to your pussy."

"Yes, yes," she chants as my punishing thrusts continue.

Faster than I would like, my balls start to draw up as the tingles of my imminent release begin.

"Clit, Demon," I bark. "Get there."

Her hand slips down her stomach, and my teeth grind when she flicks her clit and she tenses around me.

"Fuck, Demon. I—"

"Toby," she screams as she squeezes me impossibly tight and I have no choice but to fall right over the edge with her once more.

My entire body locks up before my cock jerks, filling her with everything I have.

"Fuck," she pants, her skin damp from the hot tub and her exertion, although the cold quickly sets in and goosebumps cover her body.

"Yeah," I agree, finally slipping out of her, more than spent after two mind-blowing releases.

Scooping her up in my arms, I lower us both back into the water, keeping her cradled against me. She tucks her head into the crook of my neck and lets out a heavy sigh.

I don't say anything, assuming that she still doesn't want to talk.

I understand. I don't want to talk about my life either, but the silence when I'm with her is almost as bad, the truth taunting me, tempting me.

"My boss accused me of stealing," she finally says sadly.

"What?"

"I didn't," she says in a rush, as if I was questioning that she might have done it, not that she was accused. "I'd never."

"I know."

"You don't even know me, Toby."

"Maybe I'm a good judge of character. And you don't scream 'thief' to me."

A sad laugh falls from her lips. "If only my boss agreed."

"You can get another job. It's just a coffee shop," I say, hoping she doesn't take offence to that. It's a perfectly acceptable job, she's just... worthy of more, I guess.

"Yeah, I know." She falls silent, but it's full of

unspoken words which I don't push her for. "The whole thing was a setup."

"What do you mean?" I ask, my gut twisting with her words.

She pauses. "Matt... he... He accused me of stealing from the till and demanded I open my bag..."

"It was in there?" I finish for her.

"I've never so much as opened that fucking pocket, but there was a stack of notes in there. I just... I don't understand. I thought I got on well with everyone I worked with. I thought—" A sob cuts off her words.

I squeeze her tighter, gritting my teeth when my ribs smart.

"It'll be okay. Maybe it's for the best you get out now if someone is gunning for you."

"It just doesn't make any sense," she breathes, nuzzling into me. It makes my heart race, knowing that she's finding comfort in me. The very last place she should be seeking it right now.

"I'm sorry for dragging you away. Were you in school?" she asks softly, her fingers finding the hair on the nape of my neck. Goosebumps erupt from her delicate touch and a shiver runs down my spine.

"Looking like this?" I ask with a laugh. "Nah, I was hanging out at a friend's place."

"What happened?" She pulls her head from my chest, her eyes darting to each cut and bruise on my face before she cups my jaw and gently rubs her thumb over my split bottom lip.

"Just some drunken idiots." It's not entirely a lie.

"Seems like it's not just me needing a new job."

If only it were that easy.

"So... did you bring that champagne and weed out here just to look at or..."

"Cheeky," I mutter, a smile pulling at my lips. "Not interested in the food then?"

"It's at the bottom of my list."

"And what's at the top?" I ask, wanting to know what to reach for first.

"Your cock."

"Noooo. Please. I'm sorry. Don't leave me," I scream, fear lacing each word. The slam of the heavy door of the basement rattles through my body as I'm consumed by the cold and darkness.

I gasp, my eyes flying open, quickly discovering that wherever I am is as dark as it was in my nightmare.

My heart is racing, making every inch of my body pulsate with its fast pace. I throw the covers back, my skin damp with sweat as I push from the bed and stumble toward the light of the moon shining in through the large windows.

Pressing my palms against the cool glass, I lean forward until my brow touches it, instantly cooling my burning skin.

I stand there for the longest time, sucking in deep breaths and trying to rid myself of the images lingering from my nightmare.

It's not the first time he's haunted me in my sleep, and I know for a fact that it won't be the last.

Once I'm confident I've got a little more control of myself, I take a couple of steps back and fall down onto the chaise that looks out over the trees and rolling hills in the distance during daylight.

I keep my eyes fixed on the stars as I lose myself in my thoughts, on my dark need for revenge on the man who is still controlling my life despite being locked up and unable to touch me.

My fists curl with my need to hurt him. To do all the things he's done to me and those I love over the years.

If I were at home right now, he'd have already found me standing in his cell. If he was lucky, I'd just be looming over him, taunting him. If he wasn't, then he'd already be bleeding as I unleashed the monster he spent years creating within me.

He wanted me as his little protégé, his heir in the Family. And he certainly succeeded in creating a brutal soldier. I just don't think he ever considered the fact that I might turn it on him one day.

Delusional fucking cunt always thought he was untouchable.

Big bad Jonas Ariti. Capo and son of the Consigliere.

He always believed that one day he would fill his father's shoes, becoming the Family's advisor. Hoped that I would get to do the same. Or at least, that was what I always thought.

Now I can't help but wonder what his game plan really was.

Where did he see Joker fitting into all of this?

He's the true Ariti heir, despite the fact that I have more Greek blood running through my veins.

Was his stint as a Reaper only temporary? Did Jonas plan on somehow getting him to switch teams and join?

These questions have been spinning around my mind for weeks now, and despite beating him, torturing him to within an inch of his life, I'm still nowhere closer to having the answers.

If I didn't know the manipulative cunt as well as I do, I might be starting to think that he didn't even know himself. But that's not the case. The power-hungry fuck knew exactly what he was doing. Clearly, I'm just not as fucked in the head.

I'm so lost, I don't hear Jodie get out of bed, or her soft footsteps as she makes her way over, and it's not until her delicate, warm hand slides down my back, scaring the ever-loving shit out of me that I even know she's awake.

"Hey," she says softly. "Is everything okay?"

We spent almost all night in the hot tub. Between us, we drank the champagne, smoked the joint, and polished off the food after getting the munchies for something other than each other's bodies.

It was incredible. She's incredible. More so than I ever expected her to be, which makes this whole thing a huge head fuck. As if I need any more of that in my life right now.

"Yeah. I couldn't sleep," I say quietly as I sit up straight, reach out and pull her down onto my lap.

Instantly, my muscles relax at having her close, having her scent filling my nose and her warmth against my skin.

"I'm sorry, I didn't mean to wake you."

"Shhh." She presses her fingers to my lips as she twists in my hold. Her legs encase my hips and her arms wrap around my shoulders.

"No talking. We've done more than enough."

She's not wrong. We spent all night talking about everything and nothing, finally getting the chance to really get to know each other. Although, I can't deny that I was cautious about how much information I gave her about me and my life, focusing on asking her questions and avoiding the topic of family at every opportunity. The question that I knew was coming—that really hit me—was the one about my scar on my chest. I've seen her eyes drop to it a time or two when we've been together, and I knew I was on borrowed time. You'd have thought that would have allowed me to come up with a better lie. It didn't, and I fumbled around, answering like an idiot. She blatantly didn't believe me, but thankfully, she let it go. It's not like I could tell her that I took a bullet protecting my sister from her deranged and psychotic stepbrother.

Her lips brush mine in the softest kiss that I feel all the way down to my toes.

I've never met anyone like her before. Stella came close with how she immediately made me feel comfortable in her company, as I guess she should, seeing as it turns out we share a set of parents. But being with Jodie, everything feels right. Pieces of me that I never even realised were out of place suddenly seem to fit.

"Thank you for tonight," she says against my lips. "For this. It's... everything."

"I didn't think we were talking," I remind her.

"We're not. I just needed you to know that."

I don't get a chance to respond because her lips finally capture mine and I happily hand myself over to her, my body more than ready to rediscover the electric connection between us when we collide.

18

JODIE

I was utterly spent when we finally fell back into the bed as a tangle of limbs at whatever time it was in the middle of the night.

Toby woke me, thrashing about in bed, but before I could do anything about it, he threw the covers back and got out. Despite being wasted and high, sleeping beside someone was unusual, and even though I was exhausted, I was still aware of him.

My heart ached in the darkness as I watched him fighting whatever battles he holds inside. I wanted to go to him, to help him, but something told me it was the wrong thing to do, that he needed the silence, the solitude.

But eventually, my need to comfort him became too much. And I'm glad I did. He instantly accepted my touch, my support, and despite not having a clue as to what was tormenting him, I felt like I was taking some of the weight from him just by being there.

For the first time, he really let me take charge as I sunk down onto him. It was slow, lazy, but no less intense than anything we'd experienced together before. If anything, it was more. So much more. I felt so connected to him in those few moments, surrounded by nothing but darkness and our combined pain.

I was wrecked after the day I'd had. My heart was in a million pieces, the grief overwhelming, but somehow, he'd managed to pick up all my broken, jagged parts and begin to put them all back together.

"You're almost too good to be true," he whispered in my ear after a slow but earth-shattering release had ripped through me.

He might have been the one to say those words, but I felt them down to my soul.

He was everything I needed. The light in my darkness. My escape from the never-ending pit of despair.

I know the second I wake that he's not there. The room feels empty. But it doesn't stop me from rolling over and hoping that I might find him lying beside me.

A sigh falls from my lips when I realise that I was right. Not only is he not here, but the bed is cold, like he's been gone a while.

Sitting up, I hold the covers to my chest as my eyes find the huge windows.

Clouds hang heavy in the sky, the air hazy with the rain that's pounding against the glass. But even still, the view is beautiful. I could wake to this every day and never think about the city again, I'm sure.

A crash from somewhere downstairs finally gets me moving, and after a quick trip to the bathroom and swiping Toby's hoodie from the chaise I found him on last night, I head down to find him.

My eyes linger on all the pieces of art which line the walls as I make my way from the bedroom toward the stairs. If the cabin didn't already scream insane wealth, then these certainly would. I mean, I have no idea who the signatures belong to, but they're clearly someone worthy of giving wall space to.

There's another crash as I drop down the first stair, and then the scent of frying bacon hits my nose and my stomach growls embarrassingly loudly.

I come to a grinding halt as I turn toward the kitchen. My eyes almost bug out of my head and my chin drops at the sight.

Toby is standing in front of the stove wearing only a pair of low-hanging sweats, his toned and tanned skin on display for me to eat up while he not only cooks but also dances to the music playing softly from some hidden speakers.

It takes me a few seconds to register the song because I'm so lost to the ripple of his muscles and the way his hips move, but the second realisation hits, I can't help but bark out a laugh of amusement.

He stills for a beat, the utensil in his hand dropping into the frying pan before he turns toward me.

"Oh hey," he says, the most endearing smile pulling at his lips at being caught.

A laugh bubbles up my chest as I close the space between us.

"Little Mix? Really?" I ask teasingly.

"It was just on." He shrugs.

"Sure it was," I say, running my hands up his chest and locking my arms around his shoulders. "It's okay, bad boy. Your secret is safe with me."

A hum of appreciation rumbles in the back of his chest. "I knew I could trust you, Demon," he says, dipping down to brush his lips against mine, his hands grasping my waist. "You smell like heaven," he whispers. "I wonder if you taste as good."

His lips claim mine, his tongue pushing into my mouth, and I sag in his arms, drowning in everything he has to offer me.

That is, until my stomach lets it be known

just how hungry it is, and he pulls back with a laugh.

"I think I need to feed my girl," he says, dropping a final kiss to the end of my nose.

"Your girl?" I ask as he makes his way back to the pan, a smile tugging at my lips as he none too discreetly rearranges himself.

"Well, I didn't bring you here to bin you off the second we get back into the city," he shoots over his shoulder. "Sit down," he demands when he discovers I'm still standing awkwardly in the middle of the kitchen.

"I-I can make coffee," I offer.

"Sit down, Demon. Do as you're told."

I salute him, much to his amusement. "Sure thing, boss." I swear to God he tenses at my final word, but he covers it so quickly I start to wonder if I imagined it.

Hopping up onto one of the bar stools, I watch him as he works.

"You know your way around a kitchen then, huh?"

"Did you think I was one of those rich kids who had everything done for them?"

I stare at him, a frown forming on my brow. "I... uh... Honestly, I haven't really thought anything. Your money or status or whatever hasn't really featured all that high on my list of concerns."

"So you're really not impressed by my car," he deadpans.

"I'm really, really not. This place, though... you're getting close to impressing me."

He laughs, reaching into the cupboard to grab some plates.

"It's good to know the level I need to reach in order to do so. The Maldives next time, maybe," he mutters lightly.

"So, who taught you to cook?" I ask, going back to the beginning of this conversation. I have no intention of talking about money or what he can or cannot afford. It's meaningless to me. I'd much prefer to get to the real him. "Your housekeeper?" I joke lightly when he doesn't respond straight away.

My eyes follow him as he moves, cracking a couple of eggs into fancy poaching pouches, and I can't help but notice the way his shoulders tighten.

"I taught myself, actually."

"Oh?" I ask, needing more details.

"Our... uh... housekeeper and cook stopped providing me with meals when I was a teenager."

"I'm sorry, what?" I blurt.

"It's nothing. Bullshit from my past. You don't need the details."

"Like hell I don't," I spit, a little harsher than I intended, making his steps falter as he moves to the coffee machine. "I'm your girl, remember?" I say a little softer.

"I know but... my past, my childhood... most of it isn't pretty." I grab his hand after he delivers my coffee, stopping him from retreating.

"That may be true, Toby. But it's a part of you. And I'm not scared of the dark parts." I know they're there. I see the shadows in his eyes that I'm pretty sure he thinks he hides.

"You should be, Jodie. If you saw the truth, you wouldn't be here right now."

"Bullshit," I hiss, tugging him closer, spinning the stool so I can capture his legs with mine. Reaching up, I take his sore face in my hands. "There's nowhere else in the world I'd rather be right now than here with you."

He stares at me, his eyes searching mine for something I'm not sure he's going to find. The fact that he's found anything worthwhile within me right now is a miracle when I feel like I'm going to shatter at any moment.

"Baby," he whispers, resting his head against mine. He sucks in a sharp breath as if he's about to say something earth-shattering, but the ring of a timer fills the kitchen, and with a sigh, he backs away.

"Better not ruin my rep as a chef before we've even started."

His eyes remain on me as he moves back toward

the stove, our connection holding as he allows me to see just a few more of the dark parts of his soul. I might not know the details, or even the reason why they're there. But I recognise the pain. It blends with mine and makes me wonder if it would be easier to fight if we went up against it all together.

I stay quiet, lost in my own head, just watching him as he plates up our breakfast and brings it over.

"This looks amazing," I breathe, staring down at the crispy bacon, creamy avocado and what looks like perfectly poached eggs. Clearly, he did a fantastic job teaching himself to cook.

"So," I start, needing to dig a little more into his life, "you've mentioned that your father is a giant cock. But you haven't said much about your mum."

My eyes lock on his lips as he pushes a forkful of food into his mouth, and the small smile that appears tells me all I need to know about the woman who brought him into the world.

"She's... incredible," he says after a few seconds.

"Tell me about her," I say, needing to hear about the woman who makes his face soften the way it is.

"She's the strongest woman I've ever met. The bullshit that she's endured, the pain she's suffered... and after all these years, she's still smiling."

"Are they... still together?" I ask with a wince, kind of assuming they're not.

A laugh rips from Toby as he lowers his fork and holds my eyes. "No, thank fuck. He trapped her for years, blackmailed her into being his little puppet, just like he did with me. But she's finally free."

"How did she get out?" I ask, not realising that I might be pushing a little too hard until the question falls from my lips.

Darkness flashes through his eyes before he blinks, banishing it.

"He fucked up. His lies started to unravel and the truth emerged. It helped set her free."

"And you?"

"Yes and no," he says, cryptically.

I take my first bite of breakfast, silently groaning to myself as the tastes explode on my tongue, and wait to see if he's going to continue.

"It's going to take me a little longer than her to be able to put it all behind me and move on."

"That's fair enough after everything he's put you through," I say. "I'm sure no one expects you to move on like it never happened."

He shakes his head. "I'll get there. There are just a few things I need to work through before I can close the door on that part of my life."

I smile at him, wanting him to know that I

understand without sounding patronising by telling him.

"Siblings?" I ask, my mind flicking to memories of me and Joe growing up.

"A sister. Different dad, though."

"Lucky her," I mutter.

"You have no idea. As with everything to do with families though, it's complicated."

I can't help but laugh. "My brother and I had different dads too. It never made me feel any less connected to him, though."

"How did he die?" Toby asks.

My lips part to answer, but the words don't come for a moment as I wonder if I ever actually told Toby that I'd lost Joe.

"What's wrong?" he asks, concern covering his face.

"N-nothing. Sorry. He... uh... got involved with the wrong crowd a few years ago."

"A gang?" Toby asks, lowering his knife and fork to his now empty plate.

"Yeah. The Royal Reapers. It's a motorcycle club."

Toby's brows lift. "I've heard of them. They've got quite the rep."

"Yeah." A sad laugh falls from my lips. "I was so pissed when I found out he'd joined. He was such a good kid. He had such a bright future ahead of him, and then he just threw it all away by joining that bunch of thugs."

"Why did he join?" Toby asks, pushing his plate back, resting one elbow on the counter and placing his other hand on my thigh in support. His warmth seeps through me and gives me the push I need to continue.

"Honestly, I have no idea. He was never big into bikes when he was a kid. But suddenly at fifteen, he declared he wanted lessons for his sixteenth and it went on from there. Each year he got a bigger engine, and then before we knew it, he was wearing a freaking cut and getting covered in ink. It was so unlike him. At one point, he wanted to go to uni to do engineering, and then he spent his days elbow-deep in bike oil. Not that there's anything wrong with that," I quickly add. "It just never really seemed like that was his calling in life."

"I guess people are good at hiding themselves," Toby mutters.

"I thought I knew him, you know. And then right before my eyes, he morphed into this man I barely recognised."

"That must have been tough."

"Not as tough as losing him," I mutter. "He was shot," I say, remembering that his death was how we got on to this conversation. "He got into some kind of trouble with the club and they took his life."

"Shit, babe. That's tough."

"Yeah, it's not been a great few weeks."

I pick at some more of his incredible breakfast, but after that conversation, I battle to force much more of it down.

"It's okay," he says, noticing my struggle.

"I'm sorry. It's incredible. I just—"

"I shouldn't have asked you all of that while we were eating," he says, dragging my stool closer to him, spinning me around and encasing my legs with his. "I'm sorry life's been so shitty for you. I wish I could help make it better," he says sincerely.

"You are, Toby. You have no idea how much you're helping. You appeared in my life when I needed you the most. You're my guardian angel."

He smiles at me, his eyes bouncing between mine and my lips.

"I'm no angel, baby."

I bite down on my bottom lip as thoughts of all the things we've done together flicker through my mind like a movie.

"You might be right there," I mutter, my focus dropping to the inches of bare skin before me. His bruises still look more than a little bit painful, but they have lessened since yesterday. The cuts on his face also look better despite the fact that I never actually managed to fix him up.

"I need to go shower," I say before either of us gets carried away and he ends up eating more than his breakfast in his best friend's parents' kitchen.

My cheeks blaze at the thought.

"I think I like where your mind just went, Demon."

My eyes find his and I try to dig up some kind of argument, but it falls flat.

"How about I clean up and then come and find you? You're pretty dirty; you might need help."

A lust-filled laugh rumbles up in me. "Oh yeah, totally filthy."

"Go and get naked and wet. I won't be long."

I walk away to the sound of him putting everything into the dishwasher. There's a part of me that wants to smile, because being here with him is the most incredible, weightless feeling. But then I'm hit with reality, my grief, his pain, and I feel like I'm drowning all over again.

I step onto the first floor with a heavy sigh, my eyes set on the room he claimed for us at the end of the hall, but the one sitting ajar beside me catches my eye as I move past.

I have no idea what it is, but I find myself moving closer.

Pressing my hand to the door, I push it open and step inside.

Realisation hits me almost immediately as to who this room belongs to. It's got 'teenage boy' written all over it.

The sheets are black, the dresser is covered in boys' deodorant, there are posters of half-naked women on the walls, along with a couple of signed football shirts bearing names I've never heard of. There's even a porn magazine that's been neatly tidied on the bedside table.

Jesus, I bet the staff loves Nico and his wild ways.

My eyes snag on a series of photo frames on a shelf on the other side of the room, and I immediately take off. A smile pulls at my lips the second I take in the images of a group of much younger boys all laughing and joking together.

In the earliest one, I'd say they were all about seven or eight. The oldest is recent, all of them out in the hot tub with bottles of beer in their hands.

They look... like trouble.

And if Toby and Nico are anything to go by, I bet they're a lot to handle.

I'm so lost in the images of a younger, freer-looking Toby that I don't hear him slip into the room behind me.

"I should have known you'd find these," he says, startling me as his arms wrap around from behind and the heat of his body presses against my back.

"You were so cute," I say softly, as he rests his chin on my shoulder.

"The five of us were trouble back then," he muses.

"Just back then?" I ask lightly.

"Nah, we're everyone's worst fucking nightmare now." A shudder works its way down my body at the darkness in his tone.

"Tell me about them. Obviously, I know enough about Nico already." I smirk, thinking of the night in Hades where I watched him railing Bri like it was his last night on Earth.

Toby's nose brushes up the column of my neck, quickly followed by his burning tongue.

"You really want to talk about my friends right now, Demon?"

"I-I—" I stutter as he sucks on the sensitive skin beneath my ear. "I just want to know more about you, about your life. The good bits. The fun."

"I'm all about having some fun, baby," he murmurs, making goosebumps erupt across my body.

Spinning me around, he bands an arm around my back, pinning us together and allowing me to feel just how ready for some fun he really is.

He walks us backward until my calves hit the bed, and he continues until I have no choice but to fall onto my back.

In a flash, he's on his knees between my thighs, his eyes taking in my bare pussy before raking up my body as if I'm not covered in his giant hoodie.

"We can't do this on Nico's bed," I moan

when his hands slide up my stomach before squeezing my breasts with the most delicious pressure.

"Why the fuck not? I can tell you for a fact that my bed has never stopped him."

My head lifts in shock.

"We've done plenty worse shit than fucking in each other's beds, Demon. I can assure you of that."

He drops over me and brushes his lips against mine as his hard length teases me through the fabric of his sweats.

A needy growl rumbles deep in my throat as his tongue pushes past my lips, seeking mine.

"Are you going to try to tell me that you've never had sex somewhere you shouldn't?" he says into our kiss.

"Aside from Bri's shower?" I ask on a moan as his grinding gets a little more insistent.

"Mmm... aside from that?"

"I couldn't possibly tell you all my secrets, hotshot. But I can assure you, I've never had sex in any of my friends' beds."

"Well," he starts, nipping across my jaw until he gets to my ear. "Maybe that's something we should fix. Starting right now."

His hand slips between us, and a second later, I feel the familiar thickness of his cock at my entrance.

"Toby," I moan as he slowly pushes inside my body.

"Can't get enough of this, Demon. You're fucking ruining me."

A wicked smile curls at my lips, loving how open he is when we're connected like this.

His words, his touch make me feel like I'm flying. Like I'm totally weightless when we're together and able to face anything the world might throw at us.

His movements are slow as he fills me to the hilt as his lips move against mine in the most knee-weakening kiss.

My body burns with the need for more, my core aching and trying to pull him deeper—anything to make him move.

"Toby," I moan, my nails digging into the soft skin of his shoulders.

He just starts to up the pace when something starts vibrating against me.

"What the—"

It takes me a few seconds to register what the hell is going on.

Toby's hand slips beneath me before revealing my phone that I slipped into the pocket of his hoodie before I headed downstairs earlier.

Amusement flashes in his eyes when he looks at the screen, and I'm able to read his intentions before he even moves.

"Toby, no," I cry, trying to reach for my phone. But it's too late.

He's already swiped the screen and put it to his ear.

"Brianna," he announces as if he was sitting here, waiting for her call. "How can I help you?"

His eyes hold mine, mirth dancing within them as he slowly circles his hips, making every nerve ending in my body tingle with anticipation.

"Yeah, of course she's here. What did you think I'd done to her?" he jokes. His voice is rough. To me it sounds more than obvious, but Bri doesn't seem fazed as she continues her conversation with him.

He chuckles, the sound rolling through me as he presses his thumb to my clit, the movement of his hips slowly increasing.

"Holy shit, Toby," I gasp. "Hang up the fucking phone," I hiss.

"Oh you wanted to talk to her?" he asks innocently, as if that wasn't the reason for her freaking phoning in the first place.

"Toby, don't. No. No," I warn, but all he does is smirk at me.

"Yeah, sure. I'm gonna put you on loudspeaker, okay?"

"For the love of God," I sigh as he lowers the phone and taps the screen.

"Jojo." Bri's voice fills the room. "How's your dirty weekend going with your sexy man?"

Toby laughs, his thumbs continuing dizzying circles against my clit as his thrusts pick up speed now he's released the phone.

"I-it's... uh... really... GOOD," I cry when he suddenly surges forward with such power I shoot up the bed.

"Jojo?" Bri warns. "What are you doing right now?"

"N-nothing," I pant, my entire body burning with need and embarrassment. Not that I have any reason to be embarrassed around Bri. I might not have screwed a guy in her bed, but we've pretty much done everything else together. "Oh my God," I moan, unable to keep it in when he slides a hand beneath my arse, lifting me so his cock hits that magical place inside me.

"He's fucking you right now, isn't he?" she asks, her voice a warning, but I know it's fake.

"W-we really need to go," I cry.

"You dirty little whore, Jojo," Bri mocks. "And I'm so not freaking jealous right now. I'm on a bus."

I can't help but burst out laughing at her put-out tone.

"Might be time to call in a friend for the night, Brianna," Toby growls, the roughness to his voice telling me that he's getting close to blowing just like I am.

"I am not calling Nico. He's a dick."

"Sounds like that's exactly what you need,

Bri. Dick," I cry when Toby's grip on my hips tightens and he finally loses control, rutting into me like he's a savage. "I'm hanging up," I cry, fumbling to reach for the phone that Toby placed on the bedside table.

As I twist, he pushes his hoodie up higher, exposing my chest before he leans down, sucking my nipple into his mouth and biting down until I cry out when the pain and pleasure collide.

"Toby, fuck," I cry, slamming my hand down on my phone aimlessly.

The entire thing catapults across the room with my force, landing screen down, so I have no idea if the call cut or not. Not that Toby gives a shit.

"I wanna feel you coming for me, Demon," he growls against my chest, his teeth nipping my sensitive skin before his soft tongue soothes each bite.

His hips continue their punishing blows, and long before I'm ready, heat explodes within me and I fall into a mind-numbing release as Toby continues to thrust into me until he cries out my name and collapses on top of me, his limbs twisting limply with mine.

"Oh my God," I breathe when I start to come back to myself.

Toby's hot breath tickles against my neck as he fights to catch his breath.

"Have you ever had sex during a phone call

before, Demon?" he asks, loudly enough that Bri would hear, should she still be connected.

"Pretty sure that was a first," I confess.

"And in Nico's bed. Fucking love corrupting you, baby," he says, stealing my lips and my breath in another kiss.

19

TOBY

fter discovering that Brianna was, in fact, still on the call and listening to every single thing we did and said, probably with the bluest lady balls known to man, we again suggested that she hit up Nico for a booty call and hung up on her.

Jodie still looked a little mortified by the whole thing, but seriously, after the night the four of us shared in Hades, I'm not sure anything should really embarrass her. I know for a fact I'm not in the least affected by her friend hearing just how much I want her.

Things might be complicated, my life might be a fucked-up mix of revenge and anger and my need to squash anyone who's ever hurt or tainted the lives of those I love, but there's also no denying that I need Jodie something fierce.

Every time I look at her, my need burns that

235

little bit hotter. Every time I have her, I think it'll lessen, but it never does. It just makes me want to do it over and over until I ruin the both of us.

We eventually headed for the shower, where I proceeded to dirty her up all over again before ensuring that she was thoroughly clean once more.

We spent the rest of the day lazing on the sofa, watching some sappy series on Netflix. It was shit, really, but it made Jodie smile and I quickly discovered that I quite enjoyed watching her reactions to whatever was happening on screen. It certainly seemed to help her forget everything we ran away from back in London.

I'm scrolling through Instagram when a sob rips through the cabin.

"What's wrong?" I ask, abandoning my phone and sliding over to her.

Tears fill her eyes, although she hasn't let any drop.

"I'm sorry, it's nothing," she whispers, fighting the emotion that's clogging her throat.

Ripping my eyes from hers, I glance at what she's watching, seeing a family around a hospital bed, tears streaked down their faces as they say goodbye to the man before them.

"I-I just never got to say goodbye to him," she whispers.

My heart fractures in my chest at the pain in her voice. Looking at all the hospital equipment on the screen, it's easy to forget about the man she's talking about and consider how my life could have been if Mum didn't make the recovery she has.

"That's rough," I mutter.

"It's just too much, sometimes. Too much, too close. Seeing things like this is just a reminder of those final moments that were stolen from us."

Wrapping my arm around her shoulders, I hold her tight, dropping my lips to her head and breathing in the scent of her shampoo.

"You don't have to apologise. I can't even imagine what you're going through."

"We're meant to be enjoying ourselves and leaving all that behind," she argues.

"It's not always that easy to leave behind."

She snuggles into me and lets out a contented sigh.

"Do you want to watch something else?" I offer.

She shakes her head. "I can't keep running, Toby. If I don't deal with all this, then it's just gonna keep hitting me out of nowhere and taking me under."

"It'll get easier."

"Will it?" she asks sadly.

"Honestly, I have no idea. I've never lost anyone I cared enough about for it to really impact my life. I thought I was going to, but I was lucky, I guess."

She twists to look up at me, wanting me to explain.

"Mum had a brain tumour."

"Holy shit," she gasps. "When you said she was strong... shit, Toby."

"It's been a shitty few years," I say, a sad, unamused laugh falling from my lips at just how true that statement is.

"How is she now?"

"Good," I say, swallowing past the emotions the thoughts of her not being here drag up. Jonas might have been torturing us with his presence all my life, but really, it was the two of us against the world. Things were so much more bearable before she got sick. She was always there, taking care of me, being the shoulder I craved, the support I needed when life as a baby mafia soldier got a little bit too much.

All of us were born with high expectations placed on us. Our blood alone ensured what our futures would look like. It's something none of us have ever really pushed back against, all of us wanting the life we've been born into. But that didn't mean that training our fathers put us through over the years wasn't brutal.

Mum, with her soft voice and soothing hugs, was the balm for all that violence and corruption.

But as she got weaker, I lost her support. She was still there, of course she was. But it was never the same. And it only got worse as she spent more and more time either in hospital or in bed, and I was forced to spend more time in Jonas's presence. I was forced to endure more and more of his abuse, the severity of his punishments for whatever he deemed I did wrong increasing week on week.

I put on a brave face when I was with Mum, but she could see. She knew what we were both suffering. She just didn't have a way, or the strength, to get out.

If only she'd told me the truth sooner...

If only...

I let out a heavy sigh. I've been over all the what-ifs a million times.

If I knew about Galen and Stella, we could have fled the country. Left that cunt behind. But at the end of the day, what good would it have done? He'd have always found us. And it always would have hurt more. The result could have been worse than what we're dealing with now.

I look down into Jodie's eyes, feeling her pain and grief as if it's my own, and for the first time since my entire life blew up in my face, I actually feel a little gratitude for not losing anyone I cared about. Jodie might not have any clue about who the men really were that she's grieving for right now, but that doesn't mean the pain is any less real.

If I were a better man. I might feel guilty for

what I've spent the last few weeks planning. But I'm not a better man.

I was born into a world with Jonas as a father, and I killed my first man before my tenth birthday.

My reputation might be the nice one. But my soul is just as dark and tarnished as the others'. I just hide it better.

"They think she's going to be okay. She has a good number of years yet."

"That's awesome."

"She deserves it," I say honestly. After everything my mum has endured with her husband, she more than deserves some happiness with the man who still holds her heart after all these years and the distance between them. And she needs to get time with her daughter.

"I look forward to meeting her one day."

The thought alone makes me tense.

"I'm sure she'd love that too," I say, although I already know that it's never going to happen.

I've seen the excitement in Mum's eyes as Stella and Seb fell in love, and then Emmie and Theo when she's seen them together. I know she's getting ideas for me being next, probably wondering what my girl's going to look like, how quickly we're going to send her out to buy a fancy hat and organise seating plans. Christ, she's probably already been looking at fucking baby clothes when she's been out shopping, knowing her.

She's never made her dreams for me to have a family of my own one day—a real, loving, honest family, the type she was never able to provide me with—a secret, and I know it's not something she's going to forget about easily.

"I love it here. Can we stay forever?"

Jodie snuggles into my heat, and I find myself pushing reality out once again and just enjoying her company.

It's a fucking dangerous position to be in.

"I'm not ready," Jodie says beside me as I pull up outside her house Sunday evening.

Our long weekend was both a blessing and a curse.

I bring the car to a stop and kill the engine before turning to her.

She looks like a different person from the one I found in a heap on the ground out the back of the coffee shop a few days ago. She's still fighting her battles, just like I am mine, but she seems lighter. The shadows in her eyes aren't so dark and haunting. I wish I could say the same about mine.

I've made a huge step forward in regards to my

plan this weekend, which is great. But at the same time, I've discovered something I wasn't expecting.

Her.

There's a part of me that is starting to feel more than I should.

But I can't afford to think about her in all of this.

There are always victims in war. That's how it needs to work.

And this is a battle that I'm going to damn well win.

"Can't keep running forever, baby," I say, twisting my fingers through hers.

"Come in with me," she urges. "Just for a bit. I'm not ready to let you go yet."

My eyes dart toward the house, expecting to find her mum there watching, but there are no signs of life.

"Umm..."

"I'll show you my bedroom," she says, wiggling her brows suggestively.

"I'm not sure your mum would appreciate all your calls for God."

"Maybe not. But I would like you to meet her."

Refusal sits right on the tip of my tongue. Agreeing to meet the woman who may or may not know the truth behind my lies could be the beginning of the end of my plan.

Something akin to hope trickles through my veins at that thought, but I slam it down the moment I recognise it.

Nothing is going to stop me getting my revenge, my justice.

Not Jodie, her mum.

Anyone.

"Yeah, okay," I say when the silence between us becomes too heavy. "But I can't stay long. I really need to get back."

It's not a lie—I've got streams of ignored messages on my phone from all the guys wanting to know why I've fallen off the face of the Earth and not turned up to work when we were called in this weekend, something I'm sure I'm going to be hearing about from the boss himself very soon.

No one ignores a request from Damien Cirillo, and I have no doubt I'm going to feel the pain imminently for doing just that.

Plus, I've got a ton of school assignments that I should have finished by now. I'd intended on spending some time this weekend doing them, but they soon got forgotten in favour of making the most of her. After all, I have no idea how much time we've really got.

I don't have a timeline for this plan. I'm relying on my gut telling me that it's the right time. And when it is, I'm going to pull the pin on the grenade I've been building and watch him shatter at my feet.

Pulling on my mask as I climb from the car, I grab her stuff from the boot and follow her toward the house.

The curtain is still suspiciously closed as she lets us inside.

"Mum?" she calls, dropping her handbag to the unit in the hallway. "Mum, I'm home."

Only silence follows, and Jodie's shoulders drop.

"Shit," she hisses, before darting forward and racing toward the stairs.

"What's wrong?" I ask, my eyes following her movements.

"I just need to check something."

"Okay," I mutter to myself, lowering her bag to the floor and taking off toward an open door.

My heart jumps into my throat the second I stand in the doorway and realise my mistake.

Facing Jodie's mum was never going to be the biggest problem with coming in here. Seeing the evidence of their lives, their past... that's where the torture lies.

"Jesus," I breathe, my legs moving me toward the array of photographs that cover almost every surface and the walls.

They span years, laying out every aspect of Jonas's life. One that no one knew he was living.

My hands tremble as I find images of him and

Joanne as teenagers. Joker as a baby. Jodie in Jonas's arms. And all the way up to photos of her and him probably no more than a year ago on what seems to be some kind of holiday.

When the utter fuck did he find the time to have a holiday?

Where did we think he was?

Working, probably. Lying through his fucking teeth about where he was.

How did no one know about this?

Or did they?

I try to think back to when we first found out that he was the sick mastermind behind the attempts on Stella's life. I try to recall everyone's reactions. Were they true? Or did someone, Damien, Charon, anyone already know that he had a secret life?

I find it hard to believe that no one could have known. But at the same time, we all live such fucked-up and twisted lives that I wouldn't put it past any of them to know and turn a blind eye. Hell, for all we know, they're all doing the same thing.

My hands are trembling and my heart is racing to the point I'm light-headed when Jodie's footsteps pound down the stairs.

"She's not here," she says in total disbelief as she stares at her phone. "She's... she's gone out."

"That's good... right?" I ask, stepping toward her and putting the reality of the reason I'm standing in the middle of her house right now behind me.

"Y-yeah. It's great. It's just a shock."

"She's coming back to life, baby. Everything is going to be okay." But despite my words, she still looks on the verge of breaking once more. Probably wise, considering the situation, but I'm hardly going to point that out.

Wrapping my hand around the back of her neck, I pull her into my body and hold her together.

"Thank you," she whispers. "I honestly have no idea how I'd have got through the last few weeks if I hadn't met you."

"I've done nothing, Jodie."

She shakes her head against my chest.

"You've done everything."

We stand there in each other's arms as silence settles around us. My skin prickles as if I've got a million eyes on me, and as I look over my shoulder, I realise I have. And they're all his.

When his presence becomes too much to bear, I release my arms and tuck my fingers under her jaw so she has no choice but to look at me.

"So are you going to distract me from going home by showing me your bedroom or what?"

Her eyes flash with desire despite the numerous orgasms I've given her this weekend. My girl is seriously insatiable. Something I'm more than happy to indulge her in.

Suddenly, Stella and Seb's irritating addiction to each other is starting to make sense.

"I do think you need distracting. Going home to do school work sounds boring as fuck."

"You might be onto something there, Demon."

Her delicate fingers thread through mine and I swallow nervously that she might feel the lingering tremor from standing in the middle of all this. But if she does notice, then she doesn't say anything as she tugs me toward the door and then turns toward the stairs.

We're halfway up when the front door opens, causing us both to stop immediately.

"Mum?" Jodie calls, forgetting all about what we were going to do as she spins back around and damn near pushes me aside as she runs down the stairs to get to her.

"Hey, baby. You're back. Did you have a good weekend?"

"Y-yeah. It was great," she says as I follow her back down to the hallway, hoping what we were about to do isn't entirely obvious to her mum. "Where have you been?"

"Oh... I... uh... I went out to see a friend to get some advice."

"Advice about what?" Jodie asks, concern laced through her voice.

"Um... I think we're going to be evicted,"

Joanne confesses before I step up behind Jodie and finally make my presence known.

Jodie gasps in horror as I wrap my arm around her, pressing my palm to her stomach and helping hold her up.

"No," she breathes, her body trembling.

While she freaks out, however, Joanne's eyes find mine over her daughter's shoulder, and they narrow with enough suspicion that my heart drops into my feet.

Fuck. She's about to ruin everything.

"Hello, young man," she says politely, her smile growing now her shock seems to have worn off. "I don't think we've been introduced."

"Uh... hi," I say, forcing a lightness into my tone that I really don't feel. "I'm Toby. Jodie's... f-frie—"

"Boyfriend," Jodie blurts, shocking the shit out of me.

"Oh well, hello Toby. It's lovely to meet you. I'm Joanne."

She holds my eyes, something I can only describe as suspicion crackling between us.

"We were just going to grab a drink," Jodie lies, making Joanne smirk. "We need to talk about what you just said."

"I'm sure that can wait. I doubt Toby wants to hear about our life right now."

"Um..." Jodie looks between her mum and me.

I'm about to part my lips to tell her that I'm just going to go and leave them to talk when my phone cuts through the air.

I almost ignore it, assuming that it's either Nico or Theo freaking the hell out over my disappearance, but when I recognise the ringtone as Stella's, despite knowing she's probably going to give me the same ear-bashing the guys will, I swipe the screen immediately, something deep down in my gut telling me that it's important.

"Stella?" I ask, turning away from Jodie and Joanne.

"T-Toby," she stutters, putting me instantly on edge.

"What's wrong? What's happened?"

"It-it's M-Mum. She's in hospital."

20

JODIE

"Thanks," I say as Bri passes me a glass of rose prosecco.

Lifting it to my lips, I swallow down two big mouthfuls, desperate for the numbness it can give me.

"So... there's no money? Like... none?" she says, summing up everything I explained after she let me in.

"Apparently not."

"But—"

"I know. He worked all the time. Bought all the things," I say, voicing exactly what she's thinking.

"Jesus, Jojo. What are you going to do?"

I let out a heavy sigh. "I think it might be time for my backup plan."

"That was never a serious plan," she states. "And your mum, Toby," she says, raising her brows to ensure her point hits home, "will never let you be a stripper."

"Who gives a fuck if it puts a roof over our heads?"

"I can't believe you're getting final demands already. There's no way they'd have acted that quickly after his death. It's only been weeks."

"This can't be a new situation."

"What are you suggesting? That he knew there was no money before he died?"

"Maybe. Probably. I have no idea, and I can hardly bloody ask him. Ugh," I groan, falling back on the sofa and sloshing prosecco all over my jeans. "This is a fucking nightmare."

"It's nothing that can't be fixed. Worst case, you can both crash here while you get shit sorted. Do any of you have anything worth selling?"

"Not that I know of. He had a couple of fancy watches, but I have no idea if they were actually anything valuable."

We fall into a tense silence, both lost in our own heads.

"Bri," I whisper, needing to get something off my chest but also not wanting to say the words out loud. "Do you think his death was an accident?"

She freezes mid-sip, her eyes locking on mine.

"Shit, Jojo."

My heart thunders in my chest as I think of the possibility.

"But the crash was investigated, wasn't it? The police report deemed it as an accident."

"Yeah, I know. And it probably was. I'm just letting my mind run away with itself. I've been watching too many crime documentaries."

"It does have the makings of a good TV show, I'll give you that. But as much as you might have a point, does it really matter in the grand scheme of things? It's happened, and the damage has been done. He's not coming back. The money certainly isn't coming back. You need to focus on the future."

"You're right. I know you are," I say before draining the glass in my hand. "I really thought everything was going to be okay. Maybe not okay, but bearable, you know?"

"I know," she agrees sadly. "But both you and your mum are resilient enough to get through this. You can both find jobs and start over. Everything happens for a reason, right?"

"I'm struggling with that right now, Bri. Gotta be honest."

She reaches over and squeezes my hand in support.

"Tomorrow is another day. A fresh start. The future can be whatever you want it to be. Have you heard from Toby?" she asks, moving from one depressing topic to another.

"He messaged to say that she was okay, but I don't have any more details than that."

"Well, that's something, I guess."

"Something good has to come out of all this, right?" I ask, desperate for her to find something.

She holds my eyes, a soft smile playing on her lips. "It already has. Tell me about your weekend. The bits I didn't get to listen to," she says, wiggling her brows.

"You are so bad," I laugh, hitting her with a cushion.

"Me?" She points at herself. "I'm bad? I wasn't the one fucking that boy's brains out all weekend."

I sigh, falling back on the sofa dramatically. "And it was so damn good."

"See. My point exactly. There is your good right there."

"Good, or downright dirty?" I ask with a laugh.

I tell her all about our time away, trying to describe to her the grandeur of the cabin, which I think is completely impossible, even with a few photos because it's just that impressive.

"It sounds like the weekend dreams are made of."

"It was pretty epic, all the drama surrounding it aside. I wish I knew where all their money came from."

Bri stares at me, something akin to amusement flickering through her eyes.

"What?" I ask, feeling like I'm missing something massive. "What?" I ask again, irritation flooding me when all she does is smile back.

"You're kidding me, right?"

"Uh… no?" I say, not meaning it to come out like a question.

"Fucking hell, Jojo. If I knew you were this oblivious then I'd have told you already."

"Okay, I have no fucking clue what you're talking about right now."

"Jesus, I underestimated you." I quirk a brow, quickly moving from irritated to just pure fucking angry.

"They're mafia," she deadpans.

I can't help but burst out laughing. "What the actual fuck, Bri? You really had me going there for a minute."

I continue laughing for a few seconds, but it quickly falls away when I notice she's not joining in.

"Bri?"

"I'm deadly serious, Jodie. Nico is the son of one of the most powerful men in the Cirillo Crime Family."

My chin drops and stays that way for a good few seconds.

"How did you not know this?"

"Funnily enough, I didn't actually ask if they were part of the fucking mafia on our first date."

"Of course not. You were too busy sucking on Toby's cock."

I launch the cushion at her once more, successfully knocking her entire glass of prosecco clean from her hand.

"Jojo," she whines. "That's my favourite."

"Fuck the prosecco. You've just told me the guy I've been screwing is in the fucking mafia."

"He might not be *in* the mafia. But he's definitely connected."

I sit there, gawping as memories of my time with Toby flash through my head. How they both just walked into Hades without any issues that night. His custom BMW. His bruises. Even his abusive and controlling father.

"Shit."

Bri leaves me to my thoughts as she grabs a towel from the kitchen and starts mopping up the mess I made before refilling her glass and dropping back onto the other side of the sofa.

"Does it even matter?"

My lips part to respond, but I quickly realise that I don't actually have an answer.

"He's been lying to me," I say, a frown forming on my brow. "I've spent all this time with him, told him all this stuff about my life, and I don't even know him."

"I'm not sure that's true, Jojo. You know him.

Just don't know everything about his family. And, I might not know anything about that life, but I think I understand not advertising it to everyone you meet."

"On the first night, yeah. Maybe even the second. But... things have been intense between us. Real. Raw. And he never told me. Maybe I'm wrong, but that kinda stings."

"He's a good person, Jojo. I'm sure he's got his reasons. Maybe he thought you might look at him differently if you knew."

Would I? Does knowing this change anything about the time we've spent together?

"Do you think it's like it is in the movies?" I ask after a few minutes lost in my own head.

"No," Bri scoffs. "That's all hyped up. I hardly believe they're running around the city with guns tucked into their waistbands."

"They're probably money laundering and that kinda shit though, right?"

She shrugs. "From what I've seen, the Family has a lot of legitimate business all over the city, and beyond. Their reach is quite impressive. They're powerful men, Jojo."

"How do you know all of this?"

"Google, duh."

"Did you know who Nico was that first night?"

"No. I just thought they were wealthy guys out for a good time. I mean, I assumed they had some connections based on the fact that we walked into Hades without anyone batting an eyelid. But I didn't have a clue a Greek mafia even existed, let alone that they were living on our doorstep."

"MCs, mafia families... are you sure this is real life?" I ask.

"Don't forget the Wolves," she points out.

I frown at her. "You really have been doing your research, huh?"

"Not really. I just find it all a little fascinating. The school I'm working in encroaches on the Wolves' territory. I've overheard a lot of the kids, boys mostly, talking about them."

"Hardly surprising. You've seen the news recently, right? Someone is stabbed in that estate at least once a week, and they've got dealers and hookers lingering on every street corner. It just shows you how deeply in love Sara is with Jesse that she willingly moved in."

"Well, he was hardly going to move out to her neck of the woods, was he?"

"What makes you say that?"

"Jodie, have you been living with your head stuck up your arse for the past few years? Jesse is a Wolf. You've seen his ink, for Christ's sake."

I still, not quite able to compute all this information that clearly I should have known before now. "B-but he's—"

"A Wolf," she finishes for me. "Jojo," she sighs. "You see the good in everyone, and I admire that in you, I really do. But sometimes, a lot of times actually, people aren't what you think they are."

"Apparently not," I sigh. "How did you find out about Nico?"

"Instagram. Don't tell me that you haven't stalked Toby."

I shake my head. "I haven't. I didn't want my judgement clouded by bullshit on social media. I'm assuming you have, though."

"Yeah, but there's not much on him. His accounts are all new. It's almost as if he didn't exist a few months ago."

"Great, my boyfriend is a ghost. Can this get any worse?"

"It could be a lot worse. That boy cares about you."

"Maybe so, but he clearly doesn't trust me." And admitting that hurts more than it really should.

"Jojo."

"I should go. You've got school in the morning, and I need to go and make sure Mum is okay."

"No, please, don't go. I feel awful for dropping all this on you on top of everything else." She squeezes my hand and tries to keep me on the sofa.

"No, you were right to tell me. But I wish it had come from him." Tugging my hand from hers, I place my empty glass in the sink and pull on my boots.

Normally, I'd call an Uber, but seeing as we need every penny we've got right now, my phone stays firmly in my pocket.

"Aren't you calling for a ride?" Bri asks, as in tune with me as ever.

"No. I need some air. Some time to think. You were right earlier. Tomorrow is a fresh start. I need to figure out how I want it to look."

With a sad smile at my best friend, I pull open her front door and slip out.

The second I emerge into the bitterly cold night, I pull my coat tighter around myself and head in the direction of the only home I've ever known. One that I'm soon going to have to leave to start over.

Each step is heavier than the last as the weight of my world falling apart around me takes hold.

Isn't it bad enough that I've lost the two most important men in my life? Now I'm going to have to walk away from the place where almost all of my memories were made.

That house has seen it all—the joy, the tears, the arguments, the pain. It doesn't seem right that we're ripped away from that as well as those we love.

I lose myself in my memories. The Christmases, the birthdays. The first and last days at school that always ended back at that house. The joy of having Dad come home after a length of time away working. The tears when he had to leave again.

Those images soon morph into more recent ones. Ones of the boy who's held my hand the past few weeks and helped me navigate a life that feels half empty with them gone.

The boy who appeared in my life when I needed him most, who's made me smile during my darkest times, and picked me up—literally—when things just got too much.

He's come to mean so much to me in such a short period of time.

Maybe I was foolish. Maybe my grief and pain clouded my judgement, made me see things that weren't really there, feel things that weren't really there.

No. I refuse to believe that.

When I'm with him, it is real. I feel it. I feel our connection right down to the depth of my soul. I can't be making that up because I'm sad and lonely. I'm convinced of it.

But if the feeling is mutual, then why not tell me? Why has he kept all of this a secret when it's apparently so easy to find online?

There's a part of me that totally understands. That maybe he wants to keep his worlds separate.

Keep me away from that life. And if it's anything like what we see of the mafia on TV, then of course, I can understand that. But equally, it hurts. Foolishly or not. It hurts that he hasn't been totally honest with me.

Pulling my phone from my coat pocket, I pull up my photos app and start scrolling through the ones we took together this weekend.

I stare at Toby's face, squinting as I look into his eyes as if I'll be able to read the truth within them. To discover the reason he's hiding who he really is from me.

I damn near jump out of my skin when the thing starts vibrating in my hand.

My initial reaction is excitement that it might be him, but that's quickly replaced by confusion over this whole situation that makes my stomach knot painfully.

All of that washes away, though, when I see who is actually calling.

"Hey," I say, forcing some lightness into my tone.

"Hey, girl. How was your weekend?" Sara says happily.

"It was... it was amazing," I say honestly, although it sounds anything but sincere.

Spotting the entrance to a park, I quickly head that way and lower myself to the first bench I find.

"What's wrong, Jo?"

I let out a heavy sigh. "Can I ask you a question?"

"Yeah, of course. Anything, you know that."

I suck in a breath, hating that I'm about to even say these words. "Is Jesse a Wolf?"

There's a beat of silence that instantly makes me regret the question. Nerves erupt in my belly as I wait for her response.

"Yeah, Jo. He is. You didn't know that?"

"N-no. I'm... stupid, apparently."

"No, you're not. It's not something he really talks about outside the guys, and I just kinda assumed you knew."

"I mean, I knew he was obviously into something a bit questionable given how you met, but I guess I never put two and two together."

"Why would you? It's not like you live here or have anything to do with them."

"No, but you do, and I feel like a shitty friend for not knowing this."

"Don't talk rubbish, Jo. That's Jesse's life. It's not something I really get involved in for... obvious reasons. I don't like it, but I love him and it's a part of his life, so what am I meant to do about it?"

"Yeah, I guess."

"What's this all about, Jo?"

I pause, pushing my hair back from my face as I stare up into the dark sky.

"We're losing the house. Dad had nothing. We're... fucked."

"Oh shit. I can't offer you much, I'm not exactly swimming in money over here, but I'll do anything I can. You can crash in our spare room, or—"

"Thank you," I say, my voice rough with emotion. "We'll figure it out."

"Do you wanna come over? Or I can come meet you?" she offers.

I shake my head sadly despite knowing she can't see me.

"Thank you, but I'm good. I'm just walking home from Bri's. I'm just gonna have a bath and crawl into bed. Things might look brighter in the morning."

"Oh, that reminds me. I've got a number for you for a bar that's hiring. I wanted to wait for you to be back to send it over."

"Is it in Lovell?"

"Yeah, but it's on the edge. It's not in the Valley or anything."

"Good. I might be desperate, but I'm not sure I could deal with that."

"I love you too much to do that to you, Jo," she jokes.

"I know. Thank you. I'll take whatever I can get right now, so not even the Valley is really out of the question."

"You'll figure it out. You always do."

"Who needs uni anyway, right?"

"Not me," she jokes. "I'm sure you can find something way better, but I can always use a hand. Things are really picking up for me. I was expecting it to have died down after being away, but the orders started trickling in almost as soon as I announced I was back."

"That's so awesome, Sara. If I can do anything to help, you know I will."

"You wanna stay on the line until you get home?" she asks, knowing me better than I'm sure I know myself.

"Yeah, that would be nice."

"You got it."

"So, tell me something, anything."

She starts chatting about her business, joy for what she's achieved already with her art prints and online store clear in her voice, and I lose myself to her excitement as she talks about the orders she's had and the customers she's met. It's too easy to push everything aside and just listen to her voice as I make my way home.

I just keep reminding myself that everything is going to get better because, at this point, not much else can go wrong.

21

TOBY

Stella and Seb are climbing out of her new Porsche when I fly into the hospital car park not all that long after leaving a concerned looking Jodie in the hallway of her house.

She begged me to let her come, but I'd long since shut down after hearing Stella's words.

The only focus in my mind was getting to Mum, to find out what was happening.

Pure blood-chilling fear raced through my veins as I drove like a wild beast through the city to where I know she's going to be lying in a hospital bed.

I stupidly allowed myself to believe that after everything she's been through, she might be okay. That her days of hospitals, treatment and generally being miserable were over. Clearly, I was wrong.

"What's happening?" I bark as I sprint to where they're waiting for me.

Stella is pale as she clings to Seb like he's a lifeline, and it does little to help the panic rising within me.

"We don't know. Dad rang seconds before I called you to say that she was in an ambulance and coming here. She passed out, but that's all he could tell me."

"Fuck," I bark, scrubbing my hand down my face. "Why the fuck are we standing out here then?"

Storming past them, I head toward the doors that will lead up to Accident and Emergency.

Heads lift the second I storm inside, but I don't pay them any mind as I search the mass of people for Galen.

He jumps up the second he sees me, his face wrecked, his eyes bloodshot and his hair a fucking mess. He looks nothing like the put-together man I've become used to over the past few months.

"Toby," he calls as he starts moving closer to me.

The second he's in touching distance, he shocks the shit out of me by pulling me into his arms, squeezing me hard enough to hurt as his entire body trembles in fear. The kind of soul-shattering feeling I more than share right now.

"Dad," Stella cries from behind me. Galen

releases his hold on me and pulls her into our embrace.

Despite the situation, having both of them here, having their arms around me makes it so much more bearable. Previously, I had to deal with Mum's illness with only the support of my aunt Penny and the cold and twisted fuck who called himself my father.

I know that was my fault. I could have told the guys what was happening. I could have had their support as she faced treatment and dealt with the side effects of it all, but I knew that if I opened up, they'd dive deeper into my life, and quite frankly, shit was bad enough without them learning the truth. I figured that we could all only fight one battle at a time, and Mum was the most pressing of those issues.

"What do you know?" I ask when Galen finally releases us.

Stella sniffles, and I fight not to look over at her as she lifts her hand to wipe a tear from her cheek. If I see her falling apart, then I already know it's going to break me.

"Nothing," Galen says, his voice deep and raspy as he fights with the emotion clogging his throat. "They took her straight through when we got here and I haven't heard anything since."

"Jesus," I mutter, taking a step away from the two of them and marching toward the reception.

"Toby," Stella calls. "There's nothing you can

do. Just give them time." But despite knowing her words are true, I can't stand the idea of being useless, so I continue forward and interrupt the person talking to the woman behind the desk.

"I need to know what's happening with Maria Ariti," I demand, ignoring the protests of the woman who was halfway through explaining whatever her issue is.

"I'm sorry, sir. If you could just—"

"No, I need to know what's going on. Can you get a doctor?"

"Sir, please—"

"Toby, bro. Just chill out, yeah?" Seb's voice cuts through my desperation, and his warm hand lands on my shoulder. "Just let them do their job."

"But—"

"I know, man. I fucking know." His other hand wraps around my upper arm, and after apologising for my rudeness, he drags me away and into a quiet corridor that leads to a set of double doors.

He stands before me, dipping down to catch my eye, his hands squeezing my shoulders in support.

"I know you're freaking out right now, man. But throwing your weight around isn't going to help."

"Like you did when Stella was here?" I spit, remembering all too well how he acted.

"Exactly. It got me nowhere but almost thrown out. They're looking after her. I know it fucking sucks, but you just have to wait."

"I can't lose her. Not after all this shit."

"You won't," he says confidently.

"How can you say that? She might already be —" I cut myself off before a sob erupts.

"Because she's got too much to live for. Look," he releases me and throws his arm out, gesturing where Galen and Stella are huddled together, watching us with concern. "She is not leaving them when she's only just got them back."

"Fuck, I hope you're right."

"I'm always fucking right."

"You're a prick," I scoff.

"Yeah, it's all part of my charm. Now, are you gonna chill the fuck out or am I going to have to throw you out to save the nurses a job?"

I nod, not really feeling any calmer but knowing he's right. She needs me here, not out pacing in the car park with security watching my every move.

"Great. Now go and be with them. They need you. I'm gonna go find us all some shitty coffee."

Rolling my shoulders and holding my head high, I follow his suggestion and head back to the waiting area where Galen is sitting with his arm around Stella, both of them watching me cautiously.

Without saying a word, I lower down on Stella's other side and reach for her hand.

Her concerned stare burns the side of my face, but I keep my eyes locked on the doors I've seen doctors and nurses emerge from, calling out names for loved ones of the patients they're treating.

"I'm sorry you're going through this again."

My teeth grind as I try not to allow myself to think about the worst case.

If the surgery wasn't as successful as they first thought, if the treatment hasn't worked... All of this will have been for nothing. Everything she suffered at the hands of that monster will have been pointless.

"I'm not alone this time. Whatever it is, we face it together."

Galen's hand clamps down on my shoulder.

"You got that right, Son." His words cause a giant, messy ball of emotion to form in my throat.

Seb eventually returns, amazingly with decent coffee that he passes out before dropping down beside me and attempting to get comfortable on the shitty plastic seating.

I want to point out that nothing good can come from having to wait this long, but I hold the words back. Neither Galen nor Stella need to hear my negativity.

"How was your weekend?" Stella asks eventually. "A little birdy told me you had a dirty weekend with your new girl."

"Stella," I growl, feeling Galen's interest perk up at her words.

"What? Distract us. Please," she begs, making me melt.

"She lost her job on Thursday. I took her to Evan's cabin to get her mind off it."

"Evan has a cabin?" Stella parrots, glaring around me at Seb. "I feel like this is somewhere we should have been." She quirks a brow at him and he rolls his eyes in return.

"Things have been a little... insane, if you haven't noticed, Princess."

She flips him off.

"We're going. Or if you don't wanna go, I'll take the girls."

Galen scoffs a laugh at his daughter.

"You'd love it. It's in the middle of nowhere. Hot tub, open fire." Her eyes widen further with my description. "We'll go. All of us when shit has settled down," I offer, hoping that Evan won't mind. "It's been a while since we all headed up there."

"I've seen photos, it's pretty impressive," Galen adds.

Silence falls among us. Even finding more about my weekend with Jodie is no longer enough of a distraction for Stella.

The seconds tick by, each one feeling longer than the last as I stare at the doors, my heart jumping into my throat every time someone pushes through them.

Stella's hand remains tightly locked in mine, and thankfully, I'm able to get a little bit of strength from that.

I pray that each time a doctor or nurse appears they're going to be looking for us, going to give us some news.

Disappointment and anguish flood me when they inevitably turn to someone else, but the second Mum's name rolls from the lips of a doctor, nothing but blinding fear takes hold of me.

My head spins. Blood races past my ears at such a volume I barely hear a word that falls from the doctor's lips as he explains Mum's conditions.

I pick out a few words, but not enough to fully comprehend what's really going on.

"Exhausted... stress... dehydrated... take it slow..."

I glance up at Galen and Stella as they nod, relief working its way through their expressions.

"W-wait," I say, holding my hand up. "She's okay?"

The doctor stares at me, probably wondering why he bothered explaining everything he just did for me not to listen, but fuck it. He's not the one who's been through everything I have.

"I can't say that one-hundred percent. We are waiting for her to have another scan, but from all our tests, that seems to be the case. Your mum had major surgery followed by some pretty intense treatment. Her body is still recovering. Her prognosis might be looking positive, but she is still going to need to adjust to the side effects and exhaustion."

"Holy shit," I sigh, stumbling back against the wall, my heart slamming against my chest.

Stella is there instantly, her soft, comforting touch landing on my upper arm.

"It's okay. She's okay."

"Can I see her?" I ask, looking straight past Stella and at the doctor.

"Yes, but only one of you. We're going to get her moved to a ward shortly and then she can have more visitors."

"A ward? But you just said she's okay."

"We need to be sure. Your mum has been through a lot, so the rest will be good for her. Follow me, I'll take you to her."

I quickly move forward to do as he says, but my eyes land on Galen and reality slams down on me as I see the concern on his face.

"Shit. Maybe you should—"

"No," he assures me, his voice firm and

unyielding. "You need to go. Just tell her we're here and that we love her."

I nod, unable to talk through the lump in my throat as I turn back toward the doctor.

"Toby," Mum breathes the second the doctor throws the curtain back and I find her lying there, looking weak and vulnerable.

My heart jumps into my throat as I'm once again reminded of just how serious this is. She might have been given the all clear, but I'm achingly aware that it could change at the drop of a hat.

They were less than confident at one point that we'd even get this far. Every day really is a blessing at this point.

Rushing to her side, I drop into the chair and take her hand in mine.

"The doctor said you're in here because you're exhausted, Mum," I chastise, letting her know with my tone just how I feel about that.

She stares at me, the circles under her eyes heavy and dark, her skin pale.

"I overdid things," she confesses. "I just really want to get everything sorted so we can move on."

"This happened because of *him*?"

"There are just things that need sorting with his... demise."

"None of that needs to be on you, Mum. Damien and I are sorting—"

"Toby," she cuts me off. "Let me be your

mum, please. I've lost so much time. I want to do this. I want to get our lives back on track."

"I know, but you need to not end up in here doing it."

Clasping both her hands in mine, I squeeze in the hope that she can't feel the rage that's surging through me.

"I'm sorry I worried you."

"Mum," I breathe, resting my brow against her knuckles. "I'm sorry I didn't get us out sooner."

"This isn't on you," she argues. "It was my job to protect you."

"You were ill."

"You're my baby and I failed you."

I shake my head, refusing to place any of the blame for our lives on her. She was trapped just as much as I was.

"Will you do something for me?" she asks softly.

"Anything," I promise her.

"Put an end to it. To him," she adds in a whisper so quiet I almost miss it. "I understand why you're all doing what you're doing. Trust me —if I could, I'd be doing the same. But it's killing you, Toby. He's continuing to haunt you and you're allowing it to happen."

"But I—" I start, but she doesn't allow me to continue.

"You've got a new girl in your life. Don't you

want to be focusing all your efforts on her, not your need for vengeance? It shouldn't be at the expense of your future, your happiness."

"That's not—"

"Toby," she sighs. "I can see it in your eyes. You need to put an end to it and move on before it ends up dragging you under." I hold her eyes, silently begging her to let me do this my way, but she won't budge. "Promise me. You're just dragging out the pain. For both of us."

Releasing her hand, I slump back in the chair, tipping my face toward the ceiling. She knows I can't deny what she asks of me.

God damn it.

My fist clench as I think about walking into his cell and finally putting a bullet between his brows. It's what I've wanted to do for years now. To stand over him and watch the life drain out of his eyes as he stares up at me, knowing that I was the one to end him after all the pain, the manipulation, and control.

But now, after discovering just how bad it all really was, a single bullet isn't enough. I need his heart ripped out before I finally let him go to hell. I need him to feel as betrayed and ripped apart as we have all these years.

Images of the person who's going to help me do exactly that flash through my mind. The feelings she stirs up within me might have morphed into something different compared to when I first came up with my plan, but ultimately, my end goal here is watching him lose his last shred of hope and seeing that same pain in his eyes that I've seen in Mum's for years. And that need is strong enough to make me push everything else aside.

"Fine," I agree. "I'll get it done. And I'll talk to Damien about everything else." I hold her eyes, my face a cold mask as I stare at her. "Because you need to let go of it all too. Focus on Galen, on Stella, on your future."

"Deal," she says, holding her hand out to me like she used to do when I was little and we'd agreed on a plan of action.

Reluctantly, I slip my hand into hers and we shake on it.

"To the future without that poisonous rat in our lives."

I nod in agreement, thoughts already spinning around in my mind about how I can speed things up and put an end to all of this sooner than I first planned.

22

JODIE

"I need someone who can pretty much start straight away," Courtney, the manager of the bar Sara mentioned, says as she shows me around. Well, I call it a bar, but the stages and poles make it look more like a strip club. Something that excites me and terrifies me equally. I guess the correct term is 'gentleman's club'. A shudder works its way down my spine as I think about the kind of men who might come here. Its clientele is certainly going to be different from those watching the entertainment in Hades that night.

Sara knows about my weird fascination with dancing, so I guess it only seems right that she would have found this place for me.

"Two of my girls have got themselves preggers, and I'm kinda up shit creek without a paddle right now," she confesses.

"I know that feeling," I mutter sadly.

I've already explained to my potential new boss what happened at the coffee shop, but Sara had apparently already put a good word in for me and she just waved it off. I'm not sure if it's because she trusts me already, is crazy, or just plain desperate. I'm mostly leaning toward the latter.

"I can start whenever. I really need the money, so..."

"Okay, how's Friday night sound? That will give you time to get waxed and visit a hairdresser." I lift my hand, brushing my fingers over my long brown locks. "Oh sweetie, there's nothing wrong with your hair. It's beautiful. It just needs a little... you know?" she says, waving her hand around.

"Umm..."

"A few highlights would work wonders."

"Uh... I guess."

"Listen, sweetie. I know that we're not in Chelsea or whatever, but our clients expect a certain level of... entertainment while they're here. And I'm not saying you're not it. You are. You're beautiful and have curves to die for. We just need the cherry on top, you know?

I blow out a slow breath, focusing on the hourly rate that's printed on the contract in my hand.

A few highlights and some waxing are a small

price to pay for ensuring a roof over mine and Mum's heads.

"Sure. I can totally do those things before Friday."

"Fantastic. The last thing I need from you is your personal details so I can get everything sorted."

We come to a stop beside a table and she places the folder in her hands on top of it and passes over a pen.

"Why do you need my bra size?" I blurt, although I quickly realise that it's a stupid question.

"Uniform. I'll have everything you need waiting for you Friday night."

I finish filling in everything she needs to know. By the time I get to the end of the form, I'm surprised she hasn't asked for the length of my little toe or my cycle dates, it's so freaking detailed with sizes and tick boxes of things we are and aren't willing to do.

Needless to say, most of that went unticked.

Courtney has assured me that nothing untoward happens here. But I get the feeling she might just be lying. I guess only time will tell. And really, do I care? As long as I can get some money, fix the disaster of my life, that's all that matters right now.

"Great. That's awesome. So we'll see you

Friday, say, quarter to five. Gives us time to go through everything before the punters arrive."

Nerves explode in my belly at the thought of actually doing this. It's been a running joke between Bri and me for so long that I didn't really think it would ever happen. But now I'm on the cusp of it, and not out of pure fascination but desperation, I feel entirely different from how I always thought I would.

I wanted to do it because I thought it would be liberating, but right now, I mostly just want to vomit.

"Okay, that sounds perfect," I say, forcing a smile on my face, hiking my bag up my shoulder, and holding my hand out to shake hers.

"I think you're going to fit in really well here, Jodie. It'll be like a home away from home before you know it."

I nod and pull my hand free, quickly making my way to the exit, hoping that I don't actually look like I'm running.

I want this... no. I need this. Right now, I have no other choice.

All the other jobs I've been chasing over the past few days have either already been filled, aren't starting for a month at least, or I was too honest about the end of my previous employment and they point-blank refused to talk to me further. A couple even put the phone down on me.

With a heavy sigh, I make my way out onto the street.

My phone buzzes in my pocket, and I pull it out to find a message from Sara asking me how I got on, and another from Toby.

Just like all the other times he's messaged me in the past few days, my heart has picked up speed in my chest as an internal war continues to rage within me.

I'm still pissed that he never told me who he really was, the sort of life he really lives. But more so, I just really fucking miss him.

I told myself that I'd let him have some space to look after his mum and be with his family while I tried to get my head around everything before I agreed to meet him and force him to talk. But as each day has passed, my need to just see him only grows, and my anger continues to weaken.

He knows something is wrong as well. He's figured out that I'm avoiding seeing him. His messages are coming more often, his requests to see me becoming more and more serious. But I'm scared. I'm scared that he'll either continue to lie to me, or—and possibly worse—he'll be completely honest about who he is and the things he really does for work.

I didn't want to do it, but in the end, I caved to find out more about the Cirillo Family and I read a few news articles I found online. Each one was more terrifying than the last. There were reports of violence, extortion, drug trafficking, gambling rings, fraud, just to name a few. The thought of the guy I've allowed into my life being involved in some of that makes my head spin, and not in a good way.

I know he's got a dark streak. I saw it that very first night we met, even before he tied me to that St. Andrew's cross. And I've seen it since. But I happily believed that it was his past, the abuse from his father and his fear for his mother after her illness. I didn't bat an eye when he told me that his injuries the other night were from some drunk and over-excited patrons in the hotel he works at. I realise now that it must have all been complete bullshit, and I fell for it. All of it.

Toby: Can I see you tonight?

Jodie: I'm not sure what my plans are yet. Just heading home to see Mum.

It's not a lie, yet guilt floods my veins, knowing that I'm putting off the inevitable.

Toby: Did I do something wrong? I can't help feeling like you're blowing me off.

I lower my phone as I continue walking toward the tube, desperately trying to summon the courage to just meet him, get this all out in the open, and then try to decide where I go next.

It's not like I'm living a nice calm life and messing things up with him will ruin my zen or whatever. There is zero fucking zen in my life right now.

Jodie: I'm sorry, things are just crazy at the moment.

I resist from adding any more, needing to know where his head is at right now.

Toby: Then let me help you take your mind off it. Say yes, Demon.

"Shit," I hiss as I jog down the stairs to the station and tap my card to the entry barrier.

Jodie: Yes.

My stomach tumbles as I consider the fact that I could have just made a massive mistake. But I figure that it's too late now, especially as I descend the escalator and my phone signal cuts off.

My heart pounds in my damn ears as I take a

seat in the almost empty train and drum my fingers against my thigh.

I want to see him, I do, more than I even want to admit to myself. But... shit.

Is he going to be the same person I was falling for now I know the truth? Or is he just going to be some monster that's connected to all those awful things?

Things that Joe managed to get involved with. A dark and dangerous world I have no desire to be associated with.

Jesus, what would Mum think?

I scrub my hand down my face. All she's talked about since Toby rushed out of the house on Sunday night is when I'm going to see him again and wanting to know about every minute of our weekend away. It's like she's living vicariously through us, and as much as I love the escape from reality it gives her, it also hurts.

The second my phone gets some signal, it starts buzzing in my hand as message after message is delivered.

I don't need to look down to know they're all him. And when I finally do lift it, I find I'm right.

Toby: Good girl, Demon.

Tingles erupt throughout my body as I hear him growl those words in my ear.

Toby: I'll pick you up at seven.

Toby: Jodie?

Toby: Have you changed your mind already?

Toby: Demon...

Again, it's as if he's standing right behind me as I read that final one. The hairs on the back of my neck lift and the need I've been trying to ignore since Bri told me the truth the other day surges forward.

I don't know who the hell I'm trying to kid trying to convince myself that I don't want him now I know the truth.

Part of his appeal that first night was his bad boy, give no shits attitude.

All the truth has really done is confirm that that was entirely true.

But it's not just that. He's potentially dangerous, and I dare any women to say their knickers don't get a little damp at the thought of being worshipped by a man who knows exactly how to protect them and kill, if necessary.

I shake my head, aware that I'm totally romanticising all of this, but at the same time, I'm unable to stop.

I've had images of Toby in the middle of some fight last week, throwing punches and totally owning the situation as he laid into his opponent with brutal force.

A laugh falls from my lips.

I'm so fucking screwed up, it's unreal.

Here I am, wanting to hate him, but equally, I want to jump his bones just at the thought of him.

Jodie: I'll be ready...

Toby: Where did you go?

Jodie: Tube. What should I be wearing tonight?

Toby: As little as possible and no underwear *winky emoji*

Jodie: You're such a guy.

Toby: I'm glad you noticed, Demon. Was it about the time I thrust balls deep inside you?

"Hey, Jojo," Mum calls as I push through the front door, my cheeks burning. I've sent a few dirty messages over the years, but almost all of them have been a joke. I've never had one hit me quite like that.

Unable to leave it there, I start tapping out a reply.

Jodie: Might have been about the time I *tongue emoji* your *aubergine emoji*

"Oh my God," I breathe, knowing that I really shouldn't have done that. So much for playing it cool or even trying to forget him.

"Jojo?" Mum calls again.

"Hey, Mum. I'll be right there," I shout, shrugging out of my coat and dragging my boots off my feet.

My phone buzzes once more.

Toby: And now I'm hard. Is it seven yet?

A laugh falls from my lips.

Jodie: Sadly not. I'm sure you can wait a while longer, bad boy.

Toby: It'll make the end of our night that much sweeter.

Jodie: I don't remember agreeing to a booty call, Tobias.

Toby: Fuck, I love it when you say my name. Especially when your fingers are twisted in my hair.

"Damn you, Toby," I hiss, my body heating at the picture he paints for me.

"How'd the interview go?" Mum asks, dragging me back to Earth and forcing me to get the image of Toby between my thighs out of my head.

"Y-yeah, it was good. I'm starting Friday evening," I say, a knot tightening in my belly at the fact that I haven't exactly been honest about the kind of bar it really is.

My phone buzzes once more but I ignore it, shoving it into my pocket.

"Oh, fantastic." A smile lights up her face, but I don't feel her excitement in the slightest.

"Have you managed to find anything yet? He must have had a pension, an insurance policy or something," I damn near plead, desperate for Mum not to be left with nothing out of this whole clusterfuck.

She shakes her head sadly.

"Jesus, what was he thinking?'

"Life is complicated, sweetheart," she offers by way of an explanation.

"I know, but I never expected this."

Something flashes in her eyes that makes me frown.

"What is it? What aren't you telling me?" I ask, recognising that look.

"It's..." She sighs. "It's nothing. We can't fix the past, Jojo. Right now, all we can do is look to the future."

She sounds strangely optimistic for a woman who could barely leave her room not so long ago, but I guess grief is a weird beast and I'm just going to have to roll with the punches here.

And of course, she's right. It's too late to be worried about what Dad did or didn't do. I can only assume he wasn't actually planning to die—even if I now have my questions over his death—and that he wouldn't have left us in this state on purpose. Maybe... who knows.

Just like Toby, maybe my stepdad had me fooled all this time, too.

"I'm going out tonight," I tell Mum, trying to think positively as she just suggested.

"With him?" she asks with a happy smile.

"Yep. He's picking me up in two hours."

"Then what the hell are you doing, sitting here and chatting with me? Get your backside upstairs and in the shower."

"Are you sure? I can stay in," I offer. It's a

pathetic attempt to get out of the conversation that needs to happen tonight.

"Jodie Walker," she growls, making me feel like a seven-year-old again. "You are not spending another night here babysitting me. Get out there and paint the town red."

My lips part to argue, but she cuts me a stern look that quickly stops me.

"Yeah, okay. As long as you're sure."

"I'm sure. I plan on spending the night applying for every job I can find and hunting for somewhere for us to live."

"It's not going to come to that. We'll figure it out."

"Maybe so. But we need a backup plan should the bailiffs turn up at our door sooner rather than later."

My chest compresses with the weight of that statement. "Go, child. Go," she mocks, waving her hand at me. "And do not come back down here until you're in your nicest dress and looking ready to knock him on his arse."

I can't help but laugh at her. "I'll see what I can do."

23

___

TOBY

A smirk pulls at my lips and my cock swells as I watch the screen in front of me. It's not the first time I've seen this footage, but fuck, the way it affects me it might as well be.

Jodie's back arches as I thrust into her, her arms tugging at the restraints holding her wrists. Even through the screen I can feel the connection between us crackling like two live wires ready to short-circuit as I fuck her with force.

"Fuck. Fuck. Fuck," she chants before she screams my name.

Our skin glistens with sweat, her body falling limp before I fall headfirst into my orgasm. I get to see the moment Nico and Brianna join us and the desire that fills their eyes as they watch us together.

Dragging my hand up my thigh, I rub my hard length through the fabric of my trousers.

I shouldn't be torturing myself by watching this now, but I can't fucking stop myself.

My addiction to the girl in the video has only grown this week. Since making that promise to Mum to bring all of this to an end, it's all I can think about. She is all I can think about.

And it hasn't helped that she's gone out of her way to avoid seeing me. Something I'm not all too happy with.

Of course, there are other ways to get what I want, but that's not how this is to play out. I want her willing. More than fucking willing.

The video before me comes to a stop, but another quickly replaces it. This time, we're in the coffee shop only a week ago as she once again cries out my name while I eat her like I'm fucking starving.

My cock jerks as I remember exactly how she tastes, and my mouth waters in the hope that I might get to rediscover it in a few hours.

I continue watching as she lets me take her over the counter, not even a second's hesitation about the security camera covering every inch of that place. It's the exact proof I need to confirm what I already know. I have managed to get myself firmly under that girl's skin. It's just a shame she's managed to bury her way beneath mine, too.

But she's just a pawn in my game, the final piece in a puzzle to complete my plan. And that's the way it needs to be.

"*In order to get what you want, you need to be ruthless, reckless, and unyielding.*" That prick's voice rings out loud in my ear. There was a time I thought I'd never take any of his advice seriously, but here I am, more than willing to use it against him.

And it might be reckless. I might be hurting more than the one I have my eyes set on, but that's just the way of the world.

"*You can't get to the top without stepping on a few heads.*"

Well, Jonas, I think you might very well be right. And you try stomping on my family, I'll return the favour.

Ensuring I have everything set up—assuming my plan is going to come to fruition tonight—I place my tablet on the bedside table and stand up, quickly rearranging myself when my aching cock tries busting its way out of my trousers.

My fingers curl and my heart pounds a steady rhythm in my chest as I glance around.

Oh, hell yeah. Tonight is the night that motherfucker is going to learn just how it feels, watching someone you love having their heart ripped out right in front of their eyes. And I'll do it all while looking dead into his cold, soulless ones.

I might not be his son, but he trained the monster within me. He ensured I grew up tainted, tarnished and broken, and ultimately, he is the one who is going to pay the ultimate price.

Checking the time, I quickly open my chat with Jodie.

Toby: Can't wait to see you. I've missed you this week.

It shows as read almost immediately.

Toy: See you soon. x

A vindictive smile twitches at my lips before I drop my phone into my pocket and make my way out of my flat. Hitting the button in the lift for the basement before taking the stairs even lower to our secret little hideaway where we keep all our favourite pets.

He jolts awake when I push the heavy door open and step inside. The place fucking stinks— but then I guess that's to be expected considering he's living, breathing, eating and shitting in a space that resembles a high-security prison.

Blinking against the bright light I've just illuminated around him, he looks me up and down.

"What do you think?" I ask, holding my hands out to my sides. "Will she approve?"

His lips press into a thin line as he studies me.

I hate to say it, but he's looking better than the last time I saw him. Some of the cuts and bruises I gave him for Christmas are beginning to heal, and the soldiers who have been delivering him food have clearly been spoiling him, because he seems to have a little too much strength as he pushes himself from the solid bed we gifted him with.

"I've got the perfect date lined up. Candlelit dinner, walk under the stars... and then I'm gonna bring her back here and really get the night started."

"Leave her alone," he growls, as if his words could go anywhere near stopping me.

I might have had my moments of doubt over the past couple of weeks, but standing here now, seeing this vile creature of a man I used to call Dad gives my hatred, my need for revenge, a new lease of life.

"Not a fucking chance," I mutter, stepping farther into the room and pulling a remote control from my pocket. His eyes follow my movements cautiously as if I'm about to pull out a gun. "I'm not going to shoot you yet, old man," I assure him. "Do you really think I'd have gone to all these lengths to just end you that quickly?"

"Do whatever you want to me," he pleads. "But leave her out of it. She's not involved in this life. She doesn't even know it exists."

"You know," I say, pacing back and forth in front of him, "I really wish I had time to hang around and chat, to find out how the fuck you managed to live this double life all these years and not get found out.

"I've met Joanne, by the way," I confess as the vein in his temple that used to scare the ever-loving shit out of me begins to pulsate. Now though, it does nothing. There is nothing this man can do now that will touch me. Everyone I care about is safe. Mum is home from the hospital and being looked after like a queen by Galen, my sister is upstairs with Seb, and the rest of my boys out are doing fuck knows what. For all I care, the rest of the world can burn right along with this cunt, so long as they are all safe. "She seems lovely. It really is such a shame to have to tarnish them all because of your stupid, selfish actions, don't you think?"

"You stay away from my Joanne."

"Your Joanne. Funny, I'm pretty sure the only woman you should be claiming as your own is your wife."

His lips peel back in a snarl at the mention of my mum, and burning hatred for this pathetic excuse for a man burns through my veins.

"Fuck her. She's nothing but a cheap whore."

Sucking in a deep, calming breath, I clench my fists at my sides in an attempt to stop me from ripping his fucking head off.

"So why the fuck did you marry her then? You were clearly already fucking Joanne, seeing as Joker was older than me."

"To stop him from having her," he sneers. "To give me pure bloodline heirs. You know as well as I do that we need pure Greek blood to continue our legacy, and with Joanne, I didn't have that. But with your mother," he scoffs as if she's nothing more than a piece of rubbish he's tossed away, "I could have had an army of soldiers to follow in my footsteps."

I stare at him, my brows raised almost in amusement.

"And how did that work out for you?"

He scoffs. "I should have fucking strangled you at birth."

"I'm sure Joanne had similar thoughts knowing she procreated with you. How much must it have hurt, knowing she strayed and had your precious princess with another man?"

"Don't you fucking judge me."

"Judge you?" I can't help but laugh. "You think I'm judging you right now? I pity you," I spit. "You're nothing but a worthless piece of shit who's tarnished the lives of those around him."

"My family is good. Pure. Innocent."

"So that's why Joker is dead now, is it? Because he was so fucking innocent? You set him up to kill my fucking sister," I shout, spittle flying into the space between us.

"She should have been mine," he seethes.

"Well, thank fuck she wasn't. No one deserves to be walking around this earth with your DNA."

His lips purse and his eyes harden, something that I didn't think was possible.

"Anyway," I say, taking a step back and forcing myself to lighten things up a little. It's a fucking effort when every single inch of me wants to get closer so I can wring his neck and watch the life drain out of him, listening as he takes his last few breaths on this earth. "I thought I'd set up a little treat for you tonight."

I press the red button on the remote in my hand, bringing a hidden screen behind the toughened glass on the other side of the room to life.

Jonas stares at it as if he's forgotten what a TV looks like for a few seconds before his suspicion begins to set in.

"What have you done?"

I pause for a beat, just watching him as he begins to panic.

"Quite a few things, actually," I confess. "But you'll be pleased to know that I've actually managed to record some of the better bits to ensure you don't miss them down here in the dark. It must be so lonely, thinking that the only two people in this world who actually cared about you believe you're dead."

I press another button and the empty room at Hades comes into view.

"Now, don't worry. I've got it on loop, so you won't miss anything while I'm out enjoying my night. Hopefully, it'll help distract you from thinking about what we're doing."

Obviously predicting where this is going, he gets to his feet, somewhat clumsily, and launches himself at me.

Unfortunately for him, I'm faster and have my gun freed from my waistband before he's barely moved.

"Back up, old man. I might not want you dead yet, but we all know I could aim this in enough places to keep you going for a good few days. After all, you taught me all of them. Remember?" A growl rumbles deep in his throat. "I never knew the knowledge would come in so handy."

With the gun still pointed between his eyes, I back up toward the door, leaving him standing in the middle of the room looking like a lost puppy.

"How the mighty fall, Jonas. How the mighty fall. You had such a promising future ahead of you. But now look. You're dead to anyone who cares and a deceitful, backstabbing cunt to everyone else. I press play and Jodie and I burst into the room, her eyes going wide as she takes it all in. I don't need to look at the screen to know her exact reaction. I've seen it with my own eyes more than enough times to have it memorised.

"Enjoy your night, old man. I know I will." I pull the door open and slip out as Jodie's voice rings through the hidden speakers from the video. "This is... incredible."

I've almost slipped out when I add the final blow. "If you're really lucky, at some point that might just turn into a live feed. I think it's about time she learned the truth, don't you?"

I slam the door shut a second before his body collides with it. If the room he was contained in wasn't soundproof, I'm sure I'd be hearing his roar of disapproval and anger right about now.

But as it is, I climb the stairs with a smirk on my face and accomplishment filling my veins.

Tucking my piece away, I pull my phone out once more.

Toby: On my way, Demon. I hope you're ready for the best night of your life.

She starts typing instantly.

Toy: That's some promise there, Tobias. Pulling out the big guns, are we?

"Oh, Demon. You have no fucking idea."

24

JODIE

"This place is fancy," I breathe as Toby pulls up in front of an expensive looking Italian restaurant.

"I promise I'm not being flashy or trying to impress you," he says, killing the engine and twisting to look at me.

Desire licks across my skin from the dark and hungry way he assesses me. He's told me more than once since he picked me up how much he's missed me this week. He sounds so sincere, I can't help but believe him. Especially as the connection we've shared since that very first night crackles louder than ever with our few days apart.

I study him, really study him, trying to see all the lies behind his eyes, to peel back a little of his mask that he has to be wearing. But I can't find it, leaving me to believe that it's either all bullshit, or he really is that well-trained.

"Luckily for you," I say, forcing myself to speak. "I'm starving."

His eyes drop to my lips, and everything below my waist clenches with need.

"Yeah," he agrees, his voice raspy as he runs his thumb along his bottom lip. "So am I."

He leans forward over the centre console, his hand disappearing under the curtain of hair that's hanging around my shoulders until his hand wraps around the side of my neck.

His brow touches mine as he stares down into my eyes.

A million silent words pass between us. I just fucking wish I knew if I could believe the ones that come from him or not.

My heart rate increases as his manly scent fills my nose and the warmth of his skin burns, turning my blood to red-hot lava.

His lips brush mine in the sweetest of moves that makes my chest clench.

"I need you so bad, Demon. But if I start, I'm not going to be able to stop, and I need to feed you before we get to that," he confesses, his deep voice rumbling through the enclosed space around us.

"Okay," I breathe, silently more than happy to bin off this part of the evening and just enjoy what he has to offer.

He remains still for another two seconds before he rips himself away from me and throws the door open. "Don't move," he shoots over his shoulder before slamming the door.

My head spins with desire and confusion as I watch him round the bonnet before pulling my door open for me like a gentleman.

"Wow, you're going all out tonight, huh?" I ask when I place my hand in his and let him pull me up.

"Nothing less than you deserve," he growls, tucking me into his side and wrapping his arm around my waist.

In this moment, it's so easy to believe that this is it. That this is us, no lies or cover-ups.

But I know deep down in my soul that's not true. There is more to him, I just know there is.

I just have to hope that it's not as bad as my imagination is leading me to believe. I mean, it can't be, can it?

Toby greets the maître d' as if he knows him, and I guess to be fair, he probably does. Just like all the staff at Hades.

I let out a heavy sigh as he tugs on my arm and leads me toward a table in the very back corner of the restaurant. It's tucked right behind an ornate partition, and I can't help but notice how perfect it is for the discussion we're about to have. The privacy is surely appreciated.

"Louisa, your server, will be over shortly," the maître d' assures us before taking off.

My stomach growls loudly as the scent of what I can only assume is going to be the best Italian of my life floats in the air around me.

The grin that pulls at Toby's mouth tells me he heard it.

"So, tell me about your week," he prompts, reaching across the table to take my hand.

"It's been about as shit as all the rest of my weeks recently. You really want to hear about it?" I ask, screwing my nose up.

"At least one good thing must have happened."

I discovered who you really are? I think to myself.

"I got a new job," I confess, although I'm more than happy to leave the details of said job out for now.

"Yeah?" His face lights up in excitement for me. "See, not all bad."

I think of the job and internally cringe.

"No, I guess not," I mutter as our server appears with a small bowl of olives and a pitcher of water, ready to take our drink orders and thankfully cutting off any questions about said job.

"What about you? How's your mum doing?" I ask, sipping on some water in the hope of calming my nerves once we're alone again. It does very little, and I realise that I probably should have gone ahead and just ordered straight-up vodka a few seconds ago.

"She's doing okay. She's home and being looked after by..." He hesitates, his brow pulling tight. "Galen, her other half."

"But she's okay?" He's already told me all of this over message, but I couldn't help but feel there was more to it.

"They've assured us that she is. The scans have come back clear. She just needs to rest and stop overdoing it. She seems to have forgotten what she went through only months ago."

"She's embarking on a new life. It must be hard not to get carried away, especially after all the years of crap."

"Trust me, I get it. But seeing her in that hospital bed again, it just brought it all back. She came so close to not even being here now. I just... I didn't need that reminder, you know?"

I nod, completely understanding what he means.

"So what about everything else?" I ask, my heart hammering wildly in my chest as my eyes pick out the cuts and bruises which have healed significantly since I saw him Sunday. "School? Work?"

He flips open the menu and chooses to study that instead of looking at me, and my stomach drops into my feet.

I hate myself for not figuring all this out earlier. For trusting him so blindly when I quite clearly didn't know him at all.

All the questions I've been bottling up this week spin around my head as I try to find the most pressing to start with, but it quickly becomes obvious that I'm not going to get the chance when Louisa reappears with our drinks and pulls a small pad from her pocket.

"Are you both ready to order?" she asks politely, although I don't miss the way she openly checks Toby out as if he's not obviously on a date with me.

"Ladies first," Toby says, his eyes drilling into me, basically eye-fucking me over the table. And despite everything I'm learning about this guy, I am fucking here for it.

I've barely looked at the menu, but I figure that I can't really go wrong, and I'm sure stoking Toby's ego right now will only go down well.

"You can choose, I trust you."

His eyes widen with surprise but equally, they darken with my words.

He recovers after a beat and quickly rattles off our order before Louisa disappears once more.

"You surprise me at every turn, Demon," he says, threading our fingers together once more.

"I could say the same thing about you, Tobias."

He doesn't react to my words, and that in itself speaks volumes.

My body begins to burn up, my hand starting to sweat where it's twisted with his.

"Are you okay?" he asks, the concern I've become more than used to floating through my ears. "Did something else happen with your mum or..."

"No," I say quickly.

"Okay. You've been so quiet this week, I wasn't sure if—"

"It's you," I blurt like an idiot.

"M-me?" he confirms, his brows pinching in confusion. "What have I done?" he asks hesitantly, but I see the guilt beneath. And it's all I need to see.

"Yeah. You." Pulling my hand from his, I cross my arms over my chest and rest forward on the table. My dress is low-cut enough to give him an eyeful, but clearly, this is serious enough for his focus to remain on my face. I'm almost impressed. "Did you want to start telling me the truth, or should I just walk out now?"

His eyes flare with shock as he lifts his hand to run his fingers through his hair, bringing it to a stop on the back of his neck as disbelief covers his handsome face.

He looks hot tonight. No, beyond fucking hot. He's wearing dark grey fitted trousers that hug his arse and thighs in the most delicious way, and a black button-down shirt that looks like it could have been made to measure, the way it sculpts his muscular arms and chest. He looks pretty on point for the man I've discovered him to be. Dark, mysterious, and above all else, dangerous.

"Jodie, I—"

"Lie to my face and I'll walk right out that door and you'll never see me again," I warn before he continues.

I might be a naïve little girl who allowed all of this bullshit to pass me by, trusting the wrong people, but I am done with being that person.

If there is anything here, and right now that is a very big if, then I need everything. Every dark and dirty secret he's carrying. I want to know the real him, not the act he's put on over the past few weeks to be the perfect boyfriend, because right now, that is all this feels like.

An act. Fake. Too good to be true.

"Shit," he hisses, dipping his head but still holding my eyes. "I'm sorry, Jodie."

My brow quirks as I stare at him.

"Really?"

"Yes," he assures me, leaning over the table to try to recapture my hands once more, but I sit back, needing this space between us if I've got any chance of keeping a clear head.

He pauses, I assume to let me fill the silence

by telling him everything I've figured out already, but it's not going to happen.

"I'm not the one who needs to be talking right now," I tell him with a pointed look. "I want the truth. I want to know who I've really been sharing a bed with."

"Fuck. Yeah... yeah, okay."

He drags his hands back across the table, and I swear I actually see them trembling. Is he really that terrified of me knowing the truth? My stomach twists painfully as I continue coming up with all the awful situations I've been conjuring up in my head the past few days.

After a few seconds, he seems to get a hold of himself, and he holds out a now very steady hand across the table for me. "Hey," he says with a smile, making me frown. "I'm Toby Doukas, a soldier in the Cirillo Crime Family."

"Holy fuck," I gasp, the reality of everything Bri told me slamming into me with the force of an articulated lorry.

Emotion clogs my throat and my eyes burn red-hot as his lies and betrayal fill the space between us.

"But I'm still me, Jodie. The person you've got to know, that's who I am. That's just a part of me. A part I don't go around advertising to hot girls I meet in bars."

I nod, because I understand that. I really fucking do.

"But I'm not just a girl you met in a bar anymore, am I?"

He sucks in a breath, damn near taking all the oxygen from the room with it.

"I'm sorry, excuse me."

In a rush, I push to my feet and take off.

I have a choice right now. And only a second later as I look between the exit and the bathroom sign, I have to make it.

Walk away or have a minute to take a breath?

"Shit," I hiss, squeezing my eyes closed as I follow through with my decision and pray it's the right fucking one.

25

TOBY

My jaw is damn near on the floor as I watch her walk away from me. I know I should be chasing her, stopping her from leaving, but she's just thrown me for a fucking loop.

I knew that I wouldn't be able to hide forever, that much was damn obvious. Especially with Nico and Alex's addiction to social media. But up until this point, she'd played right into my hands. She must have trusted me enough to not even go looking. I want to be pleased about that, but clearly, something has gone wrong, because right now she's running in the wrong direction.

I twist in my seat, more than ready to catch her before she manages to escape me, but I pause as she stands at the other end of the restaurant, obviously weighing up her options.

Quite honestly, I'll find her whichever route she decides to take in the next few seconds, and I can't deny that there's a certain thrill in the chase if she were to try to leave me. But equally, I mostly favour easy tonight.

My thoughts flicker to Jonas down in his dark and dank little basement. I wonder how many times he's watched those videos now? How many times he's heard his little princess call out my name?

A smile twitches at my lips, and it only grows when Jodie makes her decision, slipping down a hallway that leads to the bathroom.

Good girl, Demon.

I give her two minutes before I push from the chair and follow her lead. Eyes of the staff follow me, but I don't pay them an ounce of attention. The rest of their customers are too distracted by their meals and company to notice anything is wrong, for which I'm grateful as I march toward the door where my girl is hiding.

Pressing my hand to the door, I swing it open with enough strength for it to crash back against the wall.

A squeal of shock rips from Jodie's lips and she jumps back from the basins as if I've just shot at her.

"Toby, what are you—" Her words falter as she watches me reach back and turn the lock with one quick flick of my wrist.

"You can't run from me, Demon."

"I-I-I wasn't. I just needed to take a breath. This is... this is fucking crazy, Toby. You're... mafia," she whispers as if the devil himself might be listening.

I'd hate to break it to her, but I'm pretty sure she already knows that deep down, I'm really not the nice guy that most people have me pegged as.

No one who's been trained to fight, protect, and conquer from the moment they could walk is ever going to be 'nice'. We're monsters, all of us. Wicked, corrupt, ruthless monsters just like our fathers and their fathers before them.

I hold my hands out to my sides and I dip my head as if I'm going to look down at myself, but I never break eye contact with her.

"This is me, Jodie. Everything you already know, with a little more darkness thrown in for good measure."

"A little? Jesus, Toby. I looked online and—"

"Okay, a lot more darkness. I didn't tell you to protect you," I say, dropping my arms and closing the space between us. "You're too sweet, innocent, pure—" She scoffs, clearly not in agreement with me. "You are, Jodie. The things I kept from you... they'd have changed your opinion of me, and I wanted you to get to know me the person, not me the soldier."

With every step closer I take, she takes another back. But as was always inevitable, she eventually runs out of space and her gasp rips through the empty bathroom as she collides with the wall.

"You should have told me," she whispers. "You know everything about my life. Every dark and dirty bit, yet you held yours back. Can't you see how much that hurts?" Her eyes beg with me to understand.

I come to a stop right in front of her, leaving only a few inches between our bodies. Her chest heaves with each laboured breath she sucks in, causing her breasts to almost brush against me. My body aches for her to do just that, because I know for a fact that she'll throw caution to the wind the second we collide.

Our connection is too powerful, too potent to ignore even with the lies swimming around us.

"I never meant to hurt you, Jodie." It's the truth. In all of this, my intention was never to hurt her, to turn my need for pain and vengeance on her. She's just going to be an unfortunate victim in that cunt's final fall from grace. "I was trying to protect you. My life, it's... dangerous."

"Where did you really get the injuries last week, Toby?" she asks, her voice void of any kind of emotion.

"There was an issue with another gang in the area. We were sent in to try to keep some peace," I say honestly.

"It worked well, I take it," she deadpans, and I can't help but bark out a laugh.

"It could have been better. But I wasn't lying when I said you should have seen the other guys." She sucks in a sharp breath and my hand lands on her face, my palm cupping her jaw and my thumb brushing her bottom lip. "I'm not always a nice person, Jodie. I've told you that before. I've warned you that there is an endless pit of darkness inside me, I just don't think you appreciated just how deep that really runs."

Her eyes darken with my words and her pulse thunders against my fingers that wrap around her neck.

"But you like it. Don't you, Demon?" I press closer, our bodies aligning, and a whimper rips past her red lips. "That first night, it was my darkness that drew you to me. You saw it in me, remember? And you trusted me in spite of it."

"T-Toby, what are you—"

I lower my hand, my fingers wrapping around her throat and pinning her against the wall, cutting off her question.

Her breaths race past her lips, fanning over my face which is only an inch from hers as I tower over her, even in her heels. Her pulse thunders almost violently beneath my fingers. Questions swirl in her dark chocolate eyes as she stares up at me. There's a part of her who's looking at me like I'm the guy she's come to know, to trust. But there's this other part that is looking at a stranger.

"Ask me," I demand.

"W-what?"

"Those questions spinning around in your dirty little mind. Ask them. I'll answer you honestly. I promise."

She flinches as if that promise held as much weight as some of my darkest secrets.

"H-have you... have you... killed people?" she whispers.

"Yes."

All the air rushes from her lungs, and I take the opportunity to really make sure she understands.

"Most of the time, they're really bad men."

"M-most of the—"

"But the innocent can often find themselves in the middle of shit they're not even aware is happening around them." Just like you, my sweet and innocent little toy. My stomach clenches, knowing just how bad this is going to get for her but still refusing to stop.

"Toby, you can't—"

"It's life, Jodie. We're involved in some dangerous shit, get sent into the middle of fucking war zones. It's just the way it is."

She shakes her head, unable to process what I'm telling her.

"Go on," I prompt, knowing that she has at least a few more burning questions for me.

"Do you enjoy it?"

One side of my mouth pulls up in a grin, and my fingers twitch against her throat. "Demon," I breathe, leaning closer and brushing my nose against hers. "I fucking love it. And do you know something else?" She shakes her head again. "I think you do too."

"Toby," she squeals when I tuck my hand under her skirt and cup her pussy through the fabric of her underwear.

"You're soaked, Demon. You know why, don't you?" I ask, rubbing her clit, her juices coating my fingers even with the barrier between us.

"Oh God," she moans, her head falling back. "You fucking love knowing I'm a real-life bad boy. That I'm not just playing the game to pick up women, but that I am that person. I'm a man who will literally protect those I love with my own life, and I make those who hurt them wish they were never born. And that turns you on, doesn't it, Jodie," I growl, grazing my lips along her jaw until I nip at her ear.

"I'm sorry for not telling you everything sooner, but I know you understand. You're a good person, Jodie, and you want to see the good in others too. So I gave you the good side of me for fear you'd run if you discovered the bad too soon."

She whimpers as I continue rubbing her, her hips rolling in time with me to get more.

"Forgive me," I beg.

"Toby," she groans. "You're not playing fair."

"All's fair in love and war, baby. I might be bad, but I can also be so fucking good."

My chest heaves as desire floods every inch of my body. I've never wanted to claim anyone like I do with Jodie. My need for her is like this other beast living inside me that never settles unless I'm owning her, listening to her crying out my name and feeling the biting pain of her nails digging into my shoulders.

She swallows harshly against my tight hold, her entire body trembling with her need for release.

She moans the second I move my hand, but it's only briefly because I tuck my fingers into her underwear, the heat of her needy skin burning mine.

"Fuck, Toby."

"Tell me that you're not going to walk away, Jodie. Please," I shamelessly beg. And it's not just because I need her. There's a whole host of other reasons I need to keep her, and not just to be the final part of my revenge plan. Reasons I'm not comfortable thinking about, let alone acknowledging.

"Oh God, please," she begs as I push two

fingers inside her, grinding the heel of my palm against her swollen clit.

"Not until you tell me."

"I-I'm not," she gasps.

"You're not what, Demon?" I ask against the side of her mouth, desperately waiting for the words so I can completely own her once more.

"I'm not walking aw—"

I swallow her words as my lips crush hers in a bruising kiss that rocks me all the way down to my toes.

I curl my fingers inside her until I find her G-spot. She cries out but I steal them all, kissing her so violently that the copper taste from one of our lips fills my mouth. But if she notices then she's not fazed by it, because not two seconds later does her pussy tighten down on my fingers and she throws herself off the edge of the cliff, moaning my name into our kiss.

I don't wait for her to finish before I pull my fingers from her body and rip my trousers open.

In a heartbeat, I have her feet off the floor in favour of her legs wrapped around my waist as I drag her underwear to the side and thrust inside her.

Her scream of pleasure as her orgasm begins to ebb away bounces off the walls around us.

My fingers dig into her arse as my hips start to move.

"Fuck, Jodie. I can't even explain how much I fucking need you."

Whatever her response was going to be, it's cut off when I capture her lips again, and I don't let up until we've both ridden out our highs and she's full of my cum.

Exactly how it should be.

JODIE

I knew letting him touch me was a bad fucking idea.

My head falls back against the wall as he finally releases my lips and drops his face into the crook of my neck.

"Damn, I needed that."

I have no idea what it is, the endorphins or some shit, but all I do is laugh.

After everything he just told me, after what we just did, all I do is laugh? If I didn't know before that I was bordering on certifiable, then I certainly fucking do now.

Did I just let myself get fucked over by the devil?

My laughter dies and the only sound left in its wake is that of our erratic breathing as we come down from our highs.

Eventually, he softens inside me and takes a

step back, tucking himself away, all while holding my eyes.

"Hungry?" he asks with a smirk.

Amusement bubbles up within me again as I try to remember why I was so frustrated with him in the first place.

Yes, everything he told me is terrifying. But the boy standing in front of me is the one I got to know that first night. The one who took my grief away for a few hours. The one who picked me up last week and gave me a new reason to smile.

"Yeah. I'll be out in a bit," I say but quickly realise my mistake.

How the hell am I meant to walk back out there after that? There's no way people won't have noticed us both disappear, realised just how long we've been gone.

A smirk covers his face as if he can read my own thoughts.

"Anyone says anything, or even looks at you the wrong way, Demon, they'll have me to deal with." The smile that follows is all sweet and light, but now that I've had a taste of the monster that hides beneath, I don't miss the promise of violence in his eyes.

Jesus Christ, why does that get me so hot?

I should be horrified that he's just confessed to killing people, innocent people. But instead, I'm standing here panting like a fucking bitch in heat.

"Take your time, Demon." He turns to slip away as I close the door of the stall I've backed into.

Pulling my ruined knickers down, I lower myself to the toilet and let out a heavy sigh.

What the hell are you doing, Jodie?

I drop my head into my hands and try to talk some sense into myself. But every time I think of him, I think of all the time we've spent together. All the times he's dragged me from my grief and made me smile. The way he came the second I called him last week and literally picked me up off the street.

Does the rest of it really matter? His life is something he was born into. I doubt he'll have had any choice in it becoming his life too. It literally runs through his blood.

Would it be wrong to push all of that aside and continue because, as crazy as it sounds, I still think we could have something?

The way he lights me up inside with one look, let alone the way he makes me burn with a single touch.

That's something, right?

Right?

When I realise that I've been sitting there entirely too long, having a one-way conversation with myself, I clean up and pull my cold, damp knickers back on. They're so bad that in the end, I drop them down my legs, tug them from my feet and stuff them at the bottom of my bag.

I can feel him inside me. I don't need to be sitting in it too.

After washing my hands, I attempt to fix my makeup before holding my head high and preparing myself to walk through a full restaurant and back to our table.

Thoughts of Toby sitting there waiting for me fill my belly with butterflies and give me the push I need.

Something fluttering on the door catches my eye the second I pull it open, and I can't help but bark out a laugh.

Closed for maintenance.

I've still got a smirk on my face as I emerge into the restaurant, but unlike I was expecting, no one so much as glances my way.

So maybe there are some benefits being with a guy most of the city should be scared of.

"The ma... your... whatever owns this place then, I take it?"

His own amusement covers his face. "What gave it away?"

"A number of things," I admit. "Who did the sign on the door?"

"Could have been anyone, but my money is on Leo behind the bar."

Toby nods to the other side of the room and I follow, finding a young guy, probably a similar age to us. He notices our attention and salutes Toby.

"Mortifying," I mutter under my breath.

"Says the woman who let me tie her up in a sex club the night I met her while strangers may or may not have watched."

I shake my head, a smile pulling at my lips. "You're still not going to tell me about that, are you?"

"Maybe one day." He smirks, and my cheeks continue to burn bright red.

"You're sexy when you blush."

"Just when I blush?" I ask cheekily.

"No, you're always sexy, but even more so when you're thinking about all the things I've done to you."

I lose myself in his mysterious blue eyes, and I have to smother a shriek of fright when our server suddenly appears at my side with our food.

I don't look up at her. I can't, because there's no way she doesn't know what we did in the bathroom.

"Thank you," I mumble under my breath when she slides a plate of mouth-watering pasta in front of me.

The scent of garlic, tomatoes, and cheese makes my belly growl loudly.

"It's the best Italian in the city," Toby tells me once we're alone again. "But even still, it's not my favourite thing to eat." I gawp when he lifts his hand and sucks the two fingers that were inside me not so long ago into his mouth, his eyes shuttering as he tastes me.

"Jesus Christ," I gasp, squirming in my seat. "You're really owning this bad boy shit today, huh?"

"Mostly, I was hoping to own you."

The smile he gifts me with is pure filth and ignites an inferno inside me. And it only gets worse when I take a bite of the pasta and I can't contain the groan of delight as the flavours erupt in my mouth.

"Good, right?" he asks, his gaze focused on my lips.

"Incredible."

Spearing a piece of pasta with his fork, I watch, enthralled, as he lifts it to his lips and chews.

How the hell does he make eating so hot?

"It's a skill, for sure," he responds, shocking the shit out of me.

"Shit."

"Eat up, Demon. I've got plans for the rest of our night, and they don't involve spending too much time here."

"I can't believe you asked for that to be boxed up," I say, looking between Toby's eyes and the container full of tiramisu in his hand.

"Why not? It's too good to resist."

"Then we could have eaten it in there."

"We could," he says, crowding me until I've no choice but to back up against his car. "But I have a much better idea for how we could eat it."

"Toby," I say, pressing my hand to his chest to stop him from crushing me. "I'm meant to be pissed at you. I only agreed to meet you tonight so I could shout at you," I inform him.

"So shout at me. I'll even let you hit me, if you want. There's nothing like a bit of pain with your pleasure. Don't you agree, Demon?"

"You're so bad."

"I wanna take you back to my place. Show you where I live. Let you into my life," he tells me, brushing his lips across my cheek and sending a shockwave of desire through my body. "Say yes."

"Will you tell me more about you?"

"Anything you want to know, baby. By the time you walk out again, I swear to you, you'll know all my dark and dirty secrets."

I shudder. "Why does that almost sound like a threat?" I ask him, sobering a little.

"Because my truths are a heavy burden to

carry, Demon. You don't get to take them on lightly." He pulls back and stares me dead in the eye. My mouth immediately goes dry at his intensity. "Are you man enough to deal with the consequences?"

"Are you trying to scare me off?" I ask, attempting to do so lightly but failing massively.

"No, I'm just giving you what you're asking for. Truth and honesty. I'm not going to stand here and tell you that wanting to be a part of my life is going to be easy. It's not. It's dirty, ugly, and at times downright terrifying. But it all seems that much easier when I know I've got you."

"Toby," I sigh, completely falling under his spell but knowing that it's dangerous. More than dangerous. But can I walk away from him even knowing this? "Take me to your place."

His lips twitch, but a smile doesn't break free.

"You're sure? Because I need to warn you, I'm not going to let you go after this."

I smile, hoping to drag his own out of him.

"I'm a big girl. I think I can cope."

"Careful, Demon. They're big words when you've no idea what you're willingly stepping into."

I hold his eyes, ready to say three words that only a few hours ago I never would have believed I would be saying to him. "I trust you. Take me to the dark side."

Knocking my hand from between us, he crushes his body against mine, his hard length grinding against my belly as he loses control, and hell if he doesn't drag me right along for the ride.

Some wolf-whistling from a gang of schoolboys who pass us by eventually forces him to let me up for air.

"We should probably go before I fuck you right here for those kids to watch."

"Y-yeah, probably for the best." I might be up for an audience in some circumstances, but that seems a little much.

With a groan, he puts some space between us before reaching down to adjust himself. Heat floods me, knowing that I did that. That I turned him on so much his trousers are barely fitting him right now.

"I need to get you home. Now."

"Let's go then."

He rips the door open and damn near throws me inside in his haste.

In only seconds, he drops the container with his beloved dessert into my lap and brings his beast of a car to life.

"You know, this utterly ridiculous car makes a lot of sense now."

He laughs at me as he floors the accelerator and wheelspins out of the space.

"So where do you live?"

"It's not far."

"It's some insane penthouse or something, isn't it?"

"No, actually. I don't live in the penthouse. Nico does."

A laugh rumbles up my throat. "Can't say I'm surprised. So he's like third in line to be in charge or something?"

Toby looks over at me with amusement playing in his eyes.

"Just how much research have you done, Demon?"

"It was Bri, mostly. She was the one who dropped the bomb on me."

He nods, clearly happy about something. "What?"

He reaches over and twists his fingers with mine. "I love that you trusted me enough not to look me up."

"Seriously? There's like, nothing about you online. If I didn't know you actually existed I'd think you were recently reincarnated."

"You're not entirely wrong there," he mutters.

"What's that meant to mean?" I ask, narrowing my gaze at him.

"Don't worry, Demon. All will be revealed."

"I'm not sure I like the sound of that."

He glances over at me and winks.

"Too late. Welcome to the dark side, baby. Trust me, life is never boring."

27

TOBY

"And you pretty much have this entire building to yourself?" Jodie asks as I pull into the outside car park for our building and she stares out of the window, her eyes running up the height of it.

"Yeah. We have the top two floors."

"You are aware of how utterly insane this is, right? You should all be at home with your parents."

"We're not normal kids," I say by way of an explanation.

"You don't say," she mutters, half in amusement, half in shock.

I drive toward the building, the roller door to the secure underground garage opening as I get closer.

Jodie continues to gawp, but that's nothing

compared to the way her eyes widen at the sight of the cars all parked down here.

"This is storage for other people's cars, right?"

"Sure, you can believe that if you want."

"Just how fucking rich are you all?"

"I don't have a figure for you, but trust me when I tell you that if you were to stick around, you'd never have to worry about a penny ever again in your life." I don't want it to sound arrogant or entitled, it's just the truth.

Jonas might have done everything he could to try to strip me and Mum of everything we should have been entitled to should his untimely demise occur, but thanks to Damien and some seriously impressive work by Charon, the man I thought was my grandfather, it's looking likely that Mum will get everything she deserves.

Quite honestly, I could live the rest of my life without a penny more of his money. I'm more than capable of earning my own. Hell, I've been doing as such for years in the hope that one day we might have been able to break free. It was wishful thinking I guess, but at least if things hadn't gone the way they did and Mum didn't have Galen to fall back on, I'd have had enough to keep us going for a while.

"Wow," she breathes. "This is like a whole other world."

Pulling into my space, I don't hang around for fear of someone else appearing and trying to steal my girl off me. I have plans, and none of them involve hanging out with my friends and allowing them to get to know her, to dig too deep and ruin everything before it's come to fruition.

Climbing from the car, my eyes lock on the doorway that leads down to our secret basement. I can't help wondering just how much Jonas must be regretting his life choices right now.

It really is a shame that it's going to get worse before it gets better.

Eager to explore, Jodie is already out of the car by the time I get around to the passenger side, her eyes darting from car to car while mine linger on her.

The black wrap dress she's wearing hugs her curves in the most mouth-watering way. The deep V at the front shows off the perfect amount of skin, teasing me with what I know is hiding beneath, and the skirt kisses the tops of her knees. It's demure but stunning.

"I can't get enough of you," I tell her honestly, stepping up to her, taking her hand in one of mine and the container in the other.

"The feeling is entirely mutual," she purrs, running her free hand up my chest, causing a shudder of desire to head straight for my cock.

She grips the back of my neck and stretches up to brush her lips against mine, but right at the last minute, I take a step back and tug her along with me.

"If you let me kiss you right now, we'll never make it up to my flat before you're naked and impaled on my cock," I say over my shoulder, moving faster through the garage.

"And they say romance is dead," she deadpans.

In less than a minute, the lift doors are closing behind us and I've got her backed up against the wall, my forearm planted on either side of her head as I stare down into her eyes.

My chest heaves almost as fast as hers does, our breaths mingling as we fight the magnetic pull between us.

"Toby," she whispers, dragging her bottom lip through her teeth and tempting me like the demon she is.

"I shouldn't be doing this, Jodie," I tell her honestly, my heart aching in my chest. "You're too good for this life, for me."

Silence falls around us as she absorbs my words.

"That might be true. And I'm more than aware that I might regret this decision. But right now, there isn't really another to make."

The lift smoothly climbs through the building, my anticipation growing with each floor we hit.

"I'm glad you think so. And you're right. At some point, you'll probably end up regretting it."

"You think highly of yourself," she says, her head tilting to the side as she studies me.

"Just being realistic."

"Kiss me," she breathes, stretching up once more and trying to take control.

All I do is smile at her as the lift dings, announcing our arrival.

"Let's go. Maybe if we're lucky, you'll actually make it to my bedroom."

Before she has a chance to move, I press my shoulder into her stomach and lift her clean off her feet.

"Toby," she squeals as I all but run out of the enclosed space, praying that the hallway outside is empty and that we're going to make it to the other side of my front door without being interrupted.

And by some fucking miracle, we do.

"You can put me down now, you know," Jodie shouts, her legs kicking and her tiny fists hammering on my arse. "Tobias."

"Fuck, I love it when you say my name."

"Put me down and I'll say it again," she promises. "Come on, I want to see where you live."

"Later. There are more pressing things to deal with first."

I take off through my flat until I burst into my bedroom. I place the tiramisu down on the bedside table for later before throwing her into the middle of my bed.

My navy sheets surround her as she bounces, and I watch her with a smile playing on my lips as she laughs.

"You're so fucking beautiful, Jodie," I growl, making quick work of toeing off my shoes and ripping my shirt from my body.

"Not looking so bad yourself, Tobias," she breathes, her teeth attacking her bottom lip as she watches me strip down to my boxers, which admittedly don't hide a whole lot right now.

"I've got nothing on you. Just a wolf wrapped in sheep's clothing."

"Oh, I don't know. You can be all kinds of sweet when you want to."

"Not tonight, I'm not. I'm feeling all kinds of reckless." And vengeful.

She squeaks as I jump on her, wrapping my hand around the back of her neck and finally claiming her lips once more.

Her tongue immediately joins in as we embark on a bruising kiss, both of us fighting for dominance, although both knowing exactly who is in charge here.

Releasing her neck, I wrap my fingers around her wrists, lifting them both above her head.

I loom over her, loving the need that's reflected back at me and the way her skin is flushed with desire.

"By the time I let you off this bed, you're not going to remember how to walk let alone your own name, Demon."

"Toby," she moans, trying to rub her thighs together where they're pinned beneath me.

"So impatient. Here's how it's going to go, my filthy little toy." Dipping low, I kiss down her throat, making her whimper and writhe beneath me. "I'm going to strip you naked. Kiss you, bite you, mark you until you can't take any more. Then," I say, kissing over her collarbone and onto her chest, "I'm going to eat you until I'm confident that I'm going to be tasting you for a week. And then when you're begging, and only when you're begging, I'll finally give you what you really want and fuck you so hard I'll ruin you for any other man," I promise, needing to convince myself that she'll at least remember something good about me after tonight.

"Yes, yes. Toby, please," she begs.

Tucking my fingers under the neck of her dress, I tug that and the cup of her bra aside, capturing her nipple in my mouth and biting down until she cries out, her back arching on the bed.

"You taste like heaven, and I'm certainly headed for hell," I mutter, giving the other side the same treatment before releasing her hands and sitting up.

"Don't move," I warn, just taking her in.

The air crackles around us as our eye contact holds.

"Please," she begs. "I need you, Toby."

Slowly, fucking tortuously slowly, I reach out and untie her dress, dragging it open and taking in her—

"Where are your knickers?" I growl, staring down at her bare pussy.

"In my bag. You already ruined them."

"Is that right?" I ask, running my finger from her sternum down to the juncture between her thighs, loving the way she shudders with need from my simple touch.

Lifting my weight off her, I drag the loose fabric of her dress beneath her and tug it free of her arms before throwing it to the floor.

"Better," I murmur. But not quite good enough.

She arches for me the second I slide my hand under her back, allowing me to unhook her bra and discard that too.

"Perfect. Arms back above your head. You're at my mercy tonight." She does as she's told and I lean over her, finding the bindings that I left in position and quickly locking her into them.

"Just think of all the things I could do to my little toy tonight. All the ways I could make her mine," I mutter absently, still admiring just how incredible she looks laid out on my dark sheets. My heart races, desperately wanting to run away with itself and imagine a life where that could happen. Where she could be mine and none of the bullshit surrounding us exists.

"Anything. All of it. I don't care," she pants between heaving breaths, anticipation getting the better of her.

"Be careful what you wish for, Demon."

Before she can respond, I claim her lips before setting about completing the first part of my plan.

Reaching for the dessert we brought home, I pull the lid off and dip my fingers into the creamy goodness.

I hold my fingers above her lips teasingly.

"You want some, Demon?" I growl, my mouth watering for what's to come.

"Yes," she moans.

Dropping my fingers, I paint her lips with the tiramisu before plunging them into her mouth and letting her lick them clean.

"Fuck," I groan as her tongue circles my digits and my cock jerks in excitement.

Pulling them free, I reach for more and begin painting her body with the cool dessert, making sure I add extra to all the places that really need my attention.

"Oh my God," she groans, writhing beneath me. "Please."

When I'm happy, I finally drop my mouth to her breast, cleaning her up and letting the sweetness of the tiramisu coat my tongue before sucking her nipple deep into my mouth.

Her cries echo around the room as I continue, not missing an inch of her skin and ensuring I hit all the spots that will build her up to dizzying heights, more desperate for me than she's ever known.

By the time I've got my fingers wrapped around her calf and I'm kissing down her leg toward the spot that damn near has me drooling with need, her body is littered with hickeys and teeth marks, and I can't help but admire my handiwork.

Mine.

Her skin is flushed, her brow beaded with sweat as she moans and mewls for me. It's the most beautiful sound in the fucking world, and I can't get enough.

"Fuck, Toby, please. I need to come so bad," she breathes.

I blow a stream of air across her swollen cunt, making her jolt violently.

"But just think how good it's going to be."

"Please," she moans once more before I drop a little lower and sink my teeth into her thigh. She howls as the pain mixes with her pleasure as she tugs at her bindings above her head. But before she can come down from that alone, I drop to my front and suck her clit. "TOBY," she screams loud enough to echo around the room once more, her hips rolling with either her need for more or the need to get away from the oversensitivity, I'm not sure. I don't really care either, because there is no way I'm stopping until she's coming all over my face and her voice is hoarse from screaming.

Reaching up, I pinch her nipple at the same time I graze her clit with my teeth.

"Oh God. Oh God. Fuck. I'm so close."

"We can't have that," I growl against her sensitive skin. "Not yet, anyway."

"No," she cries, aware of exactly what I'm thinking.

Over and over, I get her right to the edge of falling before pulling back.

"Holy shit," she cries when I finally push two fingers inside of her, rubbing at the spot I know will get her right to that very tight cliff edge.

"Yes. Yes. Yes. Toby, please. I'll do anything you want. I'll suck your cock all night long if you want, just let me come, please."

"Anything?" I ask with a smirk.

"Yes, anything, Just... please. Argh," she screams when I give in and push her over the edge, watching every single second of her blissful fall as I continue circling her clit with my tongue.

Her orgasm goes on and on, proving that I was right, that it was going to be worth it in the end.

By the time she's fallen quiet, her body is

limp, her skin glowing and her eyes sparkling with satisfaction.

"Don't fall asleep on me yet, Demon. I've still got another promise to deliver."

"I'm here for it. I'm here for all of it," she says, almost as if she's in a post-orgasm haze.

"That's my girl."

Pushing my boxers down over my arse, I line myself up with her entrance and thrust forward. She's so wet that I slide inside her with ease, her burning heat sucking me deeper and making my eyes roll.

"Fuck, I'll never get enough of this."

Hitching her leg around my waist, I plant my other hand beside her head and dip down to kiss her, letting her taste herself on me as I continue to ruin her. Just like I promised I would do.

And in turn, I shred a little bit more of that cunt's heart from him.

"Oh my God," I pant. "I'm pretty sure you fulfilled all those promises," I say with a smirk as exhaustion from the last fuck knows how long with Toby begins to consume my body.

My skin is still on fire from his touch, both soft and tender and brutal and painful. Every single muscle in my body is convulsing from the three mind-numbing releases he just gave me, and my pussy is deliciously sore.

"I never back down on my word, baby," he says, releasing my wrists before planting kisses around the tender skin where I was restrained. "What?" he asks, seeing something in my expression.

"I like it when you're kinky," I confess.

"Oh yeah?" he asks, a sparkle of something wicked in his own eyes.

"Yeah. I never quite know where I stand with you, and it's thrilling."

"I'm not sure if that's a good thing or not," he mutters, rolling out of bed and strolling toward a door at the other side of the room.

"Oh, it's definitely a good thing," I call after him, stretching out the aches in my limbs and breathing in the scent of him on his pillow. "I love the thrill of not knowing what's going to happen next."

"That's good. I hope it stays that way."

"I've never been one to want a boring life."

The toilet flushes before the sound of water running hits my ears, and a few seconds later, he appears looking like a Greek fucking god in the doorway with the light of the bathroom shining behind him.

"You want a drink?"

"Yeah," I say with a laugh. "After that, I think I need more than one."

He nods. "Get comfortable. I'll be right back. I think it's time we probably talked."

My brows pinch as I study him, suddenly looking a little unsure of himself.

"What's wrong? Surely you've already told me the worst?"

"You might be wise to keep the jury out on that."

"O-okay," I mutter to myself as he disappears from sight.

Rolling to the side of the bed, I swing my legs over and test them out gingerly to see if they'll actually hold me up. When I'm confident that they will, I swipe his shirt from the floor and pull it on, buttoning it up wrong but not having the energy to fix it as I pad toward the bathroom.

"Wow," I breathe, taking in the sheer size of it.

I got a quick look at his flat before he marched me into his bedroom, and it pretty much looked like I predicted. A bachelor pad. Everything was grey, black, and white. There didn't seem to be any kind of sentimental items that I spotted. But although it might be what I expected from a young, single guy living alone, from knowing Toby as I do, I would have thought there would have been more softness, more family. It's more than obvious just how much he loves his mum and sister, so I expected maybe a little bit of them here.

It's just another reminder that really, I don't know him all that well. Something I can only hope will change now he's opened himself up entirely to me. Because I want it. I want to explore this with him in the hope that it just might be something.

Does the whole mafia thing bother me? Yeah, I guess it does a little. But I think that might only be because I'm basing my opinion of it all on what I've seen on TV and online. I might be naïve, but I'm not stupid enough to think that's anything like reality.

I clean up, wash my hands and attempt to do something with the makeup that's smeared all over my face before heading back with butterflies in my belly.

My insides somersault when I find him sitting back against his headboard with a tablet beside him and two drinks on the side. Sensing my attention, he looks up, and the most delicious smile spreads across his face, although I can't deny that there is a darkness in his eyes that makes my stomach knot with worry.

"You're too far away."

Not needing to be told twice, I take off toward him, climbing onto the bed and snuggling into his side.

He's tense beside me as silence falls around us. I can't explain why, but the hairs on the back of my neck stand on end and a tight knot twists up my stomach.

"Toby, what is it?" I ask, dread beginning to flow through my veins.

Reaching over, he grabs the two glasses of what look like whiskey and passes one to me.

"Drink. All of it," he instructs, and I do so without hesitation, the strong alcohol burning the second it hits my tongue and continues all the way to my belly.

He takes the empty glass from my hand and places it back on the side.

"There are things about me that you need to know," he confesses, his voice hard and cold and completely unlike him.

I glance up at him, a gasp passing my lips when I take in the mask he seems to have pulled on.

My Toby, the soft, kind guy I've become used to, has gone. In his place is the soldier he's briefly told me about.

Holy shit.

"Toby?" I breathe, my previously boiling blood instantly turning to ice.

"Us meeting wasn't a happy accident," he confesses, staring at a black and white piece of art on the wall opposite us.

"I-it wasn't?" I ask, thinking back to that first night when I spotted him across the bar.

"No. I'd been following you."

"What?" I shriek, not believing what I'm hearing. "You're joking, right?"

Finally, he turns his eyes on me, and I'm able to read the truth in the dark depths staring back at me.

"Fuck."

"Our lives were intrinsically linked long before we met, Jodie. You just had no idea about it."

"I-I don't understand," I say, hating the weakness in my voice.

"The man I told you about, the one who hurt me, hurt my mum. He tried to kill my sister." I gasp, the pain in his voice making my heart ache for him.

"Shit, that's—"

"He's also a man you know."

"A man I—" My words cut off as one face pops into my head.

But no, that can't be right. It can't.

My brain starts racing as pieces of a puzzle that I never realised didn't fit in begin slotting together.

"My so-called father had a whole other life, Jodie. A whole other family."

"No," I breathe, beginning to slide away from him, my stomach turning to the point that I fear I'm going to be running for the toilet at any moment.

"For years, I've been planning his downfall. I wanted to watch him lose everything, to watch as I ripped shreds off his heart and left him bleeding out, just like he spent his life trying to do to me, to Mum, to my sister when she reappeared in our lives.

"But the problem I had was that the man I knew didn't have a heart. He was a cold, abusive monster."

My heart races and my palms sweat as I

listen to his tale, praying, fucking begging for this not to be going in the direction I fear it may be.

"His need for control, his jealousy got the better of him, and he tried to have my sister killed. And he employed someone we had no idea existed to do the job for him.

"You might know him. Twenty-one-year-old recently deceased member of the Royal Reapers."

"No, Toby. Please, please don't—" My hands tremble in my lap as something akin to guilt washes through Toby's eyes.

"It was your brother, Jodie. My *father* tasked him to kill my sister on his behalf."

"No." A sob erupts from my throat as red-hot tears burn my eyes. "You killed him?"

"Me? No." He shakes his head. "Not personally. I left that to others while I went after the main man."

I can barely suck in the air I need as I wait for him to speak. But he never does. He just holds my eyes, waiting for me to ask the question he knows is on the tip of my tongue.

"Who is he?"

"Ah," he says, a sadistic smirk curling at his lips. "The man who did all of this, the man I thought had no heart, who cared about no one other than himself? It turned out he very much did.

"He went to as many lengths as possible to

hide them, but he screwed up when he involved his son in my sister's attempted murder."

I whimper, unable to stop the tremors wracking my body or the tears that finally spill over.

"For a long time, I thought he was the only one, just like the paper trail, the lies, led us to believe. But then I found another. A living, breathing person I could use to do exactly what I've been dreaming about all these years."

"Toby, p-please don't do this. Please don't tell me it was you who killed him?" I beg.

"Oh no, Demon. He's not dead."

I rear back at the amusement in his tone, my entire body shaking more violently with each new revelation.

"That would have been entirely too easy for him after the years of abuse and torture my mum and I suffered at his hands. Don't you think?"

He picks up the tablet beside him as I swallow harshly, fighting the need to puke all over his bed.

The screen illuminates a beat before he increases the volume and a voice flows through the speakers.

"Jodie, baby. You need to get out of there." His tone is strong, his warning more than clear, but the only direction I run is toward the bathroom as I bring up the dinner from only a few hours ago.

"Jodie," Dad calls from the screen, his voice cracking with emotion.

"Surprise, Demon," another voice says, one that only minutes ago sent a wave of contentment through my body. But now, all it ignites is hate. "I promised you that I'd break you, old man. I promised you that I would find that one thing you loved more than life itself and I would bring it to its knees just so you could experience exactly how it feels."

"Jojo, I'm so sorry. He's insane. You need to get away from him."

Toby's only reaction is to throw his head back and laugh.

"Insane? Really? Is that really the line you're going for here? I'm pretty sure I've got enough evidence on you to prove that the only one who is mentally unstable between the three of us is you, you twisted fuck."

The level of disgust and pure hatred in Toby's voice drags my eyes up from the floor, but I don't find him. My gaze locks on the screen he's turned my way so I can get a look at the state of the man I've thought of as my dad all my life.

"Dad," I breathe, the little girl inside me begging to forget everything Toby has told me about this man, about his abuse and just wanting to be swept up in his arms and told that everything will be okay.

"You spent all your life trying to protect

them," Toby starts. "But as it stands, they've got nothing. All your money is gone. The house is about to vanish. Poor Jodie even lost her job and is about to start working as a stripper."

Disbelief washes through me. "That was you?" I ask, desperate not to accept it.

Toby shrugs, but I see deeper. I see the pain etched onto his face that most others would miss.

"I really didn't want to hurt you, baby," he says so sincerely, I want to believe him. But I can't. He did all this. "But I promised myself years ago that I would do whatever it took to ruin this man here. And look at him. Really look at him." I do as I'm told, watching as tears cascade down his cheeks. Injuries from obvious beatings mar his face and exhaustion darkens his eyes. "This is exactly the vengeance I've craved almost all my life.

"You're lucky really, Jonas. I could have done a hell of a lot worse than just fuck your little princess. She could be locked in the cell next to you right now, after all. Her and your bit on the side. The one you loved like you should have loved my mum.

"I just have one more question, Jonas," Toby sneers, the sweet guy I've come to care about more than I should is completely gone as he stares into the eyes of the man he hates through the screen. "And I think you know exactly what it is. And I think I already know the answer." Toby looks up, his gaze burning through me before he asks whatever this final question is. "Tell us once and for all why she was always more important to you than me. As far as we can tell, neither of us actually shares blood with you." I know it's fucked up, but hearing Toby say that this man isn't actually his father sends a rush of relief through me. "But that's not true, is it? Joker wasn't your only illegitimate child, was he, Jonas? Jodie is yours too, isn't she? That's why spending the night literally watching her get fucked up hurts you so much. It's why she was the perfect pawn in my ruthless games."

My head spins to the point that I wonder if I'm about to pass out. Before I get the chance to, I retch once more, but there's nothing left to bring up.

"As fucked up as this may be, there's a part of me that feels some kind of happiness over the fact that I get to give Jodie something she's wished she could have done since the day she learned of your death, old man. I'm able to give her the gift of being able to say goodbye to the man she believed was a good, protective father. If she's lucky, she might even be able to grieve her memory of you instead of the monster I've told her you really are."

"No, please. Jodie," Dad cries, getting closer to the camera. "Don't listen to him. It's all lies. All of it. I'm going to get out of here and the three of us will be a family again. I fucking swear to you, Jojo. Please, listen to me—"

"Say goodbye, Jodie. It's over." Toby's cold voice turns my blood to ice as I curl up into a tighter ball on the floor.

I know without a doubt from Toby's tone that he's serious, and a whispered, "Goodbye," falls from my lips before the screen goes black and Toby marches from the room, an agonising howl ripping through the air as he goes.

My heart fractures. Shatters into a million pieces. And infuriatingly, it's not just for me and everything I've lost, but for everything Toby has endured in his life, too.

The bang that follows makes me flinch before something shatters and the sound of another angry roar echoes around the silent bathroom.

I try to gather my thoughts, to get a grasp on what just happened, but I can't.

It's too raw, the pain in my chest, the grief, the disbelief... it all swirls around me, threatening to pull me into its agonising depths.

Things continue to break and shatter somewhere in the flat, but I ignore it, instead focusing on trying to make my body work.

The only thing I know right now is that I need to get away. I can't be here. I can't be anywhere near Toby as I try to process everything I've just learned.

My legs are weak as I get to my feet and I

quickly stumble into the doorframe, pain exploding in my shoulder.

By some miracle, I manage to continue forward, finding the bedroom completely trashed around me. Spotting my bag on the floor where I dropped it, I swipe it up and continue on my quest to escape this headfuck.

Only an hour ago, I was blissed out on Toby's cock, and now... now I've had my world ripped from beneath my feet once more.

It's not until I emerge in a living area that movement catches my eyes and I find him standing at a wall of floor-to-ceiling windows, his palms flat against the glass and his head hanging low between his shoulders. He stills the second I take another step.

"This was meant to make the pain go away," he says, his voice low and haunted, full of years of pain and abuse.

But I refuse to feel anything for him. I swallow down any concern I have for him and clench my fists.

He did this. He brought this on both of us.

He shattered my life in all the ways Joe and Dad's deaths never could have.

"You don't deserve for it to stop hurting, you monster," I hiss.

I don't miss the way his entire body jolts at my words before I turn away from him, unable to bear the weakness in his stance and the pained groan that rumbles deep in his chest.

I move as fast as my legs will carry me toward the front door.

"Jodie, please," he begs behind me. "I'm sorry. Please. Please don't leave me."

His voice rips through me, gripping my heart in a vice and crushing it until I can barely breathe.

I hate myself for it, but a second before I rip the door open and run, I look back.

My breath catches when I find him in the middle of the room on his knees, his shoulders slumped in defeat.

"Please," he says softly, his eyes boring into mine, searching for something I'm not sure he's going to find. "I need you."

Steeling my spine, I push my shoulders back. Desperately trying to find some strength from somewhere, I pull the door open.

"Goodbye, Toby. I hope it was worth it."

Toby and Jodie's story continues in RECKLESS
PRINCESS

HATE YOU PROLOGUE

Tabitha

I stare down at my gran's pale skin. Her cheeks are sunken and her eyes tired. She's been fighting this for too long now, and as much as I hate to even think it, it's time she found some peace.

I take her cool hand in mine and lift her knuckles to my lips.

"It's Tabitha," I whisper. I've no idea if she's awake, but I don't want to startle her.

Her eyes flicker open. After a second they must adjust to the light and she looks right at me. My chest tightens as if someone's wrapping an elastic band around it. I hate seeing my once so full of life gran like this. She was always so happy and full of cheer. She didn't deserve this end. But cancer doesn't care what kind of person you are, it hits whoever it fancies and ruins lives.

Pulling a chair closer, I drop onto it, not taking my eyes from her.

"How are you doing today?" I hate asking the question, because there really is only one answer. She's waiting, waiting for her time to come to put her out of her misery.

"I'm good. Christopher upped my morphine. I'm on top of the world."

She might be living her last days, but it doesn't stop her eyes sparkling a little as she mentions her male nurse. If I've heard the words 'if I were forty years younger' once while she's been here, then I've heard them a million times. She's joking, of course. My gran spent her life with my incredible grandpa until he had a stroke a few years ago. Thankfully, I guess, his end was much quicker and less painful than Gran's. It was awful at the time to have him healthy one moment and then gone in a matter of hours, but this right now is pure torture, and I'm not the one lying on the hospital bed with meds constantly being pumped into my body.

"Turn the frown upside down, Tabby Cat. I'm fine. I want to remember you smiling, not like your world's about to come crashing down."

"I know, I'm sorry. I just—" a sob breaks from my throat. "I don't know how I'm going to live without you." Dramatic? Yeah. But Gran has been my go-to person my whole life. When my parents get on my last nerve, which is often, she's the one who talks me down, makes me see things differently. She's also the only one who's encouraged me to live the life I want, not the one I'm constantly being pushed into.

That's the reason I'm the only one visiting her right now.

When my parents discovered that she was the one encouraging my 'reckless behaviour', as they called it, they cut contact. I can see the pain in her eyes about that every time she looks at me, but she's too stubborn to do anything about it, even now.

"You're going to be fine. You're stronger than you give yourself credit for. How many times have I told you, you just need to follow your heart. Follow your heart and just breathe. Spread your wings and fly, Tabby Cat."

Those were the last words she said to me.

HATE YOU CHAPTER ONE

Tabitha

The heavy bass rattles my bones. The incredible music does help to lift my spirits, but I find it increasingly hard to see the positives in my life while I'm hanging out with my friends these days. They've all got something exciting going on—incredible job prospects, marriage, exotic holidays on the horizon—and here I am, drowning in my one-person pity party. It's been two months since Gran left me, and I'm still wondering what the hell I'm meant to be doing with my life.

"Oh my god, they are so fucking awesome," Danni squeals in my ear as one song comes to an end. I didn't really have her down as a rock fan, but she was almost as excited as James when he announced that this was what we were doing for his birthday this year. Although I do wonder if it's the music or the frontman who's really captured her attention. She'd never admit it, but she's got a thing for bad boys.

I glance over at him with his arm wrapped around Shannon's shoulders and a smile twitches my lips. They're so cute. They've got the kind of relationship everyone craves. It seems so easy yet full of love and affection. Ripping my eyes from the couple, I focus back on the stage and try to block out that I'm about as far away from having that kind of connection with anyone as physically possible.

I sing along with the songs I've heard on the radio a million times and jump around with my friends, but I just can't quite totally get on board with tonight. Maybe I just need more alcohol.

"Where to next?" Shannon asks once we've left the arena and the ringing in our ears has begun to fade.

"Your choice," James says, looking down at her with utter devotion shining in his eyes. It wasn't a great surprise when Shannon sent a photo of her giant engagement ring to our group chat a couple of months ago. We all knew it was coming—Danni especially, seeing as it turned out that she helped choose the ring.

Shannon directs us all to a cocktail bar a few

streets over and I make quick work of manoeuvring my way through the crowd to get to the bar, my need for a drink beginning to get the better of me. The others disappear off somewhere in the hope of finding a table

"Can we have two jugs of..." I quickly glance at the menu. "Margaritas please."

"Coming right up, sweetheart." The barman winks at me before his eyes drop to my chest. Hooking up on a night out isn't really my thing, but hell if it doesn't make me feel a little better about myself. He's cute too, and just the kind of guy who would give both my parents a heart attack if I were to bring him home. Both his forearms are covered in tattoos, he's got gauges in both his ears, and a lip ring. A smile tugs at the corner of my mouth as I imagine the looks on their faces.

My gran's words suddenly hit me.

Just breathe.

My hand lifts and my fingers run over the healing skin just below my bra. My smile widens.

I watch the barman prepare our cocktails, my eyes focused on the ink on his arms. I've always been obsessed by art, any kind of art, and that most definitely includes on skin.

I'm lost in my own head, so when he places the jugs in front of me, I startle, feeling ridiculous.

"T-Thank you," I mutter, but when I lift my eyes, I find him staring intently at me.

"You're welcome. I'm Christian, by the way."

"Oh, hi." A sly smile creeps onto my lips. "I'm Biff."

"Biff?" His brows draw together in a way I'm all too used to when I say my name.

"It's short for Tabitha."

"That's pretty. So... uh... how do you feel about—"

"Christian, a little help?" one of the other barmen shouts, pulling Christian's attention from me.

"Sorry, I'll hopefully see you again later?"

I nod at him, not wanting to give him any false hope. Like I said, he's cute, but after my last string of bad dates and even worse short-term boyfriends, I'm happy flying solo right now. I've got a top of the range vibrating friend in my bedside table; I don't need a man.

Picking up the tray in front of me, I turn and go in search of my friends. It takes forever, but eventually I find them tucked around a tiny table in the back corner of the bar.

"What the hell took so long? We thought you'd pulled and abandoned us."

"Yes and no," I say, ensuring every head turns my way.

"Tell us more," Danni, my best friend, demands.

"It was nothing. The barman was about to ask me out, but it got busy."

"Why the hell did you come back? Get over there. We all know you could do with a little... loosening up," James says with a wink.

"I'm good. He wasn't my type."

"Oh, of course. You only date posh boys."

"That is not true."

"Is it not?" Danni asks, chipping in once she's filled all the glasses.

"No..." I think back over the previous few guys they met. "Wayne wasn't posh," I argue when I realise they're kind of right.

"No, he was just a wanker."

Blowing out a long breath, I try to come up with an argument, but quite honestly, it's true. My shoulders slump as I realise that I've been subconsciously dating guys my parents would approve of. It's like my need to follow their orders is so well ingrained by now that I don't even realise I'm doing it. Shame that their ideas about my life, what I should do, and whom I should date don't exactly line up with mine.

Glancing over my shoulder at the bar, I catch a glimpse of Christian's head. Maybe I should take him up on his almost offer. What's the worst that could happen?

Deciding some liquid courage is in order, I grab my margherita and swallow half down in one go.

I'm so fed up of attempting to live my parents' idea of a perfect life. I promised Gran I'd do things my way. I need to start living up to my promise.

By the time I'm tipsy enough to walk back to the bar and chat up Christian, he's nowhere to be seen. I'm kind of disappointed seeing as the others had convinced me to throw caution to the wind (something that I'm really bad at doing), but I think I'm mostly relieved to be able go home and lock myself inside my flat alone and not have to worry about anyone else.

With my arm linked through Danni's, we make our way out to the street, ready to make our journeys home, and Shannon jumps into an idling Uber while Danni waits for another to go in the opposite direction.

"You sure you don't want to be dropped off? I don't mind."

"No, I'm sure. I could do with the fresh air." It's not a lie—the alcohol from one too many cocktails is making my head a little fuzzy. I hate going to sleep with the room spinning. I'd much rather that feeling fade before lying down.

"Okay. Promise me you'll text me when you're home."

"I promise." I wrap my arms around my best friend and then wave her off in her own Uber.

Turning on my heels, I start the short walk home.

I've been a London girl all my life, and while some might be afraid to walk home after dark, I love it. I love seeing a different side to this city, the quiet side when most people are hiding in their flats, not flooding the streets on their daily commutes.

My mind is flicking back and forth between my promise to Gran and my missed opportunity tonight when a shop front that I walk past on almost a daily basis makes me stop.

It's a tattoo studio I've been inside of once in my life. I never really pay it much attention, but the new sign in the window catches my eye and I stop to look.

Admin help wanted. Enquire within.

Something stirs in my belly, and it's not just my need to do something to piss my parents off— although getting a job in a place like this is sure to do that. I'm pretty sure it's excitement.

Tattoos fascinate me, or more so, the artists.

I'm surprised to see the open sign still illuminated, so before I can change my mind, I push the door open. A little bell rings above it, and after a few seconds of standing in reception alone, a head pops out from around the door.

"Evening. What can I do you for?" The guy's

smile is soft and kind despite his otherwise slightly harsh features and ink.

"Oh um..." I hesitate under his intense dark stare. I glance over my shoulder, the back of the piece of paper catching my eye and reminding me why I walked in here. "I just saw the job ad in the window. Is the position still open?"

His eyes drop from mine and take in what I'm wearing. Seeing as tonight's outing involved a rock concert, I'm dressed much like him in all black and looking a little edgy with my skinny black jeans, ripped AC/DC t-shirt and heavy black makeup. I must admit it's not a look I usually go for, but it was fitting for tonight.

He nods, apparently happy with what he sees.

"Experience?" he asks, making my stomach drop.

"Not really, but I'm studying for a Masters so I'm not an idiot. I know my way around a computer, Excel, and I'm super organised."

"Right..." he trails off, like he's thinking about the best way to get rid of me.

"I'm a really quick learner. I'm punctual, methodical and really easy to get along with."

"It's okay, you had me sold at organised. I'm Dawson, although everyone around here calls me D."

"Nice to meet you." I stick my hand out for him to shake, and an amused smile plays at his

RECKLESS KNIGHT

lips. Stretching out an inked arm, he takes my hand and gives it a very firm shake that my dad would be impressed by—if he could look past the tattoos, that is. "I'm Tabitha, but everyone calls me Biff."

"Biff, I like it. When can you start?"

"Don't you want to interview me?"

"You sound like you could be perfect. When can you start?"

"Err... tomorrow?" I ask, totally taken aback. He doesn't know me from Adam.

"Yes!" He practically snaps my hand off. "Can you be here for two o'clock? I can show you around before clients start turning up. I'll apologise now for dropping you in the deep end, we've not had anyone for a few weeks and things are starting to get a little crazy."

"I can cope with crazy."

"Good to know. This place can be nuts." I smile at him, more grateful than he could know to have a distraction and a focus.

My Masters should be enough to keep my mind busy, but since Gran went, I can't seem to lose myself in it like I could previously. Hopefully, sorting this place's admin out might be exactly what I need.

"Two o'clock tomorrow then," I say, turning to leave. "I'll bring ID. Do you need a reference? I've done some voluntary work recently, I'm sure they'll write something for me."

373

"Just turn up on time and do your job and you're golden."

I walk out with more of a spring in my step than I have in a long time. I'm determined to find something that's going to make me happy, not just my parents. I've lived in their shadow for long enough.

I look myself over before leaving my flat for my first shift at the tattoo studio. I'm dressed a little more like myself today in a pair of dark skinny jeans, a white blouse and a black blazer. It's simple and smart. I'm not sure if there's a dress code—D never specified what I should wear. With my hair straightened and hanging down my back and my makeup light, I feel like I can take on whatever crazy he throws at me.

With a final spritz of perfume, I grab my bag from the unit in the hall and pull open my door. My home is a top floor flat in an old London warehouse. They were converted a few years ago by my father's company, and I managed to get myself first dibs. They might drive me insane on the best of days, but at least I get this place rent-free. It almost makes up for their controlling and stuck-up ways... almost.

Ignoring the lift like I always do, I head for

the stairs. My heels click against the polished concrete until I'm at the bottom and out to the busy city. I love London. I love that no matter what the time, there's always something going on or someone who's awake.

The spring afternoon is still a little fresh, making me regret not grabbing my coat, or even a scarf, before I left. I pull my blazer tighter around myself and make the short journey to the shop.

The door's locked when I get there, and the bright neon sign that clearly showed it was open last night is currently saying closed.

Unsure of what to do, I lift my hand to knock. Only a second later, the shop front is illuminated, and the sound of movement inside filters down to me, but when the door opens it's not the guy from last night.

"Oh... uh... hi. Is... uh... D here?"

The guy folds his arms over his chest and looks me up and down. He chuckles, although I've no idea what he finds so amusing.

"D," he shouts over his shoulder, "there's some posh bird here to see you."

My teeth grind that he's stereotyped me quite so quickly, but I refuse to allow him to see that his assumptions about me affect me in any way.

"Ah, good. I was worried you might change your mind."

"Not at all," I say, stepping past the

judgemental arsehole and into the studio reception-cum-waiting room.

"That's Spike. Feel free to ignore him. He's not got laid in about a million years, it makes him a little cranky." I fight to contain a laugh, especially when I turn toward Spike to find his lips pursed and his eyes narrowed in frustration. All it does is confirm that D's words are correct.

"Is that fucking necessary? Posh doesn't need to know how inactive my cock is, especially not when she's only just walked through the fucking door. Unless..." He stalks towards me and I automatically back up. I can't deny that he's a good looking guy, but there's no way I'm going there.

"I don't think so."

"You sure? You look like you could do with a bit of rough." He winks, and I want the ground to swallow me up.

"Down, Spike. This is Tabitha, or Biff. She's our new admin, so I suggest you be nice to her if you want to stop organising your own appointments and shit. I don't need a sexual harassment case on my hands before she's even fucking started."

I can't help but laugh at the look on Spike's face. "Don't worry. I'm sure you'll find some desperate old spinster soon."

He looks me up and down again, something

in his eyes changed. "Appearances aside, I think you're going to get on well here."

I smile at him. "Mine's a coffee. Milk, no sugar. I'm already sweet enough." His chin drops.

"I thought you were our new assistant. Why am I still making the coffee?"

"Know your place, Spike. Now do as the lady says. You know my order."

"Yeah, it comes with a side of fuck off!" He flips D off before disappearing through a door that I can only assume goes to a kitchen.

"I probably should have warned you that you've agreed to work around a bunch of arseholes."

"I know how to handle myself around horny men, don't worry."

After finishing my A levels, before I grew any kind of backbone where my parents were concerned, I agreed to work for my dad. I was his little office bitch and spent an horrendous year of my life being bossed around by men who thought that just because they had a cock hanging between their legs it made them better than me. I might have fucking hated that year, but it taught me a few things, not just about business but also how to deal with men who think they're something fucking special just because they're a tiny bit successful and make more money than me. I've no doubt that my time at Anderson

Development Group gave me all the skills I'm going to need to handle these artists.

"So I see. So, this is your desk. When you're on shift you'll be the first person people see when they're inside, so it's important that you look good. But from what I've seen, I don't think we'll have an issue. I've sorted you out logins for the computer and the software we use. Most of it is pretty self-explanatory. I'm pretty IT illiterate and I've figured most of it out, put it that way."

D's showing me how they book clients in when someone else joins us. This time it's someone I recognise from my previous visit, although it's immediately obvious that he doesn't remember me like I do him. But then I guess he was the one delivering the pain, not receiving it.

"Biff, this is Titch. Titch, this is Biff, our new admin. Be nice."

"Nice? I'm always nice. Nice to meet you, Biff. You have any issues with this one, you come and see me. He might look tough, but I know all his secrets." Titch winks, a smile curling at his lips that shows he's a little more interested than he's making out, and quickly disappears towards his room.

It's not long until the first clients of the afternoon arrive, and I'm left alone to try to get to grips with everything.

Between clients, D pops his head out of his room to check I'm okay, and every hour I make a round of coffee for everyone. That sure seems to get me in their good books.

"I think I could get used to having you around," Spike says when I deliver probably his fourth coffee of the day. "Only thing that would make it better is if it were whisky."

"Not sure the person at the end of your needle would agree." He chuckles and turns back to the design he was working on when I interrupted.

My first day flies by. D tells me to head home not long after nine o'clock. They've all got hours of tattooing to go yet, seeing as Saturday night is their busiest night of the week, but he insists I get a decent night's sleep.

Continue reading Tabitha and Zach's story
HATE YOU!

ABOUT THE AUTHOR

Tracy Lorraine is a *USA Today* and *Wall Street Journal* bestselling new adult and contemporary romance author. Tracy has recently turned thirty and lives in a cute Cotswold village in England with her husband, baby girl and lovable but slightly crazy dog. Having always been a bookaholic with her head stuck in her Kindle, Tracy decided to try her hand at a story idea she dreamt up and hasn't looked back since.

Be the first to find out about new releases and offers. Sign up to my newsletter here.

If you want to know what I'm up to and see teasers and snippets of what I'm working on, then you need to be in my Facebook group. Join Tracy's Angels here.

Keep up to date with Tracy's books at
www.tracylorraine.com

Rebel Ink Series

Hate You #1

Trick You #2

Defy You #3

Play You #4

Inked (A Rebel Ink/Driven Crossover)

Rosewood High Series

Thorn #1

Paine #2

Savage #3

Fierce #4

Hunter #5

Faze (#6 Prequel)

Fury #6

Legend #7

Maddison Kings University Series

TMYM: Prequel

TRYS #1

TDYW #2

TBYS #3

TVYC #4

TDYD #5

TDYR #6

TRYD #7

Knight's Ridge Empire Series

Wicked Summer Knight: Prequel (Stella & Seb)

Wicked Knight #1 (Stella & Seb)

Wicked Princess #2 (Stella & Seb)

Wicked Empire #3 (Stella & Seb)

Deviant Knight #4 (Emmie & Theo)

Deviant Princess #5 (Emmie & Theo

Deviant Reign #6 (Emmie & Theo)

One Reckless Knight (Jodie & Toby)

Reckless Knight #7 (Jodie & Toby)

Reckless Princess #8 (Jodie & Toby)

Reckless Dynasty #9 (Jodie & Toby)

Ruined Series

Ruined Plans #1

Ruined by Lies #2

Ruined Promises #3

Never Forget Series

Never Forget Him #1

Never Forget Us #2

Everywhere & Nowhere #3

Chasing Series

Chasing Logan

The Cocktail Girls

His Manhattan

Her Kensington